AMONG THE CURSED AND DIVINE

NICOLE BAILEY

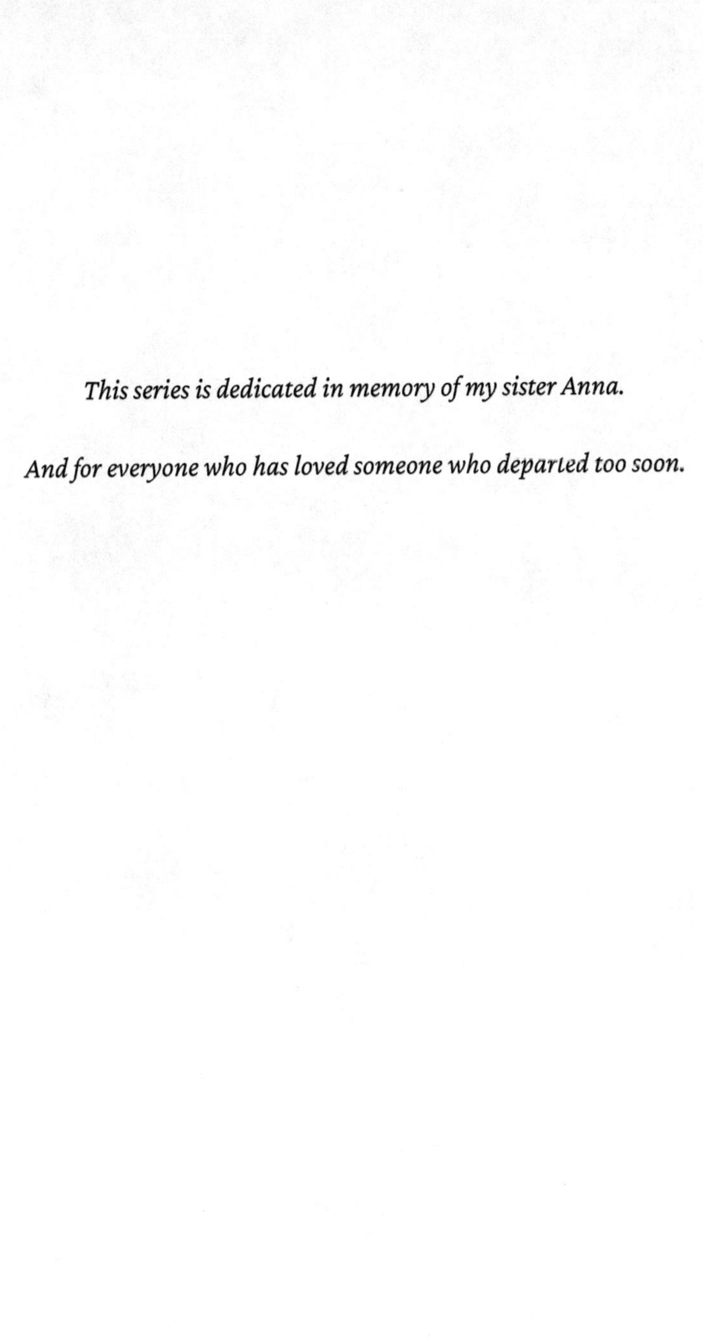

This series is dedicated in memory of my sister Anna.

And for everyone who has loved someone who departed too soon.

CONTENT WARNINGS

Please note these content warnings may contain mild spoilers for this book.

Among the Cursed and Divine is based on a story that deals intimately with grief, loss, and death. This book depicts the loss of animals, humans, and divine creatures of all ages. It explores grief in an intimate, detailed manner.

Enkidu's curse is, in some ways, analogous with a partner who has received a terminal diagnosis. The denial, grief, and anger both Enkidu and Gilgamesh experience as well as their relational struggles while facing these emotions are explored.

This book contains the depiction of battles including death and mild gore as well as an on-page animal sacrifice.

The story also contains strong language and sexual content.

I hope readers will find that I've handled these topics with sensitivity. However, I wished to include a note for anyone who may find this content triggering.

MAP

Anu
Nippurash
Entrance to
the Divine Realm
Humbaba's
Lair
ID-UGINA River
Umma
Uruk
THE CEDAR FOREST
UTU
Inanna
N
nanna

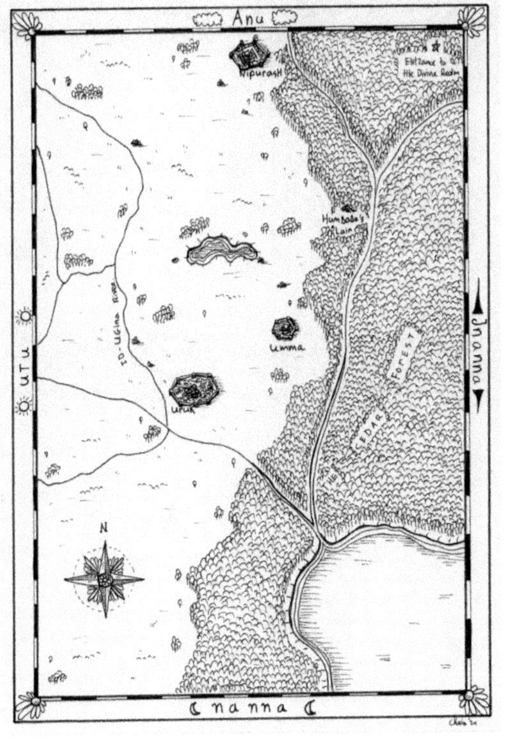

CHARACTER REVIEW

Main Characters:

Gilgamesh: Two-thirds god and king of Uruk.

Enkidu: A man created by the gods to balance Gilgamesh.

Shamhat: Queen of Uruk.

* * *

Gods:

Inanna: Uruk's primary deity. Goddess of romance, sex, fertility, beauty, war, and justice.

Ninsun: Goddess of cattle, dreams, and prophecy. Gilgamesh's mother.

Anu: God of the sky. Inanna's father.

Utu: God of the sun. Inanna's brother.

Enlil: God of storms.

Nanna: God of the moon.

* * *

Secondary Characters:

Usun: Gilgamesh's and Shamhat's son.

    Hirin: Gilgamesh's closest political advisor.

    Abgal: Gilgamesh's head solider.

    Meritkara: One of Shamhat's partners and Gilgamesh's wives.

    Akkiru: One of Shamhat's partners. A musician.

    Utnapishtim: Gilgamesh's ancestor who saved the world by building a boat during a flood and was granted immortality by the gods as a reward.

REVIEW OF BOOK I

In **In the Midst of Omens**, King Gilgamesh rules the grandest city in the world, Uruk. But that isn't enough for him. He wants a legacy that will outlive him and he's willing to stop at nothing to get it.

The goddess Inanna wants Gilgamesh to make his sole divine vow with her and have a child together so she can place a son on Uruk's throne. Gilgamesh struggles to outmaneuver her.

The Queen, Shamhat, asks Gilgamesh's goddess mother Ninsun to intercede with his insatiable desire for legacy.

Ninsun gives Gilgamesh a prophecy: *You shall gain what you desire but lose that which matters more.*

The gods answer Shamhat's request by creating Enkidu. He lives in the cedar forest with a wolf as a companion until Shamhat seeks him out.

When Enkidu comes into Uruk, he finds the palace and city overwhelming. Gilgamesh is attracted to Enkidu but unimpressed. The man can fight but has no history, connections, or desire to dominate.

They grapple with each other but slowly start to understand each other and fall in love.

When an attacker attempts to assassinate Gilgamesh's and Shamhat's son, Usun, Enkidu helps save the boy.

Enkidu joins Gilgamesh on a campaign against another king and intercedes when Gilgamesh acts cruelly. In a fight after, Enkidu shares that someone attacked Usun and calls the King out for his thoughtless actions.

Gilgamesh is distraught over how little control he has. He decides he and Enkidu should fight the dragon, Humbaba.

Doing so nearly costs them both their lives, and Gilgamesh realizes his mother's prophecy was about Enkidu. Desperate to save him, Gilgamesh calls on his mother and vows to give up his legacy if it will spare Enkidu.

After they've recovered, Gilgamesh asks Enkidu to make the divine vow with him. He knows this will anger Inanna and expects her to take his life.

On the night they're celebrating the New Year and their vow, Inanna attacks. Her father, Anu, sends the Bull of Heaven into the palace's courtyard. Gilgamesh and Enkidu work together to defeat the bull.

Inanna, angered, says death is too easy a punishment for Gilgamesh. Instead, she curses Enkidu saying he will die in one year's time.

GLOSSARY

- **Lugal**: King
- **Nin:** Honorific for an esteemed woman such as a goddess, queen, or princess
- **Ensi:** Honorific for a prince or governor
- **Dumu:** Son
- **Adda:** Father
- **Ama:** Mother
- **Shed:** Sumerian curse word equivalent to 'shit'
- **Urmah:** Lion

"Hold my hand in yours, and we will not fear what hands like ours can do."

-The Epic of Gilgamesh

CHAPTER ONE

CURSED

ENKIDU DASHED AWAY from a slashing blade, slamming into the stone wall with a grunt. The ache in his hip told him he'd pulled the scars from Humbaba's attack. That wouldn't stop him, though. He dove forward, knocking his opponent's sword away.

Usun dropped, rolled, and crashed into the wall before snatching up his practice weapon. He jumped back to his feet and charged towards Enkidu.

A smile slid up Enkidu's lips as he caught the boy's blow with his blade. They circled each other, the clatter of their weapons and their heavy breathing the loudest sounds in the empty courtyard.

Enkidu had worked with Usun on sword work for weeks, always in that quiet space where few others from the palace roamed. The humming chatter of a thousand lives beyond the courtyard walls reached them, but it did nothing to tame the wildness inside. Vines tangled around each other, violet flowers bloomed, and a fountain trickled behind overgrown bushes.

Usun sprung forward and slammed Enkidu's fingers

with his weapon's side so he dropped the sword. Enkidu caught the weapon with his opposite hand and slammed it forward so the edge pressed to the boy's throat.

For a moment, the child breathed heavily against the practice blade before he smirked and took a step back. Then he bowed, nose to knee, and rose with an arm swiping sweat away from his forehead. "That was impressive."

"Same to you, Usun. You're a strong swordsman."

The boy's cheeks colored, but he looked away, his dark eyes reflecting the sky's pale blue. "Not as strong as the King."

He turned and walked over to a set of mugs they'd left on the fountain's edge. Usun lifted one and took a swallow. Enkidu paused a moment before joining him. Usun was so much like his father. He had the same broad shoulders and thick, dark hair. And the same stubborn-ass response to avoiding his emotions.

"I'd say the King has had a few more years' experience with a blade than you have."

Usun nodded but his gaze remained distant. "Plus, he has god's blood."

Enkidu dropped against the wall so he leaned next to the child. Hurt tinged the edges of the boy's voice, and the smooth surface of his eyes shone. "Your father considers god's blood to be a curse." They'd discussed that several times since Inanna's revenge had been announced. Since she'd decreed Enkidu would die after one more year of life. Enkidu shuddered. "Whether or not you surpass your father, you'll best me within a year."

Which was a good thing as Enkidu didn't have more time left than that. Already days had slipped away. Each one felt like a gift and a curse. They never lasted long enough. No amount of sacrifices, gifts, or pleas had roused

Inanna to speak with Gilgamesh. After he'd vowed himself to Enkidu, destroying her plans to have an heir to Uruk's throne, she'd unleashed the Bull of Heaven on them and seethed when they'd defeated the beast. She'd keep her word and kill Enkidu before another year bloomed.

A season passed him by that he'd never experience again. He'd tasted meals he'd never have again. Watched sunsets that were gone forever. Spring already unfolded, new plants blossoming that would fall fallow again soon. Plants Enkidu would never see again.

Usun crossed his arms. "I shall never outmatch the King."

The boy's posture was stiff, his gaze far off. He didn't believe himself worthy of being Gilgamesh's son, or maybe doubted his father loved him. Gilgamesh avoided the child out of his fear that Inanna would harm him as she'd done Enkidu. So, his father's fears weren't misplaced.

Privately, though, Gilgamesh's gaze would go distant when he spoke of Usun, his tone shifting deeper and more reverent. He loved the child but refused to express it. The cost of Inanna's potential wrath was too steep a price. They both suffered for Gilgamesh's refusal to pay it.

"I wouldn't be too certain of that." Enkidu bumped his shoulder into Usun's. "Let yourself come into your full adult strength before you judge."

"I won't find out, anyway. My father never spends time with me." The boy stood, pulling away. Enkidu frowned. He wasn't usually so distant or prickly. Time passed for him as well. His childhood clung to him like a spider web he passed through. Soon the last remnants would fall away.

Enkidu jumped up and closed the gap between them again. Selfishly, it was a relief to not worry about his impending doom for a few minutes, to focus on someone else's troubles. He gripped Usun's shoulder. "Your father seems distant, but it's not because he wants to be. He wishes to protect you."

Usun jutted his jaw up the same way his mother did. "Can't he see I'm not a child anymore?"

"I'm not a father." Enkidu took a deep breath. "I imagine, though, that one's offspring will always feel somewhat like a child to his parents no matter how old he grows. Your father loves you, Usun. I wish he could say it to you himself."

Usun softened, his arms dropping. He nodded and shifted away then ran fingers back through his tangled curls. "Thanks, Enkidu."

He smiled as the boy lifted the practice sword and tucked it into the shelter where they stored them. "I have to go. My stupid scribing lessons are today."

"Best not be late."

Usun shrugged but bounded forward, only to stop and turn back. He waved and a wide smile stretched across his face before he tumbled ahead. Childhood and adulthood yanked on Usun, both wanting dominance. Moods rushed over him then washed away, leaving the eager-eyed boy once again.

Enkidu chuckled and placed his practice sword in place as well. Moving back out of the shelter and into the sunlight, Enkidu sighed. He'd never had a childhood. Fate had only allowed him to experience a thin slice of life. There were no comforting memories to reflect on, and now no future to look forward to either.

Mosaics shimmered in gleaming sunlight. Enkidu lifted his face to the sun's warmth, Utu's light shimmering over his skin. He'd helped Gilgamesh and Enkidu after Humbaba nearly killed them. Enkidu's fingers rose to his tunic, and he scraped them across the scar through the fabric.

No god would intervene now, though. Inanna was the daughter of the sky deity, Anu, and therefore untouchable.

Her will would play out, and Enkidu could do nothing about it besides resign himself to his damned fate.

Gilgamesh couldn't stop it either, but that didn't keep him from trying. Where Enkidu was content to float with a current, allowing it to take him where it might, Gilgamesh would fight until his muscles gave out.

They'd end up in the same location either way.

Enkidu reached the courtyard's damaged section where the Bull of Heaven rampaged. Already workers had erected a new wall. It stretched across the yard, yet undecorated. While construction happened, gardeners let it grow wilder. They'd removed the shattered tiles and smashed plants. If Enkidu bent down and ran his fingers through grass, though, he could still find glimmering specks that lingered from that night's destruction.

It had started as such a perfect evening. Gilgamesh had vowed himself to Enkidu—forever. They'd stumbled into the courtyard drunk and warm and happy. Gilgamesh had pressed him against a wall, kissed him sloppily, and Enkidu had slid fingers down his back.

Then Inanna appeared. She'd ripped Gilgamesh from his grasp, sliced into his love's flesh like sand. Blood coursed down his muscles. Then they'd fought the bull creature.

They won.

Or so he'd thought.

Enkidu reached the wall and stretched his fingers over it.

"There you are."

Enkidu turned to face Akkiru who walked towards him, the layers of his kaunake kilt whipping around in the wind. His clean-shaven head gleamed in the midday light.

"Have you been looking for me?"

Akkiru grinned. "I have. Palace gossip says you're helping train Usun here. He's becoming quite the fighter."

"His father's proud of him." It needed saying. Perhaps he should have said as much to Usun. The boy wouldn't believe it, though, not if he didn't see it in his father's actions. Enkidu's gaze followed the trail Usun had taken out the courtyard. "Even if the King can't say so."

Akkiru nodded as he stepped into a shady spot beneath a palm tree. "Are you free this afternoon?"

"When am I not free?" Enkidu huffed a breath but tried to stop it with a smile which probably gave the effect of him baring his teeth in a growl rather than the peaceful expression intended. "I suppose I understand what you meant now, when you shared about giving up your role for love."

Before, Enkidu had filled his days with working as an advisor for Gilgamesh. Now that they were known lovers, he couldn't do so without causing issues. Gilgamesh had sat on the bed when he'd explained the situation to Enkidu, then jumped up to pace, then dropped on the mattress again. When he finally spoke, Enkidu had only chuckled. Of course he couldn't have his lover among his advisors. It was much like Akkiru giving up his position among the musicians when he began a relationship with the Queen and their other partner, Meritkara.

Akkiru leaned on the tree. "I suppose the King can't have the man he shares a bed with publicly helping him make decisions for the city."

Warmth swept across Enkidu's nose. "Of course not."

"What if I teach you music?" Akkiru grinned as he vaulted up.

"You mean how to play something?" When he nodded, Enkidu frowned. "I'm not sure. I doubt there's any point being that I have such little time left."

Silence drifted between them. In the distance someone shouted, drums pounded, a donkey brayed. Enkidu had given voice to the unspoken—the thing everyone talked around. He'd grown tired, nearly dizzy with how others avoided it. *Just speak honestly.* He'd die at the end of the year. Neither his stubborn lover's relentless pursuit to avoid it nor others pretending it wasn't true changed that.

Enkidu was hungry to drink up every taste of life he could swallow. The only thing after life was the Great Below. In less than a year, Enkidu would become a shade of his former self, doomed to spend eternity in a cold, dark cave filled with sorrowful souls. A shudder slipped down his body and he curled his toes in his boots to fight it. Thinking about the dreadful future didn't change it.

Akkiru cocked his head. "Who can say how much time any of us have, really? I mean, I could drop dead from heart weakness tomorrow. Would that make learning a new skill today a waste?" Enkidu's lips pinched into a frown, but he couldn't argue. People died unexpectedly. His fate had given him the gift—or curse—of time. "Life is for the living, Enkidu. Not one of us can number the days we have remaining."

I can. He kept that thought to himself, however. Along a far wall, a broken mosaic of the dragon-creature, Humbaba stretched out. The bull's attack had broken bits of its body away, but its fiery eyes remained. Enkidu thought he'd die when fighting the creature; had planned on it. He hadn't regretted his choice for a moment. He would have thrown his body over Gilgamesh's a hundred more times without hesitation.

Akkiru's voice went soft. "I just believe we should make the most of the days we have." He jerked his face up, and his expression brightened again. "Besides, with the way the King relentlessly pursues avoiding this curse, I think you'll remain among the living for a long time. He is worrying Shamhat to an early tomb, though."

Enkidu breathed a laugh. Gilgamesh always pushed forward with his ambitions, and Shamhat attempted to smooth down his edges. He wasn't one to be tamed, though. The smile lingered. Akkiru's eyes twinkled and the hopelessness that had surrounded them flitted away. It was no wonder Shamhat loved him so dearly. He had a point, besides.

No god had offered a promise of life when he'd thrown his body over Gilgamesh, sacrificing himself to save the man when Humbaba attacked. Yet fate—the directions the gods wove the world with—gave him several more seasons with the man he loved. Perhaps the same kind divinity watched him now and prepared to intercede once more. He had to cling to that hope and not allow his impending death to shape the entire year.

He turned his face towards Akkiru. "What instrument do you think I'd be good at?"

Akkiru grinned again and gestured for Enkidu to follow him back towards the palace.

CHAPTER TWO
BLOOD OMENS

BLOOD HIT THE GROUND, splattering Gilgamesh's boots and staining the hem of Shamhat's tunic. Gilgamesh frowned as the diviner finished slitting the lamb open, its entrails spilling out onto the stone. He crossed his arms. Already his injury had healed from the Bull of Heaven's attack thanks to his divine heritage burning through his veins.

The sun set in the distance, bleeding red across the sky to match the temple roof's gory setting. Guards stood at the corners, their eyes trained towards the city. The rest of the roof's expanse was empty, and it made the blood's splashing seem louder. A wrinkle curled Shamhat's nose, but she otherwise didn't react as the diviner plunged his hand into the creature and pulled out the liver, his eyebrows pushing together as he weighed it.

The diviner continued shuffling through the blood and tissues. His eyes dashed up once. Then a second time.

"Well?" Gilgamesh asked.

"It's difficult to comprehend Anu's will sometimes, my king."

Gilgamesh stared down at the pitiful man. Gods did he

hate diviners. They'd always affronted him with their paltry attempts to speak to the gods. As if Gilgamesh, divinely born, would need their intercession. Now he found himself desperate. If the last weeks had been more fruitful in his search—his desperate hunt for any method to break Enkidu's curse—he never would have employed one. The diviner sat up. His elbows dripped blood as he stared at his king. A bead of sweat coursed over his brow and he swallowed.

"That sounds suspiciously like you don't wish to tell me what you've seen, diviner." Gilgamesh attempted to keep his voice level. Attempted it but failed. The words came out clipped, snapping like bones breaking.

Shamhat moved, closing the gap between their arms, bumping into him. She wanted him to go easier on the man. Gilgamesh had paid for this *holy* man to give him a word from the divine, though. Now he withheld unfavorable news—or he had nothing to say because he was a fraud.

Gilgamesh's hold on his god's powers loosened, and the man trembled beneath their weight.

"The g-gods," the diviner choked out, "act as they please, Lugal. All I can do is interpret what I see. Us mortals can't control gods' actions."

"Mortal," Gilgamesh whispered. "Have you forgotten who you stand before?"

Shamhat poked him in the ribs. He clenched his teeth but didn't meet her gaze. This impertinent charlatan was going to give him some godsdamned answers.

"Of course not, my king." The man stumbled and bowed over the lamb several times. Blood coursed down his arms, reaching his tunic's sleeves and staining them. "I would never forget how blessed I am to work for the great god-king Gilgamesh, son of the mighty Lugalbanda and the eternal Ninsun, builder of grand walls, and defeater of divine monsters. I'm not worthy to stand in your presence, Lugal. Forgive me—I hesitate only because the answer is not what you hope for."

Gilgamesh sighed and let his eyes drift closed. Enkidu had once teased him with the same addresses, with his status he'd loved to drape like a shawl around himself. He'd deserved the mockery. For too long, he'd seen himself as divine. Now he felt as mortal as the man accused him of being, so helpless. When he'd angered Inanna, he'd expected his death. That he could have accepted. Enkidu's demise, though? His breath caught in his chest. His foolishness would cost him a person he loved far more than life.

He opened his eyes. Shamhat stood with her chin raised, her gold-decorated headpiece glimmering over her forehead. Her gaze remained fixed on the diviner who still glistened crimson.

Gilgamesh had a reputation.

Once that had meant everything.

Now it was river mud. Sloughed away by cruel gods.

"Are there no other gods willing to intervene?" Gilgamesh asked. Shamhat shifted again. It was like she positioned herself to support her husband. What a ridiculous notion. But he didn't pull away.

The diviner looked back towards the sunset then returned to his king and queen with trembling, stained hands. "From what I can see," he said carefully, "even immortals fear the goddess who has cast this curse. Who might defy her and live?"

Shamhat's forehead furrowed. Gilgamesh had said to her a few months before that things could only change when someone would stand up to Inanna. He'd meant that regarding Usun. He longed to spare him the goddess' wrath. Then Gilgamesh intended to sacrifice his own life. Never did he think Inanna would curse Enkidu instead.

The diviner's mouth gaped and closed, his skin graying which gave him the appearance of a dying fish. Shamhat jabbed Gilgamesh's side again. He blinked. He'd been glaring at the man like he prepared to cast divine judgment.

"Very well, diviner. Hirin waits for you with payment."

"T-thank you, Lugal." The man's hair swept forward with his stumbling bow. "My queen." Another nod to her then he turned and nearly ran.

The entrails stained the roof, blood creeping across tiles and spreading between the cracks. What a waste of a creature. Shamhat kept tight eyes on the diviner until he'd disappeared, then she crossed her arms.

"Speak whatever is on your mind, my queen."

Her gaze didn't break. "I didn't say anything was on my mind."

"Not with your words. Your posture, however, screams at me." She dashed her face in his direction. "And if your eyes were weapons, they would cleave meat from my bones. Perhaps you could pull my liver free and find answers the gods refuse to offer."

Her lips furled in, and she turned back towards the pink-tinted city. Darkness spilled across the top of the sky, promising night's impending arrival.

A wind whipped her shawl around her shoulders. It was three breaths later, and with a wrinkled brow, that she turned back to him. "Have you considered what happens if we don't discover the answer you seek?"

Her words smacked into him, and he gasped. "What do you expect me to do? Give up?"

Bowing her head, she removed her headpiece and

twirled a golden disc on it between her fingers. "We've angered a goddess. Her words are law, Gilgamesh."

"I'm aware." Inanna had breathed that damn curse, rewoven fate, and the world shifted. No other gods would answer Gilgamesh's prayers. When he'd made an offering at Nanna's temple in gratitude for his help with defeating the Bull of Heaven, the incense burned brighter. But Nanna didn't show himself. Not even Gilgamesh's mother, Ninsun, would reply to his pleas. She wouldn't even speak to him currently.

Inanna enacted a curse.

Other gods wouldn't get in the way.

They had their own relationships and dramas to balance. One mortal life meant little if it kept Inanna appeased. To the gods, Enkidu meant nothing. Even Gilgamesh's rage and wrath held little sway. They could crush him in an instant and the people wouldn't dissent. They were gods, after all, it was expected that they dominated mortal lives, sometimes with devastating impacts. Yet, other gods were stronger than Inanna, older. If any of them would speak against her, they could change fate. Not one was willing, however, so Gilgamesh would have to find a way to shift it himself.

Shamhat's lips parted. They shimmered coral in the light. "What if," she whispered, "you accept things as they are?"

"You mean accept that Enkidu is going to die?" he growled. The world had tilted sideways since Enkidu's curse. Since he'd watched realization spark in the man's eyes and his shoulders hunch as he understood the damning Gilgamesh had caused him.

Raising her face, Shamhat swallowed. "Yes." A wobble had entered her voice, a gleam spreading across her eyes, but she didn't look away. Gilgamesh's nose flared, and he curled his hands into fists. How dare she suggest he give up and allow the curse to play out. She lifted her chin and continued. "I'm so sorry for it. But what if you enjoy the time you have left instead of chasing hopeless cures that don't exist?"

"You're serious?" He lifted his hands before him like he could show her how empty they were. Life would lose its meaning if he lost Enkidu, and she suggested he embrace that hideous future. How could she possibly believe that was an acceptable response? "I will not. If you think I wouldn't fight just as relentlessly for you, you're mistaken. How can I stop trying if I have breath left in my lungs? How can I sit back and give up if there's even a scrap of hope, Shamhat?"

"I understand grief," she said through her teeth. "I lost my entire family when I should have had years left with them. My parents should have known their grandson. Instead, they're gone." Tears filled her eyes and one slipped down her cheek, curved along her lip. Wind cut across the empty roof, fluttering her curls. "Maybe there's a hope embedded in this. You can love Enkidu while he's still with us and not live with regrets of things left unsaid."

Gilgamesh heaved a breath. His tunic grated his flesh, and he wanted to rip it off or punch a wall. "Because I love him, I will fight for him."

Shamhat cleared her throat and swiped fingers over her cheeks. "You're not the only one who cares for him, you know? Akkiru has grown closer to him. And Usun spends some time with him every day. He's grown rather fond of the man."

Gilgamesh looked away, back towards the palace that hunched beneath the sunset. How he wished he could spend time with his son. This was the reason he'd avoided doing so, though. Inanna only cared for her glory, and she slaughtered anyone that stood in her way. If she'd thought for a moment he favored his son, she'd end him too. At least Usun had a family in Shamhat and her partners, support from mentors, and teaching from warriors like Abgal and now Enkidu. Usun had a community even if Gilgamesh couldn't be part of it.

His entire life, Gilgamesh had sacrificed everything. As much as he loved Shamhat, he'd married her for the city's sake. He had no relationship with his son, few friends, and his connections with people in the palace were mostly based on fear. He kept himself distant from everyone to protect them. Then the gods gave him Enkidu whom Shamhat had prayed for. Now she wanted him to release the man, the only person he'd ever been able to love intimately in every way. She mentioned their son who could be in the same position if Gilgamesh had ever turned a glimpse of attention in his direction.

"This is exactly what I wished to avoid for Usun. If Our Lady in Heaven"—he spat Inanna's title and didn't care what divine heard his rage—"had cursed him, would you ask me to stop seeking a cure?"

Shamhat turned fully to face him. She wore gold and purple fabric that whipped around her form. She held her posture upright, and her jewelry gleamed. "How can we fight the gods, Gilgamesh?"

"I must try."

A sigh left his wife. Turning her face away, she leaned towards the sun as though she reached for the god who gleamed the last of his light across them. A dozen heartbeats passed, the city's chittering filling the space. Then Shamhat walked over to her husband and took his hand. The gentle weight of her thumb swept over his knuckles. "All right. If you must do this, then know I'll support you. If you need this next year to attempt to defy the gods, I'll give you my blessing to pursue it. But I think it's foolish, Gilgamesh."

He clutched her palm. She disagreed. She'd always been the wiser of the two of them, the one less willing to take brash risks. However, she'd stand beside him while he took one. She loved him, even when he acted the fool. "I've killed two divine creatures. Maybe, if I try hard enough, I can achieve the impossible again."

Her shoulders rose with a breath and she loosed it like trees gave up leaves. "Maybe." She reached up and brushed his cheek then turned and walked away.

* * *

A headache pinched at Gilgamesh's temple, and he unclenched his teeth as he stopped before his bedroom door. Torches flickered down the hall, glistening along mosaics. Guards stood with spears in hand.

The King took a slow breath that lifted his chest. He needed to bring his emotions back under control. He couldn't let defeat show with slumping shoulders and a pinched brow. The curse had already come between Enkidu and him. Now everything they said seemed to have double meanings and they danced around discussing the future like it was made of flames. If he walked in demoralized, it would ignite the painful feelings, causing fissures.

He stepped into the room and clicked the door shut behind him. Enkidu sat on a couch with one leg tucked under the other. Despite his bulk, he moved through the world gracefully. Gilgamesh's focus would have remained on Enkidu's thick muscles, how the dark hair on his arms gleamed, the curve of his horns sweeping back into his curls, and the long line of his neck.

Except the man was playing a flute.

Terribly.

Enkidu mercifully stopped the squealing attempt at music and lifted his eyes.

Those godsdamned beautiful eyes which held the forest's colors—dark cedar and shimmering lakes and spring grass.

Gilgamesh leaned on the wall. "Where did you get that?"

A laugh huffed out of Enkidu, and his hair rustled around his shoulders. Gilgamesh would love to tangle fingers into the locks, use the leverage to pull Enkidu's lips to his.

"Akkiru has convinced me to learn to play."

Gilgamesh couldn't help the smile sliding up his face. He shouldn't have bothered with trying to improve his mood and putting on a facade. Being in Enkidu's presence lifted him naturally. "Did he?"

Enkidu looked up from under his brow. "You think it's a waste of time don't you? I thought so myself but let Akkiru talk me into it."

Pain twisted through Gilgamesh's chest like a god's hand clenched his heart. Enkidu thought it a waste because he believed he'd die in less than a year. Soon, the gods would rip him from Gilgamesh's grasp, throwing him into the ghostly Great Below to suffer alone. Gilgamesh wanted to rage and scream and break temples. He wanted to destroy every god who was complicit. Losing Enkidu was going to take something from him that he couldn't regain.

That wouldn't happen if Gilgamesh had any ability to alter fate, though.

"I think it's a good use of time."

Enkidu frowned down at the flute. "I sound ridiculous, be honest."

Gilgamesh stepped across the rug and pressed a hand on the wall so he looked down at the man. "Actually, I'm thinking of the number of jokes I could make currently."

"Because my attempt is awful." Despite his words, Enkidu's voice had grown thick. The space between them warmed.

Gilgamesh leaned closer but didn't touch him yet. He wanted to tease them both, draw out their twining desires as long as he could. "No, love. It's because your lips look wonderful wrapped around that instrument."

Color flushed Enkidu's cheeks as Gilgamesh had expected. Enkidu chucked the flute to the other side of the couch. "Well you've ruined that activity for me forever."

Gilgamesh's brows shot up. "A shame for me if that's the truth." Enkidu laughed then clenched his fist into the King's tunic and pulled him closer. Their mouths nearly touched, a whisper of breath spreading between them. Enkidu didn't move, though. He seemed to want to drag it out too, to let the heat build until they burned.

"You weren't at dinner." Gilgamesh's voice had filled with gravel.

Enkidu's fingers slipped, sliding over his collarbone. "I ate with Akkiru and Meritkara, actually."

"Have you abandoned me for Shamhat's partners?"

Enkidu trailed thick fingers into Gilgamesh's beard. All the King wanted was for the man to undo the curls in it, tug at it as their bodies slid together.

"I heard you spoke with a diviner today." Enkidu's eyes

flashed, and he dropped the hand. Losing his touch was like the curse playing out. Gilgamesh leaned closer to stall his retreat. He couldn't bear it.

Enkidu wanted him to stop searching for answers.

But Gilgamesh wanted forever with the man. His legacy, his fame, his deeds? Those could perish. Everyone wanted him to give up challenging the curse, but he wouldn't. Even if he was the only one willing to fight.

Enkidu's long lashes batted his cheeks, and he shifted away, his voice going soft. "Did you learn anything?"

Something curled the edges of his words, made them as delicate as a lake's surface. One stone of discouraging information and he'd shatter. So, Enkidu hoped after all. He'd acted in the last days as though he accepted his unfair fate. He'd told Gilgamesh they should give up. Yet, his voice betrayed him.

Gilgamesh swept an errant strand of hair behind the man's ear. "I've learned diviners are every bit as useless as I suspected them to be before the meeting."

Enkidu's shoulders dropped, his eyes darkening. He parted his lips to speak again. Whatever he'd say would be filled with bitter acceptance, the sorrow-tinged tone he'd used since Inanna had cursed him.

Gilgamesh grabbed his jaw, lifted his face, and kissed him. He didn't want to hear defeat coarsen the silky rumble of his voice. He'd save Enkidu if he had to fight the gods himself to achieve it. No one and nothing would cause him to believe otherwise.

Enkidu's lips parted until his mouth warmed Gilgamesh's. He leaned closer and curled fingers behind his neck. Heartbeats pounded into Gilgamesh's palm.

But how many of those did Enkidu have left?

An innumerable amount for the moment, but there

would come a point where only a hundred remained, only a dozen.

Would Gilgamesh know when the last beats echoed against his skin?

Enkidu sighed and leaned back. His eyes sparkled, and he tangled his fingers into Gilgamesh's beard, pulled him forward to bruise his mouth once more.

"No more talk for now," Gilgamesh said as he disentangled himself and grabbed Enkidu, pulling him to his feet. Those forest-colored eyes watched him with the devotion of a high priest. Gilgamesh wanted to devour him. To not speak or think of death but only feel the man warm and alive against him.

He tugged him past his sitting room and towards the bed.

CHAPTER THREE
A MESSAGE

ENKIDU TUCKED his hands behind his back as he and Gilgamesh passed guards in the palace halls. Gilgamesh's eyes slipped to him and glistened with desire. Or love. Maybe both. For a moment, his expression was free from the desperation and hopelessness that crowned him since the curse. Enkidu's stomach warmed.

They'd only left Gilgamesh's room moments before, but already he longed to grab his hand, lead him back. The King's freshly styled curls in his beard gleamed as they passed a torch. His earrings and necklaces shone.

Undoing all his finery would cause another hour of attendants putting it together again. Gilgamesh hated others styling him, despised sitting while they twisted the coils and rubbed lotions into his skin.

So, Enkidu kept his hands to himself. One touch from him and Gilgamesh would capitulate. That would push his agenda back, though. They walked towards the soldiers' training grounds, and it occurred to Enkidu that Gilgamesh could use the exercise's release.

"You should join me," he said, "the next time I spar with Usun."

Gilgamesh's eyes darted towards Enkidu again, this time with a sharpness that made Enkidu feel a pinch of annoyance. Their footsteps echoed around the hall. "You know I cannot. In fact,"—he turned his face towards Enkidu, and the sadness returned—"you've experienced why I can't. I was foolish to risk you."

His lips furled into a thin line, and his expression darkened. Enkidu reached for his arm. Bringing up Usun held the risk of stoking Gilgamesh's anger. That Enkidu could face. He hadn't expected him to follow it back to his grief instead.

"You weren't. I wanted to be with you—still want to be with you. It's worth the cost." Gilgamesh's frown deepened, and Enkidu continued. "Even knowing how things have turned out, if I could go back, I'd still choose to love you."

His words were true. If given the opportunity to slide back through time's currents, he would change nothing. He'd throw himself before Humbaba to save Gilgamesh again without hesitating. Even on the night of the curse, Gilgamesh had told him to go but he'd stayed. If he had a chance to repeat the evening and alter his actions, he'd remain there and face the goddess' wrath. It was as Akkiru said, after all. He could die tomorrow from some mortal malaise. Whatever time he had, he wished to spend with Gilgamesh.

However, he nearly preferred the arrogant, preening Gilgamesh who faced a goddess with fire in his eyes to this anxious, distracted version. Gilgamesh would spend the next year ceaselessly searching for answers to save him. That was a miserable prospect.

"Usun is a child." Gilgamesh stared straight ahead. His

voice had belted itself up, straightened its back. He used the tone that directed his men into battle or levied punishments. It was his tone that implied he wasn't to be argued with. There was nothing in the world that made Enkidu desire to argue more than that tone. "He isn't old enough to make foolish decisions that get him damned by some vindictive goddess."

"He won't be a child much longer." Enkidu's words came with a bite he didn't intend. If Gilgamesh wanted to criticize Enkidu's choices, he could do so directly. That argument had teemed in the background for days. Enkidu wasn't giving in to the distraction and shifting the conversation away from Usun. "And what he wants—what your son wants—more than anything is a relationship with you."

Gilgamesh's brow bunched, and he parted his lips to speak, but an advisor turned the corner, walking in their direction.

Hirin stopped then bowed low twice. During his prostration, Gilgamesh's gaze glided towards the doorway that led to the courtyard. They'd been so close to making it to their destination before something disrupted them. Hirin rose. "Lugal, forgive me for interrupting you, but I think I've found an answer."

Gilgamesh snapped his chin up. "To the curse?"

Hirin nodded and glanced at Enkidu who had grown as still as a statue. He'd never imagined they'd actually find an answer. It had all felt like a tremendous waste of time. Now hope dangled before him. If he could gather time, then he could find some purpose in his life, something that might make him worthy to be Gilgamesh's partner, might make his existence worth its weight.

He held his breath as Gilgamesh spoke. "Good, good. Tell us at once."

Hirin pulled a clay tablet from a bag. The gold discs adorning his sash clattered together. "It's a conjecture, my king. I hope I haven't lifted your hopes prematurely. But we've unearthed an ancient tablet that tells the direction Utnapishtim traveled after the gods bequeathed him with eternal life."

Gilgamesh accepted the tablet. It was rough edged, the marks softened with age. Enkidu continued holding his breath, unwilling to give in to any feelings yet, as Gilgamesh skimmed the writing. The only human the gods had ever given the secret to immortality to was Utnapishtim. Gilgamesh hated that ancestor of his and found the man's life a waste. The gods granted Utnapishtim and his wife immortality after they'd built a boat and saved humanity, animals, and seeds from a great flood. All they'd done with their eternity, however, was travel away and hide. Gilgamesh could never respect someone who ran when they could do something, especially his distant relative. Perhaps Utnapishtim might hold life's secrets, though.

"More importantly," Hirin continued, "this tablet implies that Utnapishtim received more than just immortal life. The gods also bequeathed him with divine powers."

Gilgamesh released a breath that echoed in the hall then brushed his thumb along a line. "If we find him, he could help Enkidu. He's my ancestor, my blood."

Dread crawled up Enkidu's throat, burning it. Utnapishtim lived in the gods' territory. Even knowing only a little about it from the songs the musicians sang in the children's courtyard, he understood it was dangerous, a place no human ever traversed.

"It seems possible, Lugal. At least, it's the best hope

we've had so far." Hirin cleared his throat. Readjusted his sleeve. "You can see, though, that he retreated into divine lands. No mortal can travel there."

Gilgamesh lifted his face. "Ah, but Enkidu and I are not mere mortals."

"Just as I thought, my king. You could both travel there and—"

"No."

The advisor and Gilgamesh turned towards Enkidu.

The journey into divine territory sounded dangerous and would consume precious time Gilgamesh didn't have to spare. Hirin spoke true—this was conjecture and a wild one at that. Utnapishtim was Gilgamesh's blood, but that didn't ensure he'd help them. It was possible the man didn't have divine abilities at all. Besides, the chances they'd survive a journey into divine territory were low.

"You can't leave right now and certainly not for my sake."

Gilgamesh's countenance darkened. He stared at Enkidu. Someone stepped into the hall, froze as their gaze met the King's, bowed hastily then turned and walked away. Torches flickered. Gilgamesh took a deep breath and handed the tablet back to his advisor. "Let Enkidu and I speak alone, Hirin."

The man accepted it, wrapping it in a cloth as he bowed low. "O-of course, my king."

He scurried away as Gilgamesh stared at Enkidu. A fire burned in his eyes. Not the roaring flames of something fresh, but hot coals that had simmered for days. With a few nudges they could spark into something greater, something that could consume the world.

When the hall had grown silent again, Gilgamesh's jaw

worked. "What do you mean, no? This is the closest thing we've had to finding an answer."

Enkidu fisted his hands then flexed them. "How long would this journey take? If we could even find the location."

"I don't know. If the distance is what I'm estimating, perhaps three to four moons to get there then—"

"You'd lose another year of your son's life." Traveling and risking everything didn't guarantee Enkidu's salvation. If anything, it gambled Gilgamesh's life as well. Chances were they'd never make it to Utnapishtim but languish at the hand of some divine monster along the way. Even Gilgamesh's mother wouldn't intervene after Inanna's curse. If they took this journey, they'd do so alone.

"As I told you," Gilgamesh bit out, "that relationship will never happen. I can't connect with him without endangering him, and I won't risk it. Had I been wise, I never would have endangered you, but I did. Now I must try to fix my error."

Enkidu straightened to his full height and looked at him directly in his flashing brown eyes. "I believe I have a right to say what I want out of this relationship. I've told you several times that I knew the risks and chose you anyway."

"Is that supposed to comfort me? Is it supposed to bring me peace, understanding that you believed I would destroy you when we met?"

"That is not what I said." Their voices echoed as they rose in volume. Enkidu wanted to grip the man's arms and shake him. Or maybe press their mouths together until he swallowed his arrogance and prickling pride away. Gods, was the man infuriating. And gods, did Enkidu love him despite that.

"What do you want, then? Do you wish to give up? To lie here in defeat and let the gods win?"

"We aren't gods, Gilgamesh." Enkidu stepped closer. "We've come up against those we cannot defeat. It's not foolish of me to acknowledge our limitations."

Gilgamesh bared his teeth in a growl and turned away. "You're just giving in to fear. This isn't like you."

The comment hit with an intensity, like Gilgamesh had smacked him and blood fought its way to the surface. "You don't even know what I'd choose on my own. I've vowed to follow you, which I've done." Gilgamesh turned around, his brows pulled together, but Enkidu didn't let him speak. "I've stood at your side facing impossible odds and divine creatures. But this is about me, and I have a right to decide. Wasting a year of your life to—"

"It wouldn't be a waste." Gilgamesh moved closer to Enkidu. Close enough that even in the hall's dim light, Enkidu could make out the fine lines on his lips, the curl of his lashes.

Their breathing echoed between them, and Enkidu leaned closer so their noses brushed. He wanted to give in to the touch, but he couldn't forget why the time mattered. "For your son it would be a waste. For Shamhat. Even for the city. Are you thinking of anyone else's desires?"

Gilgamesh's nose flared. "I'm thinking of yours."

"Are you? Because it sure as shed doesn't feel like you're hearing a damn thing I'm saying."

Gilgamesh stepped forward, pressing Enkidu back against the wall. Their knees grazed, their hips, their chests. The coals in his eyes sparked to life. "Oh, I've been listening. I keep hearing you say you're going to quit. That you aren't even willing to try."

Enkidu wouldn't burn and yell like Gilgamesh. Instead, he whispered. "If that is what you hear, then you truly haven't listened to one fucking thing I've told you."

Gilgamesh took several deep breaths, growled through his teeth, then turned and stormed down the hall. Enkidu watched him go but didn't follow.

*　*　*

Enkidu moved through the palace like a boulder. People shifted out of his path, and he didn't acknowledge them. They were used to having a divinely touched being of his size storming through the halls—it wasn't usually him, though.

Now he burned like Gilgamesh had touched him with his fury until it bled into him. Gods, he loved the man, but he was stubborn and unable to look beyond his fucking nose.

Enkidu's hands trembled, and he longed to have something to fight, a tree to rip from the ground, a monster to slay.

Unfortunately, the palace surrounded him and Uruk beyond that. He couldn't wrestle or destroy without doing damage. Instead, he stormed through the endless halls like the god Enlil, crackling with energy he couldn't disburse.

He wove through the main courtyard, taking side paths. He never enjoyed crowds and especially not when emotions filled his chest until they spilled over with breaths that hissed between his teeth. Moving around the soldiers' practice yard, he found the quiet courtyard behind the palace.

The gardeners might consider it a travesty that it was so much wilder after the Bull of Heaven's damage, but Enkidu loved the change. It wasn't as peaceful as the forest, but it was still better than the rest of the palace and the damned noisy, unrelenting city.

Enkidu's head throbbed. He reached the middle of the

yard where knee high grasses grew and stepped between them, sinking into their cool touch.

Gilgamesh was ceaseless. This was what the gods had sent Enkidu to cure, and he'd failed. Now he'd die and Gilgamesh would continue roaring and gnashing his way through life. A prickling sensation crawled down Enkidu's arms, raising hair. In the end, he had no purpose. He'd failed the one aim the gods had given him.

A sound like rushing water had Enkidu looking back over his shoulder. He'd been caught in his own fury and worries, not paying attention. Once, Inanna had arrived when he'd been equally distracted.

He jumped to his feet as a goddess landed before him.

She took her human-like form, her dark curls resting on her shoulders as she lifted her chin to look up at Enkidu. Her hooved feet sank into the grass beneath them.

"Ninsun," Enkidu said.

Gilgamesh had called on his mother, prayed and begged for her to intercede or even just to appear. At night, in his and Enkidu's room, he'd growled over his frustrations with her. Now she stood before Enkidu, blinking in the sunlight.

"I can't intercede with another goddess' curse." Ninsun's voice was soft. "Gilgamesh wants something I cannot grant him. Seeing me will only hurt him more." She dropped her eyes towards the ground. Aside from those deep brown eyes, Gilgamesh hadn't inherited the features she maintained in her human-like body. Where she was slight and elegant, her movements flowing like the river, Gilgamesh drove through life like a beast, with decisive footsteps that shattered things beneath them. That's how he planned to continue forward in life, smashing and breaking and demanding.

A headache throbbed in Enkidu's temple even as

Ninsun's gentle voice echoed through his mind. "I'm not here for Gilgamesh's sake this time but for yours."

Enkidu lifted his face, his heart floating into his throat. Perhaps she'd found some way to break the curse. If he had time, he could change things, help Gilgamesh, find some purpose beyond being the King's tragic lover.

Ninsun's form shrank, like a riverbed drying up. "I'm sorry, Enkidu, that's not what I'm here to tell you."

Enkidu released a breath that whispered past his lips. He didn't know why he kept clinging to hope that there might be some answer. If even the gods wouldn't intercept, even Gilgamesh's mother wouldn't speak to her son because of the curse, then it was hopeless.

"The Wolf dies this week."

Enkidu snapped out of his thoughts like a whip cracked his flesh, pulling him back to the present. "Do you mean the wolf who—"

He didn't know how to finish that sentence. The Wolf hadn't raised him, precisely. Enkidu had been fully grown and able to provide for himself, to help the pack even. Yet, the Wolf had been his first mentor.

"Yes, that wolf."

Enkidu stepped back, crushing grass beneath his heel. "How can I prevent it?"

Ninsun blinked at him. Her features blurred, shifting into the wind before refocusing. "You cannot. His future is already woven."

A surging heat burned in Enkidu's stomach, rising up his throat. "Then why tell me this?"

"If you leave before sunset, you'll have time to see him again." The goddess rippled like she was fading.

"Wait. What of your son?" Enkidu didn't have time to process the news she'd brought him, but he could speak up for Gilgamesh's sake. Ninsun's eyes shimmered—with emotion or just a result of her vanishing into the elements Enkidu couldn't say.

The next moment Enkidu stood alone again, his arms outstretched towards an empty blue sky.

Shoulders dropping, he turned around. The shrubs and greenery tangling together in a breeze no longer comforted him. Ninsun had arrived to usher ill tidings he apparently had no ability to alter.

He should ignore it, stay in Uruk at Gilgamesh's side, and find some way to make the man understand the importance of avoiding this trip. Shifting around, Enkidu stretched on his toes where he could see outlines of hundreds of houses beyond the palace walls. The sun rose above it all with its rattling, buzzing noises.

Beyond the milling mass of humanity, an old friend faced his doom.

This was the last chance Enkidu would have to see him. Memories whispered through his mind. Lazy mornings, the lake sparkling like gemstones, dragonflies dancing over it, the Wolf with his red-streaked coat yawning and stretching out beside him.

The creature had given up much to look after him.

Enkidu couldn't forgo a last opportunity to see him.

He left the courtyard, returned to his and Gilgamesh's room, and packed a small bag. With it hefted over his shoulder, he walked to the throne room and approached one of the guards standing at the door. The man nodded. Beneath the helmet, his eyes glinted with recognition.

The guards and soldiers knew Enkidu now. Most of them had watched their king and Enkidu spar.

"I need to speak with the King." Enkidu tightened his grip on the bag.

"Of course." The guard turned towards the door.

"When he's finished, I mean. I don't need to interrupt."

The guard swiveled away from the massive doors and readjusted his spear. "As you wish, Ensi."

Enkidu nodded and moved farther down the hall to wait outside the guards' direct view. He readjusted the bag. He'd only packed a change of clothing and soap to freshen up with before returning to the city. In the forest he could find food and water. Beneath a star-studded sky, he could locate comfortable places to sleep.

Sunlight that fell in from high windows slowly moved across the floor. Enkidu shifted his weight from one foot to another. A guard walked up. "The King is ready to see you now."

Enkidu nodded and followed him then stepped through the massive doors. Gilgamesh sat on his throne next to Shamhat. They both gleamed in gold and purple. They'd already dismissed the advisors. As Enkidu walked up the long path, Gilgamesh jumped to his feet. "Enkidu?"

He stopped at the same spot all petitioners did, a respectful distance from the royals. Bowing then rising, he stood in the sunset's orange glow that spilled in through the open roof.

Gilgamesh nodded at Shamhat, who met Enkidu's eyes, bobbed her head, and exited with the remaining guards.

The King of Uruk removed his crown and shawl, placed them on his throne, and walked to meet Enkidu. He gleamed in the light's golden radiance. It was no wonder he saw himself as equal to the gods. With Utu's light illuminating his dark hair and glowing across his eyes, his muscles' curves revealed without the shawl, and the room emphasizing his height, he appeared divine. Despite their argument earlier, Enkidu's stomach warmed. He'd made love to his man, knew his body, listened to his worries and fears.

He saw Gilgamesh as no one else in the world had.

"Enkidu," he sighed, "about earlier—"

"I need to leave."

Chin snapping up, Gilgamesh's eyes flashed, and it wasn't from the sun's reflection. His gaze swept towards the bag Enkidu carried then back. "Have I angered you so much? I spoke foolishly, yes, but it's—"

"No, of course not." Enkidu winced. They stood close enough to touch yet both kept their hands at their sides. The distance between them felt as cold as he imagined the Great Below was. "Your mother appeared to me—not to offer any help with the curse." Gilgamesh's face brightened then shadowed in a heartbeat. "She informed me that an old friend of mine will die soon. I wish to see him."

"Then I'll go with you."

"No." Enkidu's daily time was flexible. Too flexible, in fact. He had nothing to fill the hours. Instead, he could practically hear time slipping away like leaves dropping from a tree. Gilgamesh, though, couldn't leave without causing hundreds of people issues. His trips required preparation and planning. "I leave within the hour." Already late afternoon light splashed over the walls. Ninsun had said if he left by sundown, he'd see the Wolf again. He couldn't risk wasting time. "You're needed here."

Wrinkles swept across Gilgamesh's brow. "You're leaving me?" Despite whispering the words, they carried, echoing off the massive statues that lined the hall.

Enkidu grabbed his hand, and he unfurled his fist slightly. "I vowed to you that I would stand at your side until the end. Have I ever broken a promise I've made to you?"

Gilgamesh's deep brown eyes glistened and his nose flared as he took a deep breath before answering. "Never."

"And I never will." Enkidu clenched his grip tighter, and Gilgamesh curled his fingers over his knuckles. Despite the touch, he felt distant. So many unspoken things swept between them—ghosts of things to come that Gilgamesh couldn't face. Maybe Enkidu was afraid to acknowledge them too. If they opened the jar they'd shoved all the fear and grief into, perhaps so much would spill out it would drown them. It would cause them to lose each other amid the ravaging waves. Better to keep it bottled up and hidden. Even if it left this awkwardness between them. "This is something I must do alone. Allow me that, please."

Features scrunching together, wrinkles spreading across his brow, Gilgamesh shifted his jaw back and forth then gave a sharp nod. "If you must."

His body had shifted closer to Enkidu's, like he feared to release him.

"I'll return to you. I promise it."

Gilgamesh nodded again, but his expression didn't change. Perhaps that was what he'd look like when Enkidu died and he grieved him. Would he hold himself together like the King or roar and fight like when they'd faced Humbaba?

It didn't matter.

Enkidu wouldn't be there to see it.

He pressed a kiss to his lover's mouth and tried to forget about the future.

CHAPTER FOUR

A DISGRUNTLED KING

Someone poured more wine into Gilgamesh's chalice, and he took a swallow. Eyes lingered on him, despite the occasion being about others. The King didn't enter a space without the crowd noticing regardless of the situation. He dropped his gaze to the drink, uninterested in playing the political games that night.

Across the room, beneath dozens of hanging silks and cloaked in candle smoke, Shamhat laughed as she spoke with the bride who flushed and turned her face away. Her new husband stood at her side, eyes wide as he stood before the Queen.

Hirin took a seat on the sofa next to Gilgamesh's. "Lugal, it is a great honor to have you here with us this evening."

"Congratulations to you, Hirin. It seems your daughter has made a fine match."

The advisor clasped his hands together and bowed towards Gilgamesh twice. "With thanks to you."

"I believe that was Shamhat's doing more than mine."

"And I will thank her again, Lugal." Gilgamesh didn't doubt he would. Shamhat would keep her fixed smile on as she graciously accepted the man's flourished gratitude. Hirin annoyed Shamhat, and at another time Gilgamesh would revel in finding some way to poke at her over it, but not that evening.

Another swallow of wine didn't turn his mood.

Enkidu had left him. With a deep breath, Gilgamesh set the chalice down. Getting drunk wouldn't help, and after Inanna had attacked him and Enkidu when they'd been intoxicated, he wasn't eager to risk having less than his full senses available. Enkidu had said he would return. He kept his vows. Yet, time slipped away from them, and Enkidu chose to spend some of their precious days apart.

Everyone always left Gilgamesh in the end. When Enkidu returned, it would only be for the gods to rip him from Gilgamesh's arms before a new year began. Even his mother had abandoned him. She appeared to Enkidu, giving him some prophetic vision that made him leave, but she wouldn't speak with her son.

Wincing, Gilgamesh readjusted, bracelets sliding down his wrist. Many at the wedding feast rarely got to see their king up close. He needed to keep his image in place. They wanted to observe the god-king who defended Uruk, who had killed not one but two divine beasts. The shepherd who protected them.

With Enkidu gone, Gilgamesh struggled to care.

He dreaded lying in bed that night, the blankets cool, the massive mattress empty.

As it would be if Enkidu died.

Once, Gilgamesh had been satisfied living a solitary life. He had a friend in Shamhat and otherwise used all his energy pursuing a legacy. Now he'd rip his name from history's embrace if it would spare Enkidu.

All he wanted was to grow old with the man. Love him for each of those days. Care for Uruk together. Have a permanent companion and lover for once in his life.

Was that too godsdamned much to ask?

The bench cracked beneath his tightening grip, the wood splintering, and Gilgamesh released his fingers from it. Damn it. He'd have to make sure he had a replacement sent. Hirin would never request it, but he needed to keep those loyal to him close. Damaging their homes wouldn't do that.

All his life, Gilgamesh hadn't fit the world. He'd stormed and fought through it all but what else was he supposed to do? God's blood burned through his veins, his body towered over other mortals, and nothing satisfied.

Then he met Enkidu.

His heart gave a painful lurch.

Musicians shifted to a different tune, lighthearted and filled with flutes. Shamhat turned towards them and offered one of her full-cheeked, benevolent smiles. They beamed beneath their queen's approval.

"Your daughter must be a clever woman to keep the Queen so engaged." Gilgamesh forced himself to abandon his moping. He could sit and spin his worries and grief around Enkidu endlessly. He wanted to save the man; one day apart from him already ached. If Enkidu refused to travel into divine territory with him, then Gilgamesh couldn't go. If he failed, he'd have spent the limited days they had left apart from Enkidu. He'd have to stay here in Uruk and wait for the man he loved, his entire heart, to die. With that depressing thought firmly clenching into his gut, Gilgamesh nodded to the bride.

Hirin's cheeks flushed, and he buried his smile behind his chalice before answering. "She is clever, Lugal, if you don't mind me saying so. She must have inherited that from her mother."

Gilgamesh chuckled. That was a sentiment he could appreciate. He felt similarly about the half-grown boy-child he and Shamhat had brought into the world. Usun with his glistening, hopeful eyes and the same stately bearing his mother possessed.

"I'll miss her a great deal." Hirin sighed the words. Before Gilgamesh, Hirin always remained reverential and formal. Yet, staring at his daughter wrapped in a bridal shawl, deep into the night after several servings of wine, and with the darkness, music, and smoke obscuring their conversation from others, the man's eyes grew misty. "She's always been attached to me. Always arguing with me over philosophy and law." A low rumble of laughter escaped him.

Offering a nod, Gilgamesh returned his gaze to the girl who spoke animatedly with Shamhat. A truth hit him as intensely as the tree trunks Humbaba had flung at him, thudding hard enough to bruise. Hirin had everything Gilgamesh didn't.

He could be close to his children, have a loving and close family with no fear the gods would give a damn about his life. Hirin wouldn't have a legacy that outlived him, but in this lifetime, he had everything Gilgamesh didn't. Couldn't.

It was what Shamhat had spent their entire marriage trying to show him.

The gods had made certain Gilgamesh never had that opportunity. Inanna had always stalked him, full of her own motivations and designs. Gilgamesh had spent every breath attempting to outmaneuver her. Now here he sat, stuck, with no moves left to make.

"I took the liberty this week, Lugal, to read more tablets stored alongside the one discussing Utnapishtim. I don't know if you feel now is an appropriate time to discuss it?"

Gilgamesh sat up straighter and turned towards the man. The conversation didn't matter if Enkidu wouldn't take the damned trip. No, Enkidu would rather stay in Uruk and allow death to tumble him down without a fight. Heat flared in Gilgamesh's stomach again, but he attempted to push it down. "Tell me what you know."

"Utnapishtim and his wife were ferried to an island deep within the divines' realm, as you know. Someone removed the precise location. Another writing suggested they longed to escape mortals who pleaded for Utnapishtim to use his divine powers on them. It would likely require the help of some divine to find them."

The party roared around them, the music reaching its peak, people raising their voices to speak over it, dinner plates emptying. He'd need the help of useless gods to get to this ancestor who held divine powers. Gilgamesh ran his hand over the couch's broken edge. They had the time if Enkidu was willing. Plus, Enkidu was good at speaking with even the most stubborn of asses. Gilgamesh was proof of that. If anyone could achieve this task, it was them.

"I've been thinking, Hirin." As soon as the words left his mouth, Gilgamesh didn't know why he would share this except that he desperately needed to allow his thoughts to form into something more structured. "Who can actually best an immortal, all-knowing, eternal goddess?"

Hirin released a breath and rubbed his hands together, crouching over, crinkling his navy tunic. "That is a difficult question, my king."

"I'll take your honest answer." Gilgamesh swallowed the last of his wine. Shamhat nodded to the bride and groom and turned in his direction, her guards following.

"I suppose, the one most suited to defeat a goddess would be another god."

Gilgamesh smiled at the man and tipped his chalice in his direction. "I think you're right."

"If you don't mind me asking, Lugal, do you wish to go into divine territory to beseech another god?"

A hum rumbled Gilgamesh's chest. "Something like that, perhaps."

Ideas tumbled through his mind. If only Enkidu would agree to go, to take the risk and try something. How could a man brave enough to face down the Bull of Heaven, to stand before the snake, Inanna, hesitate at this opportunity? Gilgamesh's thoughts didn't shift even as he walked alongside Shamhat back to the palace later.

"I thought you wanted to stop grinding your teeth," his queen said, her gaze fixed ahead on the path where guards' torches splashed light.

He side-eyed his queen to find her smirking at him.

"Are you worried about Enkidu's safety?" she asked when he didn't reply.

"Not presently." After all, Inanna couldn't punish Gilgamesh by dangling Enkidu's death over him if the man were to die before the year ended. No, she'd keep him alive until the New Year, the day they'd made their vows, when she'd promised his demise. "I miss him, though."

Gilgamesh whispered the last words, and Shamhat slipped her hands into the crook of his elbow, her small, soft fingers tucking comfortingly around his forearm. He pulled her closer and lifted his face to take in the stars he and Enkidu had lain under together before.

He wanted another year to do so.

A hundred more years.

And he would defy the gods to achieve it. But he could only do so if Enkidu would join him. Gilgamesh stared at the glistening sky above and felt hopelessly out of control and mercilessly mortal.

CHAPTER FIVE
AS THE HEAVENS WATCH

Enkidu had spent his first day running, leaving the city's noisy clatter behind with every footfall. He veered away from the farmlands and villages and ran through wild, unmanned territory. Wind cooled his sweaty brow, his heart thundering pleasantly.

Out in the wide world where he could see nothing but swaying grasses, the distant bunch of cedar trees, the sky a colorful stretch above him, Enkidu felt alive again as hours passed.

He wished Gilgamesh was with him.

Perhaps it was foolish to take the trip alone. If Gilgamesh were there, Enkidu would laugh as the man teased him and sleep wrapped in his arms. The tension buzzing along his form and his growing fear for the Wolf might dissipate.

Not if Gilgamesh kept discussing some plan to fight the gods, though. That would only add to Enkidu's misery. He didn't know how to help Gilgamesh see reality. They were mortal beings, caught in the divine's webs. As much as they might struggle, it only tangled them deeper, made it easier for the gods to kill them.

Reaching the forest's edge, he slowed and ducked his head beneath low-hanging branches as he stepped into the woods' cool embrace. If Gilgamesh was there, the awkward tension that lingered between them, the ghost of all the things both refused to speak of, would poison it. Enkidu was tired of the discomfort hanging on them like ill-fitting shawls. Tired of being the reason for it.

With a huff he lifted his face to the forest's glistening beauty. Sunlight spilled through branches, dappling leaves like jewels. Mushrooms grew on a fallen log, bunching alongside moss. A butterfly stretched its wings. Distant bird cries echoed, and a breeze rushed through the glen, crackling dry leaves together.

Enkidu closed his eyes, let his booted feet sink into the earth as the wind tangled through his beard and whispered over his cheeks.

There were two periods of his life the forest brought to mind.

His time with the Wolf, the peacefulness of it.

And his journey to face Humbaba with Gilgamesh, the tension between them. That was a different type of unrest. His greatest stressors then were feeling the push and pull attraction he had with Gilgamesh and his wariness of facing the divine dragon.

If only life were that simple now.

With a sigh he started moving, following a familiar trail that curved around the lake and passed through a thick grove of trees. Yips and growls sounded out, curling through the air and raising hairs on the back of Enkidu's neck.

As he turned a corner towards the Wolf's den, a streak of fur dashed towards him, claws extended.

Enkidu rolled and avoided the impact. Jumping to his feet he gasped. Dozens of wolves were fighting, blood-matted fur littering the clearing. A she-wolf stood at the den's entrance, her golden eyes fixed on the fight, the pups behind her watching with trembling snuffles.

The wolves were under attack from another pack.

Enkidu jumped in, grabbing an enemy wolf and flinging him across the clearing. The creature whined then was cut off as its body snapped against a tree trunk.

The Wolf had once experienced trouble with another pack that wanted their choicer territory with the lake that drew a variety of creatures. However, the pack had been strong when Enkidu left, the Wolf firmly in control.

He slammed towards another group of snarling, drool-drenched wolf teeth and yanked the strange creature away, following with a growl of his own. Enkidu hesitated, though. Already he didn't recognize all the creatures. He didn't want to harm a pack member unintentionally.

If only he hadn't lost the ability to understand the animals' language when he left the forest.

Half a dozen other fights continued. Growling rumbled loudly enough to tremble through Enkidu's chest.

A muscular wolf dashed from beneath his challenger and tumbled the creature over.

The Wolf.

He lifted his face, his golden eyes widening as they took in Enkidu.

"Behind you," Enkidu shouted.

A pair of enemies used his distraction and pounced.

The Wolf turned and plowed towards them. Snarls and

yelps sounded out. Enkidu leapt in their direction as blood's bitter tang swept through the air. Pups whimpered.

Slamming two attackers aside, Enkidu made it across the clearing, his lungs aching for breath.

The Wolf snapped an enemy's neck and threw his body down into a pile of lifeless bones and flesh. Enkidu slammed into the second creature. Its sharp claws found aim and ripped through his chest. Pain sheared along Enkidu's muscles, gliding down his arms until even his fingernails hurt.

He held tight to the creature, though, and tossed it a dozen trees away.

The enemy wolf looked up at him with wild eyes, his chest rising and falling as his injuries dripped blood. With a yip and growl, he called off the others of his pack and they ran out of the clearing.

Enkidu turned back towards the Wolf who took a few unsteady paces towards him. The Wolf keened something then growled. Enkidu shook his head as he kneeled before him even as his muscles throbbed with the injury. "I don't understand you, friend, but I'm glad I could be here to help."

The Wolf took another uneasy step then collapsed. Enkidu dropped beside him and gasped. The Wolf's stomach was slashed open, dark blood spilling down his legs and soaking into the leaves.

"No," Enkidu gasped. He reached for the wound, stretching his own injured flesh and sending sticky blood to course down his stomach. Enkidu pulled his bag aside and searched through it. If only he'd packed something useful. Even if he had, he wouldn't know what to do with it. He had no healing skills. He had no ability to do anything but crouch there before his first friend and watch him paint the forest floor scarlet. His spare tunic was the closest thing he had to a bandage, so he pressed the material to the wolf's stomach. The creature shuddered, and it did nothing to staunch the bleeding. Instead, crimson warmth flooded over the material, dying it nearly black.

Enkidu's heart tightened like it might burst in his chest. The other wolves gathered around, some limping. The Wolf's mate left the den, ran to him, and dropped to lick his nose. He snuffled and growled something to her before turning his perceptive golden eyes on Enkidu.

Enkidu placed a hand on the wolf's head, felt the coarse texture of his fur. He was young. He should have lived far longer than this. The Wolf didn't try to speak to him again, he only watched Enkidu with glistening eyes.

I've achieved my duty, he seemed to say. There was pride in the tilt of his chin, determination in the set of his lips even as he gasped breaths past the pain.

"You've lived well and protected your pack, Wolf. Your life has had great meaning."

The wolf blinked, nudged his head into Enkidu's hand, turned back towards his mate for another nose lick, then heaved a great breath before his body went still.

Blood still poured over Enkidu's hands and dripped off his wrists. He trembled and refused to release his breath or draw another. If he did, then this would be real. The Wolf, his first friend and mentor, would be dead.

A pup whimpered, and some creature in the distance snapped a stick.

The clearing otherwise remained silent, as though all the wolves held their breaths alongside Enkidu.

Then the Wolf's mate lifted her face and released a howl. It rang out, loud and resonant, grief woven into the aching whine. Enkidu moved away from the blood and the Wolf—his friend he hadn't been able to help.

The she-wolf released another haunting howl as the other pack members watched Enkidu. Sorrow rippled across their eyes, but they nodded to him. He'd arrived in time to help save the Wolf's family.

His skin crawled as others joined the she-wolf. The forest had gone silent in response to the wolves' song, and Enkidu couldn't stand to be there another moment. He snatched his bag with bloody hands, turned, and ran.

He crashed through the forest, smashing shrubs beneath his heels and startling moths. Lungs burning, he didn't slow but pushed himself harder. The impact of his footfalls ricocheted through his body.

He wanted it to hurt, to feel the pain.

Gilgamesh's mother had given him enough warning for him to see the Wolf but only moments before his death. She'd avoided Gilgamesh, avoided helping them. The only thing she offered freely was pain.

Perhaps worse, Enkidu had a divine creator as well, and she'd never even spoken with him. No, she'd created him to temper a king at Ninsun's request then abandoned him. The gods really were cruel. To satisfy Inanna's anger, they'd let Enkidu die although he'd done nothing to deserve a curse.

Not one god would stand up for him or Gilgamesh.

Just like the Wolf. Ninsun could have interfered and spared his life.

Instead, she stood back and did nothing.

Enkidu stopped suddenly enough that the jolt ached his knees. He lifted his face and roared, screaming through his teeth so spit speckled his lips.

Birds burst from trees, squalling and flapping their wings, feathers twirling down around Enkidu.

Dropping to his knees in moss, his fingers sank into dirt. Dirt the wolf would soon join. Enkidu would soon join.

His chest ached. He longed to lie down and die and get it over with. Or fight alongside Gilgamesh and demand a fair judgment from the gods.

He couldn't do this in front of Gilgamesh. He couldn't scream and rage and feel this much. That would spur Gilgamesh on to more foolishness—more putting himself at risk and thinking of nothing but Enkidu's curse.

Inanna's revenge had hit true.

She'd torment Gilgamesh by making him look into Enkidu's eyes each day and watch his death approach.

She'd torment Enkidu as well, but she probably didn't give a damn.

Enkidu had always been expendable to the gods. He'd come into the world alone and soon he'd leave it alone. Who would howl his remembrance when he was gone? Perhaps only a furious king who would get himself killed fighting the divine over it. At least the wolf had lived well, died with purpose.

What purpose did Enkidu have?

All the anger spilled out of his body like blood gushing, leaving him exhausted. He curled onto the forest floor and fell asleep.

* * *

Returning to Uruk, Enkidu lingered on the journey. Gilgamesh waited for him, and he'd grow anxious if Enkidu was gone too long, but he needed time to grieve.

Once the anger had mostly burned off, he started back

towards the city, hopelessness filling him until his stomach ached with it. He'd lost his change of clothing at the wolf's death and people eyed his torn and blood-speckled tunic. Then they lifted their gazes to his horns and took unsteady steps back.

When he finally reached the palace, his limbs felt as heavy as stone. He wanted nothing more than to sleep. But after washing up, he sought Gilgamesh, happy to find him alone aside from Hirin who Gilgamesh quickly dismissed. The room was shadowy, and golden sunlight spilled from high windows in stripes over the colorful rug. Gilgamesh's crown sat on a table in the corner, the jewels gleaming.

Closing the door behind Hirin, Gilgamesh's brow furrowed. It didn't change his beauty. Days of not seeing him had been too long. Enkidu wanted to drag fingers along his arm, smell the oils in his beard. His perceptive, dark eyes flicked towards Enkidu's collarbone. Despite wearing a clean tunic, the scars stretched above the fabric.

"You're injured. What happened?"

Enkidu clicked his tongue. The raking wolf's claws had already mostly healed into raised pink scars. What was one more scar on a body that wouldn't live much longer, anyway? "It's nothing."

Gilgamesh couldn't even say hello without jumping to fear again. Enkidu was divinely formed. He could handle a few minor injuries.

Gilgamesh's lips parted, then pressed together. "It's something. If I'd known you'd gone to face danger, I wouldn't have left you to go alone and—"

"Do you expect me to ask you permission for every move I make?"

Gilgamesh frowned, his eyes darkening. His beaded

shawl clinked as he shifted. "Am I not allowed to worry about you?"

"All you do anymore is worry about me!" Perhaps Enkidu hadn't lingered long enough on his trip back. The anger bubbled up again, burning his gut. All he'd wanted was to find the comfort of Gilgamesh's arms, tell him about his journey, and possibly share his grief. They were back to this unsurpassable something that lingered between them. Enkidu longed to crunch it beneath his fingers, break it until it didn't exist anymore.

"Should I not?" Gilgamesh's voice bounced around the room.

The heat of the argument they'd had before Enkidu's trip returned. His body ached to close the gap between them, find his hand, kiss his mouth. But the fury that had left him running through the woods covered in his friend's blood refused. "You say you want me to join you on some doomed trip into divine territory, but you can't tolerate me experiencing some minor mortal injury? Which one is it?"

"I want to go there for your sake."

Enkidu stepped closer. "Even if it gets me killed?"

"You act as though sitting here in Uruk and waiting for Inanna's retribution won't do the same damn thing." All the relief and love that had shone in Gilgamesh's eyes when he'd stepped into the room had drained, making space for hot, burning emotions. The way he threw the words at Enkidu drained the warmth from his face. It wasn't his fault that Inanna cursed him. It wasn't Gilgamesh's either, though he knew the man wouldn't believe him if he said as much.

"I should have rested before coming to speak with you," he whispered. Gilgamesh took a step forward, an arm outstretched, but Enkidu stumbled back and shook his head. "Please, let me have this."

Gilgamesh's face fell, his eyes welling with emotions and turning a rich, soft brown. Enkidu wanted to fix the issue between them, but he needed rest first, needed to untangle his own thoughts before he could deal with Gilgamesh's anxious questions. He turned and walked out of the room, shutting the door quietly behind him.

Being in the man's presence for a few minutes, despite the interaction, had his heart lifting and a warm surge of energy twisting down his limbs. If only Gilgamesh would stop letting worry and fear taint every interaction. Perhaps it would be best to reconnect in their room, to meet him physically first, have some sort of release from the emotions tumbling through Enkidu before he tried to put words to them.

He turned into a hall and nearly stumbled into someone.

"Enkidu?"

He froze. Shamhat stood next to her attendants, her gold headpiece catching light that bounced over the walls. Her lips puckered in a frown. "I'm glad to see you returned. Do you have a few minutes you could spare?"

A deep breath filled his lungs before he trusted his voice. He bowed. "Of course, Nin."

She shooed away her attendants who eyed Enkidu warily but obeyed their queen. She led Enkidu into a dark room and lit candles at a table before gesturing to a couch. Enkidu took the seat and readjusted. His knees raised to his chest as he sank into the furniture. It was another reminder that he wasn't created for this world. Truly the only living creature he matched was Gilgamesh. He'd never belonged here. Gilgamesh should have known Enkidu wasn't designed to live a full life. Enkidu should have known it. He was nothing more than a scheme crafted by malicious gods.

His stomach ached and not from his scar. When he pressed into his grief, pushed the wound so blood rushed forth, he knew the pain's source. He didn't want to give up Gilgamesh. He longed to see years pass, to argue over a hundred different things, to watch gray sweep through his beard and kiss wrinkles that would form at the corners of his eyes.

Those things were gone. Gilgamesh wanted them to chase that dream into the divine realm. The gods wouldn't allow the two of them to infiltrate their world and steal secrets or undo Inanna's curse. They were both dead if they went on the journey.

Better to live the next year and embrace his fate—even if that meant dying without purpose—than spending it chasing ghosts of things that didn't exist.

Shamhat poured wine into a chalice and handed it to Enkidu. The metal's cool touch brought him back to the present. She stood in the room's shadows and served herself some as well, the wine sloshing softly. He couldn't make out Shamhat's expression, just the upright posture of her form, her careful movements as she set the wine down again. Glimmering in the candlelight along the wall were crude night sky mosaics crafted from chips of deep blue lapis lazuli and pale stones.

"Gilgamesh did those as a boy." Shamhat sat on the couch next to Enkidu's.

Enkidu stretched his arm out so he could spread a hand over a sky map. They were unsophisticated compared to other mosaics within the palace, but for a child with limited experience they were exquisite. As his eyes adjusted, he discovered dozens of mosaics flowing around the space. Each one portrayed a different time of the year. Gilgamesh had named the stars for him once and promised to teach him all their names as the seasons passed. Now they only had one of each season left to share.

"He's never shown me this room."

Shamhat took a sip from her chalice. "He wouldn't. He hates these mosaics because they're not perfect. When we were first married, he wanted them torn down, but I wouldn't allow it." She smiled. "Now, what's wrong? Did your trip not go well?"

Enkidu shifted and brought the drink to his lips to stall speaking. He couldn't discuss his journey into the forest or watching the wolf's life slip away. After swallowing, he sighed. "I angered Gilgamesh before I left, and my first act in returning was reigniting the argument. I wonder if I've created a chasm between us."

Shamhat crossed her legs into an elegant line. "Welcome to the reality of loving Gilgamesh. Trust me, it often feels like that. I'd be glad to listen if it would help. For years, I'd have appreciated having someone who understood my warring frustration and love for the man. Akkiru and Kara have endured more than a few ranting sessions from me."

"I can't imagine you ranting, Nin. You overstate things, surely."

Shamhat smiled, and her eyes sparkled. She leaned back on her couch and waited.

Enkidu stretched his toes within his boots. "Hirin suggested that Gilgamesh and I could locate Utnapishtim in the divine realm. He thinks the man might possess divine powers. I argued it was a foolish idea." Enkidu set the drink down. After watching the wolf die, his life wasted, he burned with the desire to fight his own fate. But he couldn't forget the reasons this journey would be a terrible idea. "A waste of time and dangerous. What about Usun? What about you?"

Shamhat shrugged. "Hirin may have a point, though. There's a reason Utnapishtim and his wife disappeared after ascending to immortality. After all, I don't think I'd want people bothering me seeking favors or the gods' secrets for eternity."

Enkidu scoffed. "Surely you aren't entertaining this as well?"

Shamhat was the level one in their marriage. If she encouraged Gilgamesh with this idea, Enkidu would never convince him against it.

"It's far-fetched, but I see potential in it." She placed her chalice next to his. "Do you not wish to travel?"

Enkidu spread his hands upturned before him. "Others need Gilgamesh here more than I need him to waste a year and endanger his life for what would certainly be a hopeless task."

Ninsun had told him he couldn't prevent the Wolf's death. And he hadn't. Gilgamesh would do the same, travel and fight and end up with injuries if not worse only to find himself in the same place. With a dead body and no hope. Enkidu shuddered.

Shamhat leaned forward and grasped one of his hands. Her gentle touch reminded him of their first meeting, when she'd smoothed lotion over his skin and oiled his hair. Before he'd known she was a queen. Before he'd known his destiny to love a king.

"Gilgamesh has endangered himself in far more foolish ways. This would probably be good for him. At least he'd feel like he's done everything he can. Inanna doesn't mean for Gilgamesh to die before he endures her punishment, anyway. My guess is she'd even protect him to make sure he lived through the pain she has in mind for him." She bit her lip, and it unfurled slowly. "Plus, it would give you both time that you wouldn't have here in the palace."

Enkidu hadn't considered that Inanna might go as far as safeguarding them in the divine realm solely to achieve her retribution. That changed things. If they could travel with minimal danger to Gilgamesh, perhaps it wasn't foolish. But there was still the city to consider, the people he left behind.

"Wouldn't it harm you, Nin, to be without your husband and king?"

Shamhat laughed and dropped his hand. "Half my marriage he's been off conquering other cities or negotiating. It wouldn't be that different for me." She raised her eyes. They were so similar to Usun's. A wide, warm brown that searched everything as she spoke. "Do you not want this, though? If you don't, you shouldn't do it. Even if Gilgamesh fights and gnashes his teeth. What is it you desire, Enkidu?"

Enkidu fell back against the couch with a huff. He'd scarcely thought of his desires. His focus had been on Usun, the city, Shamhat, the Wolf, and the gods. He'd barely lived long enough to have fully formed desires. Perhaps with years he'd discover he loved music or art or stories. The little time he'd walked the mortal world, he'd yet to discover the things that made his heart patter, the tools that might allow him to leave a mark on the world.

Shamhat had cleared space—allowed him to consider with no wrong answers. He dragged a thumbnail along the cushion before lifting his face again and speaking bone-deep truth. A truth he'd been afraid to speak aloud. "I want to live. If there's any hope, I'd like to try. I just don't want to harm others in doing so."

"Well, you won't. So you should go."

The way she said it, so evenly as though it was obvious, ripped all the uncertainty aside. Gods, perhaps Gilgamesh wasn't the only stubborn one. Shamhat made a good point, too. If they traveled together, they'd get time. Time that politics and messengers and gods would consume if they stayed in the city. Pressures of that lifestyle ate away at Enkidu, adding to his misery. He remembered the night of their vow, Gilgamesh's voice husky and low when he'd said he wanted to have Enkidu in the wild again.

Enkidu shivered and jumped to his feet. The fight had been a stupid one. He needed to find Gilgamesh. As he reached the door, he turned back to Shamhat. "Oh—"

"Go, find him." She smiled and nodded to the exit.

He bowed. "Thank you, Nin."

She smirked and returned to her wine.

Enkidu went to the room he'd left an unhappy king in first. It was empty, Gilgamesh's crown remaining on its stand. From there he went to the soldiers' yard. Practice swords clattered together, and several men nodded at him, but Gilgamesh wasn't among them. He left and walked to the throne room, then the dining halls, the courtyards, and even their bedroom. Night had fallen by the time he prepared to give up, then he had a thought.

He went to the place Gilgamesh had brought him before and climbed the ladder to the roof. Gilgamesh sat, his arms wrapped around his legs, his face lifted towards the heavens.

Enkidu held his breath. He'd seen Gilgamesh shimmering and polished, angry and covered in blood, flesh bared and passion in his eyes. But this—this twisted Enkidu's heart. Gilgamesh sat in pale blue light, his skin softened, his face fixed on the heavens. Of all the beauty in the world—including the thousands of stars sparkling around him—nothing could surpass Gilgamesh sitting there with his beard half undone, his tunic rippling over his muscled form, his eyes full of wonder and sorrow.

The ladder shifted, creaking against the building. Gilgamesh looked over then jumped to his feet to meet Enkidu who finished the climb. As soon as the King reached him, he grabbed his elbows and pulled him close. "Enkidu." Relief was an oasis amid the desert in his voice. "I've been overbearing and foolish and inconsiderate. Forgive me."

Enkidu released a shuddering breath and tucked his nose to his neck. Gilgamesh sighed and curled against him. Everything felt right in the world again.

"Of course." Enkidu tangled his fingers into the loose hair Gilgamesh's attendants hadn't twisted into braids. "You're not the only one who's been foolish. I spoke with Shamhat this afternoon." Gilgamesh leaned back. Moonlight puddled in his dark eyes, making them glow. There was no anger or fight left in them. Only the sadness his fury attempted to shield. Enkidu traced down his jaw, his fingers slipping into Gilgamesh's beard. "She convinced me you're right. We should seek Utnapishtim. See what we can learn."

Gilgamesh sucked in a breath he held for a moment before releasing it and shaking his head. "We don't have to. It's your life, and I'm being too demanding. You made a fair point that I'm attempting to control your life too much. If you'd prefer—"

"I'd prefer to find an answer if possible. I've just been afraid to admit it. Afraid to take up space or give into hope. I want to go."

The words escaped him like birds taking flight. Now they were out in the world, unwilling to return to their nest.

Enkidu wanted to live. He didn't wish to join the Wolf in dying young. He longed to have time to seek his purpose and years to spend sleeping next to Gilgamesh, time to form friendships, the ability to watch Usun grow into an adult. The desire burned in him the way he'd longed for beer when Shamhat had given him the first taste. The moment before, he hadn't known it existed, but with one taste he never wanted lake water again.

Gilgamesh shuddered and Enkidu clutched him tighter. He wanted this as well. Wanted a chance to defy Inanna and her wretched curse, to have a say in his fate and future. Perhaps, together, they could achieve it. Gilgamesh brushed their noses together and held Enkidu as the heavens watched.

CHAPTER SIX
FAREWELL

LIGHT WAS EVERYWHERE, burning so Gilgamesh blinked against it. His bare feet sank into soft grasses, but he couldn't see them. Stars burst across his vision, turning the world foggy.

A shudder trailed down Gilgamesh's spine. He loathed when he dreamed. It only happened when he received an omen.

The gentle breeze pushed hair off his neck and brought a sweet smell. There was nothing to do but endure the dream and see whatever wretched prophecy came with it.

Gilgamesh's heart raced as he fumbled forward with an outstretched hand. His palm met rough bark at the same time his vision could make out a hint of the tree's outline amid the light.

"Gilgamesh."

The King bowed beneath the voice's weight. It rippled with authority. More light flooded into the space, making everything pearlescent. Even within the dream's realm, he felt nauseated, bile rising up his throat.

"Utu," Gilgamesh whispered as though the name flowed from his mouth without him forming it.

He stood beneath a god unveiled.

"Not quite unveiled. You cannot see me fully or you would die, mortal king. Walk with me."

Gilgamesh rose. The world still glistened but he could make out a few steps ahead where a path led. The light gleamed from behind his shoulder, causing lapis lazuli gems set in the walkway's stones to shimmer. Flowers that Gilgamesh had no name for grew along the road. Beyond, everything glowed so brightly it hurt to look.

"You saved my life." Gilgamesh forced his gaze to stay ahead, to not look back at the god walking behind him. Even within a dream the action could kill him. His eyes burned from the mere reflection of Utu's presence. "You saved Enkidu's life. I owe you thanks."

If it wasn't for Utu and Ninsun, they both would have perished in Humbaba's lair. His mother told him that Utu was glad for the creature to die. The monster had embodied darkness. Now his mother wouldn't speak with him because of Inanna. Gods were fine with Humbaba being destroyed, but no one would stand up to Inanna and her ridiculous behavior.

"You've angered a goddess, mortal king. My sister is young yet and has attributes she still needs to outgrow. However, the gods do not meddle in another divine's matters. I assure you, you do not wish to see the gods at war."

Honey-sweet and incense-rich smells reached Gilgamesh as he walked. The sun had consumed the sky, yet the air remained cool. Flowers grew along vines that flowed with the path, never crossing it. Each petal held a unique color, some like rainbows, translucent and bright.

Gilgamesh tried to look beyond the path, but it was too bright for him to make out more of the garden. Wherever this dream was set had to be located in the divine realm.

"You shall see it in person, though you will have to find the peaks of Mount Mashu and cross through a mountain of death first. For now, I come bearing an omen, Gilgamesh."

Gilgamesh scraped his fingers over wool-soft leaves and didn't answer. He hated godsdamned omens, despite having braced for it the entire dream. Omens were riddles that never helped. Utu's casual discussion of death didn't increase Gilgamesh's hopes that this would be any different.

"I'll withhold it if you prefer." The light brightened.

"This omen is not what I hope for, is it?" Gilgamesh wished he'd never sought the answer to the prophecy his mother had interpreted. He could hear her gentle voice speaking doom. *You shall gain what you desire but lose that which really matters.*

He'd give anything to undo that, stop his restless seeking and the path that led him to damning his lover—to hold Enkidu in his arms and know the man's heart would continue pounding. That Enkidu didn't face the arrow of Gilgamesh's choices.

"Omens are rarely what mortals desire."

"Mortals have so little to hope for." Gilgamesh continued walking but his words came fiercer than they should have when standing before a god. When walking under a divine's burning light. He couldn't help it, though. The man he loved faced an early demise, and the only thing that came after that was the Great Below. A world of shadows and darkness. He wouldn't even have the comfort of a long life with beautiful memories to warm him there.

"All we have is a brief existence and that's often cut short. Gods hold our fates but see us as disposable servants. Only the misery of death embraces us in the end."

The crunching of Gilgamesh's footsteps covered silence. When Utu spoke, he was quieter. "You make fair points. Do you wish to hear the omen or not?"

He didn't, but if it offered any hint to help Enkidu, he'd be a fool to avoid it. "Yes."

"You will have a grand adventure and discover answers, but this eternal life you search for is not yours to find. I shall not stop you as other things will come to pass from your journey—important things. But the secret desire burning in your heart is not yours to claim."

Eternal life wasn't his greatest hope, though. Even bringing Inanna down wasn't. He only wanted Enkidu to live a normal, mortal life with him. He'd gladly give up his private hopes and plans if they'd just let him keep Enkidu. That was the question he needed to ask. The answer he sought. "Will I at least save—"

Gilgamesh woke with a gasp. Sweat dripped down his forehead and his heart thundered. Enkidu pressed soft kisses over his cheek, brushed fingers through his hair, and whispered soothingly.

He wrapped his arms around Enkidu, pulling him close.

Utu withdrew before he'd answered his question. Could he save Enkidu from Inanna's curse? She'd given him a single year of life left to live but Gilgamesh had to break the curse or find some way to outwit her.

Enkidu shifted, moving the blankets, and Gilgamesh readjusted so his head lay on Enkidu's chest and he could glide his fingers back and forth across the smooth surface of his horn.

Having Enkidu at his side again, he felt foolish over the

argument. How he wished he'd swallowed back his demands and just loved this man instead. All he needed was to secure his salvation and he'd let every other ambition go.

"Was it an ill omen?" Enkidu whispered.

"I don't know."

Like all prophecies from the gods, it was a riddle that offered no help. Gilgamesh was part god. Perhaps mortality would ultimately undo him, but while he lived, he burned with god's blood.

Utu said his journey was important. Gilgamesh could change things like no mortal could. Maybe it wasn't hopeless. If he could stall Enkidu's death, could spend the rest of his life with Enkidu's body warm against his, he could face anything.

* * *

Shamhat's room had more color than Gilgamesh's. It was also more unorganized. She held herself together in every area of life, but her private living space had clothing draped across furniture, tablets on a desk with an uncleaned reed resting on a speckled cloth, and Akkiru's musical instruments tucked in corners or stacked on stools.

Gilgamesh paced across the jewel-bright rug from his mother's temple. It was an item Shamhat brought with her into their marriage. His boots trampled the material, pressing their brilliant colors down as he looked up at his wife.

She was already dressed for their presentation before the people, her makeup shimmering over her smooth skin, her grandest headpiece in place, her shawl embroidered with gold disks. Everything in her bearing exuded leadership. Uruk was safe in her hands and the people would know it as soon as they saw her.

"You've arranged everything for the next few months as far as I can tell." Shamhat smirked. "I should have urged you into a divine journey years ago." She laughed, but it came out higher than normal, forced despite her steady appearance.

Gilgamesh grunted. "Glad I'm finally proving useful. You'll remember that I arranged things before we left to face Humbaba. Should the worst happen—"

"Don't." The word came like a blow, slicing into his speech. Shamhat stepped across the rug's crimson and golds and gripped Gilgamesh's arm. Her hand skimmed over his skin, and she watched her fingers trace trails over his hair. A shadow of all the things she didn't say crossed her eyes, all the fear and doubt and worries. Gilgamesh parted his lips, but she raised her chin, Uruk's unyielding queen sliding back into her countenance. "You stay safe and protect Enkidu. I expect you to return to me, my king, bearing good news for our city."

Her gaze was intense, her eyes dark and glittering. Her grip tightened. She was afraid but not backing down. She believed they could defy the gods and succeed. Gilgamesh didn't intend to disappoint her. "As you say, my queen."

Posture loosening, she released her grip. "I'll see you in a few hours."

Gilgamesh nodded. He and Enkidu needed to dress the part before standing before their people and saying good-bye. He needed to check their supplies and discuss final details with Hirin. Standing before his wife, he hesitated to leave. He wanted to promise her he would change things, that he would save Usun from the damned fate he'd inherited from his father, that he'd overthrow Inanna if he achieved it with his dying breath.

She'd wanted him to promise to return.

The one thing they'd never done was lie to each other. And he wasn't sure that was a vow he could keep.

Gilgamesh leaned forward and pressed a kiss to her forehead, tucking the promise into his heart. He'd find a way to succeed, to secure her and Usun, protect Uruk, and save Enkidu. He'd do it no matter the cost.

Later, after Gilgamesh and Enkidu dressed in richly dyed tunics, bejeweled shawls, and clattering bracelets, they stepped together before a gathered crowd. Their clothing was a waste as they prepared to take a long journey where it would all prove useless. Gilgamesh clenched his teeth to keep from frowning.

They stood before half the city who'd gathered before the palace to see the King and Enkidu off.

Already he'd made his speech. Now they said goodbye to the advisors, soldiers, and family who were lined up along the palace as others watched.

The people wanted to see their king gleaming and golden and strong.

When they returned from this journey, from the divine lands, they wouldn't need jewelry to shine before the people. They'd create a legacy that surpassed any mortal adornment. If everything went as Gilgamesh planned, they'd do more than just have a grand adventure. They'd return with Enkidu's salvation, yes, but also with better terms for humans who dealt with cruel gods. People who sacrificed and labored for the divine, only for them to meddle with their lives out of spite.

Gilgamesh nodded to his wives and children as he passed them. He didn't even know all their names. Then again, most of the children weren't actually his. Already his most recent bride, the woman Enkidu had gone head-to-head with him over, had the rounded stomach of pregnancy her tunic scarcely concealed. Another child arrived that would bear his name but belonged to someone else. He'd always been a ghost within his home, not able to get close to others. Until he'd met a man who changed everything.

Enkidu stood speaking with Akkiru who said something that made him laugh. Gilgamesh smiled. All he wanted was for him to laugh like that for decades, to have the man at his side for a lifetime. They went on this journey to achieve that, and he'd fight the gods to see it happen.

Gilgamesh reached Usun.

What your son wants more than anything is a relationship with you.

The boy lifted his chin to meet his father's eyes. The city's pale buildings reflected in his dark irises and his mahogany curls fluttered across his forehead. Gilgamesh wanted to reach out, place a hand on the boy's shoulder.

But it could cost him.

His jaw had sharpened, and he'd gained height since Gilgamesh had last interacted with him. Here was a child who truly belonged to him, yet they were strangers as much as any other. Of anything Gilgamesh had done, what little he'd given to his son was one of his greatest deeds, and he wouldn't risk the boy's life.

He nodded to Usun then stepped up to his wife before kneeling before her. She was even more majestic standing with the palace stretching behind her and sunlight glowing in her braids. "My queen."

"My king." She offered her hand, and he kissed it. The city's focus fixed on their leaders, and Gilgamesh smiled as he rose back to his full height. Shamhat's eyes were as sharp as a well-honed knife. This was a performance they put on for the rest of the world. They needed to remember that she had Gilgamesh's full authority no matter how long he was gone. Or even if he didn't return.

"You didn't visit your mother's temple before leaving."

Gilgamesh had to fight an eye roll. She apparently hadn't exercised all the admonitions in private. "She won't see me. Time is precious, and I have little of it. I'm tired of squandering it by waiting on her."

Shamhat winced. She'd always been closer to his mother and more devoted to her as a goddess. "I understand." She reached up and brushed his shoulder, smoothed a wrinkle from his tunic. Her fingers traced down his arm again then she grabbed his palm and squeezed. It was more public affection than they usually expressed but he tucked her petite hand within his. "I love you, Gilgamesh. Stay safe and protect Enkidu as well. Hmm?"

Enkidu had moved closer and was speaking with Usun. The boy shook his head, but a smile pulled up his lips.

Gilgamesh returned his attention to Shamhat. "I have no requests for you, my queen. We both know this city rests well in your hands."

She smirked. "True. I'll miss you arguing with me, though. I'll be spoiled with always having my way by the time you return."

"I'll store up a slew of arguments for when I do."

"Something to look forward to." She tilted her chin as if she prepared to challenge him. He couldn't help his responding grin as she spoke. "I'll see you by the New Year, Lugal?"

He nodded but pulled her into his arms. She startled then melted into the hug and he bent down to whisper into her oil-sweet hair. "I love you too, Shamhat."

Her grip tightened, and it took a moment before she released him. They stared at each other for another trio of heartbeats, then he turned and found Enkidu. The two of them waved goodbye to the palace attendants, the soldiers, the advisors, the politicians, and family.

Then they began the path through the city where they continued waving and Gilgamesh yelled out promises of victory and glory. He shouted them without a beat of hesitation. They'd succeed or they'd die trying.

CHAPTER SEVEN
AMONG RUINS

"I don't want to go into the forest." Enkidu's voice was soft, his eyes averted. Gilgamesh readjusted his pack and studied the man. The entire walk so far, he'd been distant and quiet.

Gilgamesh had thought they'd overcome the tension when Enkidu found him on the roof. That night they'd made love for hours, Gilgamesh running his fingers over Enkidu's flesh like he'd memorize the man's every dip and hair. When their mouths met, Gilgamesh felt like he could taste his soul.

Enkidu had agreed to go on this trip, to try.

And Gilgamesh would fight until his heart ceased pumping to save him.

Hope had flushed back through Gilgamesh. The two of them together could achieve anything.

Even after the dream with Utu's omen, Gilgamesh had tucked alongside Enkidu and felt like the world's chaos settled. Since their journey began, however, he'd pulled away again. Something weighed on him. Now he stared at the forest with a sheen muddying his hazel eyes.

Gilgamesh scuffed a boot over grass. Each time he attempted to breach whatever ate at Enkidu, it seemed to push the man further away. Gilgamesh took a deep breath, down into his stomach, the axes on his hips shifting. "I know a different way. It's somewhere you've never been before, above Humbaba's lair."

Enkidu frowned down at a moth that flitted through petite ivory flowers. "Will it delay us?"

"Only by a few days. There's somewhere I'd like you to see on that path."

Enkidu raised his face. His gaze met Gilgamesh's for the first time in what felt like days. His lips lifted a touch. "All right, I'll follow you."

After pressing a kiss on his cheek, Gilgamesh turned away from the forest and walked north alongside it. This trip hadn't been Enkidu's plan, he'd hated the idea from the outset, and even after agreeing he seemed to go along with it begrudgingly. But he'd shared a truth. He wanted to live. Gilgamesh would do anything to force that hope into existence, make it reality.

Days passed until they reached closer to the Id-Ugina River again, farther north where it widened and the waters rushed rapidly along. Gilgamesh pointed as they approached what he looked for. "There."

Enkidu walked with him onto a sand-covered street surrounded by half a dozen dilapidated buildings. Vines crawled out from square windows where plaster crumbled. Most roofs had fallen in. A tree grew in the middle of one, its bough brushing over broken walls.

Enkidu studied all of it slowly. "What is this place?"

"We don't know." Pressing a hand to Enkidu's lower back, Gilgamesh walked them through the village the wild slowly consumed. "It's some civilization that existed before

Uruk, though, and was lost. There's not much remaining here aside from a few crumbling pots and broken pieces of furniture."

They stepped into a building. Grasses swallowed most of the floor, some of them nearly thigh high. Running a hand along a wall, Gilgamesh whispered. "The first time I came across this was with my soldiers. It made me realize how a place can become forgotten by history. Maybe one day Uruk will be unremembered as well."

"Uruk is far larger than this village." Enkidu stepped ahead into the room. He never hesitated in a wild place. Gilgamesh would have used a stick to see if any snakes or other beasts hid in the grasses. But Enkidu moved through them like he swam through the greens, as if he belonged among them. "It's comforting in a way, though."

"Comforting?" Gilgamesh had always found the place haunting. His ears strained there, like they listened for people long gone.

Enkidu looked back over his shoulder. "The forest is slowly taking it back. Everything begins in the earth and ends there as well. I do find that comforting."

Heat swept through Gilgamesh's pounding heart. He turned his face to take in the place again and saw it with fresh eyes. A spiderweb in a corner glistened, the dew on it like jewels. Wind sighed through the structure, a soothing song. And the colors of the place were the same as Enkidu's eyes—warm browns, rich greens, gleaming golds.

Maybe it wasn't the crumbling tomb he'd imagined, but a sign that life carried on. That there was hope.

He stepped behind Enkidu and curled an arm around his waist. "You're always saying such profound things." Enkidu's breath lifted his hand. "Perhaps you're meant to be a philosopher."

A chuckle rumbled Enkidu's stomach and trembled through Gilgamesh. "Look at me. Do you think the gods created a man like me for philosophy?"

Gilgamesh turned Enkidu to face him. He moved his eyes slowly down him, taking in the elegant sweep of his horns, the softness in his eyes, the graceful way he held himself. Those lips that kissed with heat but parted to speak such wise, thoughtful things all the damned time.

"Yes."

Enkidu's nose flared then he moved towards the damaged wall and ran his hands over the same place Gilgamesh had touched. He stood beneath a broken section of the roof so light spilled over him. He glowed ethereally. Gilgamesh took a step forward. He wanted to touch the man, make sure he was still there and whole. He seemed like a ghost colored with such eerie light amid the broken house.

"I think you're full of shed." Enkidu turned towards him, grinning, life dancing in his eyes again. "You're blinded by love."

Gilgamesh returned the smile and stepped forward. "Or I speak the truth and you're the one who isn't seeing things clearly."

"Mhmm. What would your advisors think if they saw you here, standing among ruins discussing philosophy?"

Gilgamesh moved so they nearly touched. The atmosphere crackled with tension. Enkidu's gaze rested on Gilgamesh's lips, and he shifted closer. Gilgamesh liked where this was going very much. Fuck philosophy and thinking about life and death and the meaning of it all.

"They'd think their king was not only god-born and fearless but also brilliant," Gilgamesh said in the tone that he knew would make Enkidu's eyes flash, his lips part to argue.

Gilgamesh captured his mouth in a passionate kiss before Enkidu could do so.

Enkidu dug fingers into his ribs, curling his thumbs over his hips. Upon pressing him against the wall, plaster cracked, dusting the grasses beneath them. A boom echoed, and Gilgamesh lifted his face. A fat raindrop hit his cheek. Another followed.

The heavens opened. Rain fell so fast they couldn't move quickly enough to avoid it. The dry ground didn't absorb the downpour, and they splashed through rapidly forming puddles, huddling together beneath the corner of what remained of the roof.

Gilgamesh flung his hands out. His tunic clung to his body and dripped cool water into the dirt. "Fuck."

Enkidu lifted his face, his nose and cheeks red, his beard dripping. He smiled. "Now, there's the king I know."

"Angry and grumbling?" He wrung his tunic out and water trailed his leg. "It's a wonder you put up with me."

Enkidu removed his tunic and balled up the fabric. He lifted his face, smiled, then threw the sopping wet material at Gilgamesh. It hit his cheek with a wet thunk then dragged down his arm, leaving moisture where he'd just dried. Gilgamesh clacked his teeth together. "Do you have some odd enjoyment you derive from throwing shed at me?"

Enkidu laughed hard enough that his stomach shook. He was nearly bare, only his loincloth remaining. Rain rushed beyond them, and the world had gone dark, but Gilgamesh would know Enkidu's shape in endless darkness. He could certainly make it out in the shadows, muscles flexing as Enkidu prowled towards him, the way his chest hair had darkened in the rain, pasting to his flesh.

He grabbed Gilgamesh's fingers and whispered against his neck. "I wish to spend the next hundred years bringing that defiant expression to your face."

"Wonderful," Gilgamesh grumbled, but he could scarcely keep the annoyance in his voice. There'd been so much lingering between them, so many things Enkidu kept silent and tucked away. Gods, all he wanted was for the man to live that century he spoke of and harass him every day of it. Never had Gilgamesh met someone who kept him as enthralled. He knew he never would again.

Enkidu bit Gilgamesh's neck softly, and he groaned. Grasping Gilgamesh's hand, Enkidu drew him a step back.

"Follow me?" Enkidu breathed so goosebumps rose over his flesh.

Anywhere, he wanted to reply, but he was too fixed on Enkidu's lips brushing his neck, the man's hands sliding over his hip.

He followed as Enkidu moved them across the room. Rain fell so hard it murmured into a cacophony that drowned the world. Everything became Enkidu's elegant fingers gliding across damp skin, Enkidu's scent turned wild in the rain, Enkidu's voice rumbling approval as Gilgamesh returned the touches.

They stopped moving, and Gilgamesh was so hungry with love for the man, he might starve. Enkidu grabbed his arms, grinned at him, his eyes wild, and whirled them.

World spinning around him, Gilgamesh stumbled to keep his balance, then found himself in the downpour, rain drenching him. He hissed at the deluge's impact then glared at Enkidu whose smile had spread across his cheeks.

Gilgamesh swiped a hand over his beard, flung rain away. "Oh, you—"

"Person you're willing to risk your life to save?" Enkidu asked with a laugh, half yelling over the pounding rain.

The gray world enveloped them, but Gilgamesh no longer cared that he stood sopping beneath a deluge. Because Enkidu was before him. Beautiful, fierce, gentle, brilliant, passionate Enkidu.

"You are my life." Gilgamesh couldn't even match the teasing tone of Enkidu's words. Standing there with Enkidu watching rain glide down his form, his eyes twinkling even as they blinked away the drops, Gilgamesh knew he'd never spoken truer words. He'd risk everything for him, give anything. Once they made it to the divine realm, he probably would have to sacrifice. He'd do so without hesitating.

Enkidu's smile slowly disappeared. He reached for Gilgamesh's hand before resting his forehead on his shoulder. Gilgamesh pulled him closer and scraped a cheek along his horn. They stood like that until the rain slowed, then they shrugged down against the wall and Enkidu leaned on Gilgamesh.

"A friend of mine died," Enkidu whispered. "I saw it myself."

Gilgamesh's breath caught, and he pulled Enkidu closer. The story spilled out of Enkidu and Gilgamesh listened and rubbed his back rhythmically. When Enkidu finished the telling, he sighed like it had taken something from him. Gilgamesh shifted where he could hold more of his weight but couldn't fight the snarl wrinkling his nose.

The gods were cruel. Even his own fucking mother.

He and Enkidu had come together to change things. That truth fizzled down Gilgamesh's nerves and blossomed into his bones. Utu said this journey had a greater purpose.

Gilgamesh would find a way to save Enkidu, then he'd make the gods account for their actions.

Burying his nose into Enkidu's hair, he vowed it to himself.

And for the time, he'd treasure every minute of the months it took them to reach the divine's territory. He'd love this man like his heartbeat depended on it. When they returned to Uruk victorious, Enkidu's salvation in hand, Gilgamesh would do whatever he could to keep him safe for the rest of their lives.

CHAPTER EIGHT

AMONG THE DIVINE

SHAMHAT HAD BEEN RIGHT. If Enkidu gained nothing else from the journey, if he still died at the end, he would be grateful for the time traveling through the wild with Gilgamesh again.

Once they'd left the ruins, they journeyed into woods Enkidu had never been, somewhere north of Humbaba's lair. They'd gathered food, lain together beside fires, and made love beneath the stars as they once had.

For a few blissful weeks, Enkidu was so happy he wondered if he was dreaming. Even when they discussed more difficult things, Gilgamesh's ominous dream or Enkidu's grief, he was next to Gilgamesh, tucked in his arms. At his side, he slept peacefully despite how dark the world seemed.

Then the landscape changed, growing quiet. For days they walked through silence so intense it ached. Enkidu curled his fingers around his bags' straps. It wasn't normal for the world to be so still. Usually, birds chittered at each other, bugs whined, something crackled dry leaves in the distance.

Here, the world held still, not even a breeze coming to ruffle the long, thin, mournful shapes of trees.

"This has to be the doorway into the divine realm." Gilgamesh snapped twigs as he moved between a pair of pines and swiped his hand before them. The air rippled, glistening with colors, and a spicy scent Enkidu had never smelled before rushed in the wind.

Enkidu nodded but his gaze slid back and forth over the stark landscape of slim, unmoving trees against a dark, cloudless sky. According to Akkiru, scholars believed mortals died if they crossed the line between the human and divine realm. Enkidu doubted many had tested the theory. No human would have been foolish enough to travel several days through silent, barren woods that hunched away from wind that didn't exist.

They were not human, though, and certainly not wise, so here they were.

Gilgamesh pressed through the shimmering gap between the trees, his arm dipping like he reached into a lake. Enkidu jumped forward and grabbed for him, but Gilgamesh pressed forward, falling into the world beyond.

Enkidu gasped as he disappeared.

The barrier's surface stopped rippling.

Enkidu's heart pounded. Traveling through woods with Gilgamesh was one thing. They could protect each other from beasts, gather food and water, and locate safe places to sleep. Stepping into an unknown world made Enkidu's throat tighten, but he couldn't abandon Gilgamesh. Would never. He closed his eyes and pushed through the barrier. Something slimier than lake algae wrapped around him, making his stomach churn and cheeks tingle like he might lose his breakfast.

Gilgamesh grasped him, tucked him under his arms. He

smelled like fresh pine, but there was always a refined city-scent that lingered on him too from various oils and spices. And a hint of sweet cedar that curled around the edges of all the other tones. It was like breathing fresh air after swimming in tepid water.

Stomach slowly settling, Enkidu raised his face and frowned at the surroundings. "This is the gods' territory?"

Gilgamesh loosened his grip and slowly appraised the dry, rocky land, the jutting, knife-sharp cliffs, the dark clouds that sat frozen in the sky. "It's not like in my dream."

He'd discussed the dream a few times, but he always seemed to leave details out. Enkidu's gut twisted whenever it came up. It had to hold more than what he'd shared with the way Gilgamesh frowned about it, but Enkidu couldn't find the courage to insist Gilgamesh tell him. Instead, when he discussed it, Enkidu remained silent. He tucked his face into Gilgamesh's shoulder. Gilgamesh slid fingers over Enkidu's horn but kept his gaze fixed forward.

"Most creatures like Humbaba remain in this realm, away from humans. We need to stay aware."

Enkidu pulled away to stand upright, but his heart ached. They'd stepped into the divine's realm and would face immortal dangers. Together they'd killed the Bull of Heaven with minimal injuries, but taking on Humbaba had nearly ended them both.

If he knew this journey resulted in Gilgamesh dying too, Enkidu would have refused to go. Hope was a poison. It filled his lungs until he couldn't turn his head without his vision blurring.

If there was a chance he might survive the curse, he couldn't give up.

He slid his hand over his blade's hilt at his side and nodded to Gilgamesh who had axes on both of his hips and more weapons in his pack. For what little good human blades would do when facing immortal beasts.

They started moving down the hillside they stood on, along a rocky trail.

The world remained silent. It ached in Enkidu's mind. He could manage without sight, but the lack of sound felt like having his skin peeled back. He kept searching around, certain something had to move and make a noise somewhere.

But it was just the King and the wild man walking through sacred territory, their footsteps echoing against eternity.

Cresting another hill, they reached a scattering of caves and boulders. The sun shone low and tired behind clouds, coating everything in a foggy orange.

Flapping wings caused Enkidu to look towards the sky.

Vultures circled.

One cried out.

He walked towards whatever they flew above, and Gilgamesh followed but slid his axes loose and whirled them in his hands.

They passed through a narrow gulch and came out the other side.

Bones shot from the earth like they'd unburied themselves. A dozen lions lay half-eaten with exposed ribs and blood-matted fur. Death was everywhere.

Enkidu released a breath and clenched a boulder's ragged edge to keep himself upright.

The stink of blood and rot hit him, and he retched. All the nausea that passing between the realms had caused him surged back into his stomach.

Gilgamesh wrapped an arm around his waist and traced

his gaze over the gnarled, half-dead plants growing amid the slaughtered pride. The dark mouth of a cave stretched beyond. This pack had died in their home, some stronger beast ending them even in a highly defensible place.

"Gilgamesh," Enkidu whispered, "what if this is a mistake? We've come seeking life, but what if we've stumbled into our deaths?"

Gilgamesh turned so his beard grazed Enkidu's cheek. He pressed a kiss to his temple. "Then we shall go down fighting. But I do not think, together, we will die. Let's get away from here."

Enkidu nodded. A weak squeal pierced the aching silence, and he froze.

"Enkidu?" Gilgamesh looked back over his shoulder.

"Something is hurt." Enkidu moved forward into the mosaic of death that had terrified him moments before. Another pitiful mewl rang out from within the cave.

Enkidu approached the cave's opening. Vultures at a nearby carcass flapped their massive wings and flew away. Their shrieking filled the uncomfortable silence.

Gilgamesh's steps sounded behind him. When Gilgamesh reached him, he grabbed his arm. "What are you doing?"

"Some creature needs help."

Gilgamesh's eyes went wide as they fixed on the cave. "It could be a monster."

"It's not." Enkidu knew it in his gut. He couldn't leave some animal to die slowly of an injury he might help.

Gilgamesh sighed but readjusted his grip on the axes and nodded towards the cave's opening. Enkidu led the way, walking in slowly. Shadows hung like cloaks, and the space stank of rot. Enkidu covered his nose but continued farther into the darkness when the whimpering cry echoed again.

Gilgamesh heaved a breath as Enkidu charged forward.

A lioness lay torn apart, her mouth open so her fangs glistened in the dim light.

Beneath her half a dozen cubs remained perfectly still.

They were gone.

Enkidu hit his knees and gently pushed the lioness aside. The babies were uninjured—they'd apparently starved. The lioness had thrown herself over them, protecting her young at the cost of her life.

Gilgamesh kneeled beside Enkidu and rubbed his back.

Enkidu's nose flared as he reached for the lifeless creatures. Why did fate have to be so brutal? They barely looked old enough to have opened their eyes. Had their paws even touched dirt outside the cave? Had they felt a cool breeze ruffling their fur or the sun's warmth before cruelty stole them?

Something shifted among the pile. A head lifted and released the pleading cry Enkidu had heard. The cub attempted to rise but stumbled.

Gilgamesh leaned in towards the creatures, squinting in the darkness then he grunted. "It has an injured leg, and the wound is festering. A pity, we should put the thing out of its misery."

"No." Enkidu snatched the baby into his hands, being mindful of its limbs. "He's not dying."

The lion cried out at the movement but curled into Enkidu's arms as he drew him closer.

Gilgamesh clicked his tongue. "He will with no family to feed him paired with that injury."

The cub tucked against Enkidu's chest, burrowing its face

into his beard. He was golden with tufts of dark hair on his head and tail and fine ribs smaller than Enkidu's fingers that showed through his side. A slash wept blood along his leg and it was swollen and hot, but it was something that could heal.

"We can protect him," Enkidu said.

Gilgamesh's face snapped up. "Enkidu, look at the thing. It's bound to die in a few days' time. Even if it didn't, how are we supposed to continue this journey with a lion cub?"

Enkidu brushed his thumb over the creature's wild patch of hair. The cub was so small compared to him. So needy. But it had bright, intelligent eyes that blinked up at Enkidu without a hint of fear.

What a foolish beast to fight for life in such a cruel world.

Enkidu brushed down the cub's back again. It still had the softness of youth.

Enkidu was doing the same—fighting and journeying and facing gods to beg for a few more years. It yowled within him. Even if the world around him fell apart, even if life was brutal and unjust, he wanted a chance. Wanted his portion of it, at least.

He'd done no worse than any other mortal to deserve a life cut short.

Gilgamesh was right about the cub. If they left him, he'd die within the day. A cruel death filled with pain and suffering. The creature raked soft claws over Enkidu's fingers.

"I want to keep him."

Gilgamesh stood and angled away. "We cannot keep a lion as a pet."

Enkidu rose as well, slowly to keep the cub steady.

"Mosaics and statues of you around Uruk always have lions in them."

Gilgamesh crossed his arms. Uncrossed them. Waved them at the little creature that gnawed on Enkidu's finger. The cub's tongue was rough as it grazed his thumb's pad. "Yes, to make a point. Lions are dangerous."

"This one isn't dangerous." Enkidu readjusted the cub enough to pull his bag free. He removed a blanket to tie as a sling and some honey which he poured into a cloth, twisting the top before offering an end to the little lion. He lapped at it a few times then hungrily sucked.

"Don't feed it!" The King of Uruk looked at Enkidu like he'd announced he planned to keep a venomous viper on his person.

Enkidu ignored him and stepped out of the cave. When fresh air hit his face, he took a deep breath and walked past the cub's dead family, back towards the direction they'd come. The lion feasted eagerly, sucking the honey down greedily as tiny paws kneaded the fabric. Its eyes had a ring of blue around them in the light. Enkidu stopped and turned back towards Gilgamesh who still had his mouth parted.

"Is it because I won't live?" he asked.

Gilgamesh snapped his mouth closed and frowned before speaking. "What are you talking about?"

"If I save this creature,"—he brushed the lion's coat—"and he becomes attached, he won't be able to return to the wild. If I die, you'll be stuck caring for him. Is that why you don't wish for me to take him?"

Gilgamesh's jaw worked, but he didn't speak. His eyes dashed between the cub and Enkidu, a sheen sweeping over them. His silence blended in with the unnatural world. For a moment he seemed more divine than mortal.

"No. It's because we can't drag a lion along with us. Fine, though. Keep him but clean that wound and bind his leg, or he'll struggle to walk." Gilgamesh growled. He slammed his axes into their holsters, storming forward. He stopped to look back and emphasized his words. "When we return to Uruk, however, he's your responsibility. Don't expect me to become attached to that little beast."

Enkidu smiled down at the cub and ignored Gilgamesh. The creature needed Enkidu. By the time a year had passed, he'd be old enough to survive on his own. For now, Enkidu could make a difference. He could leave a mark on the world, a smear in clay that might harden and outlast him. "I'm going to call him Urmah."*

"That's a bit to the point," Gilgamesh grumbled without looking back.

Enkidu's grin widened. "Would you rather name him something else?"

"I'd rather not name him at all."

Enkidu had caught up with his lover, but he whispered down to the little golden cub, to Urmah, "Don't worry. Gilgamesh is moody and takes a while to come around, but he will."

"Don't begin your relationship with that creature by lying to it."

Enkidu leaned over and kissed Gilgamesh's cheek. "Thank you."

Gilgamesh heaved a breath and grumbled. Color had swept high on his cheeks. Enkidu chuckled but kept his thoughts to himself. Urmah needed them, and Gilgamesh usually did the right thing. Sometimes it required a nudge, or a shove down a cliff side, but he'd be glad they'd saved

----

*   Urmah is Sumerian for lion

the creature one day. Even if the animal only lived a few more days, at least they'd tried. They'd shown the gods that amid a cruel reality, they wouldn't become vicious themselves.

Enkidu tucked the cub tighter into his sling. When they stopped for the night, he applied a salve to Urmah's wound and fed him more honey and eggs they found. Gilgamesh ate his meal angled away from them both, as though he couldn't tolerate looking at the lion. Enkidu chuckled and cracked another shell.

A few days passed and the creature hungrily yowled and jerked around within the sling. Gilgamesh kept grumbling about him drawing monsters to them, but they'd encountered nothing but the endless silence. Urmah's coat had become glossier, and he had the increasing energy of a young cub. Enkidu smiled more and worried less with each passing day.

They'd finally reached the mountains. In the distance the duel peaks stretched up towards the clouds that hung low in a gray sky. The entire world felt leeched of color, even the boulders studding the sand between them and the mountains were a dreary mud-brown, the color of a dried up lake. As they crested a final hill before reaching the mountain's base, Enkidu smiled down at Urmah. He was golden with crystal blue eyes and bursting with enough energy to make up for the landscape's dreariness.

Something zinged through the air. Enkidu raised his face away from the cub.

"Gilgamesh!" he cried.

But it was too late.

The flying boulder slammed into Gilgamesh and knocked him to the ground.

CHAPTER NINE
SENTRIES

BREATHS CAME PAINFULLY, a slicing sting that caused Gilgamesh to grit his teeth. The stone that covered his torso scraped his skin. Enkidu cried out as Gilgamesh pushed it off his chest and rolled across the ground, jumping to his feet again when he found a boulder to shield himself behind.

Enkidu met him there, and his hands were everywhere, grazing Gilgamesh's cheek, brushing his shoulders, coursing along the edges of his chest as gently as petals. He didn't flinch even when another stone flew past them, clipping the boulder and landing with a thud onto the ground, dust flying. "How badly are you hurt?"

The cub stared out of its wrap at Gilgamesh, its eyes wide and searching.

"I'll make it," Gilgamesh said. "We need to focus on overcoming whatever we've stumbled across." He grabbed Enkidu's hand and pressed a kiss to the knuckles. Enkidu moved closer to him, tucked his nose into the dip of his neck.

The lion cub whirled around within its sling, banging

Gilgamesh's injured chest. He gritted his teeth and hissed from the pain but said nothing. Nurturing the half-dead animal had awakened something within Enkidu, washing away the sadness that had lingered around his expression. Gilgamesh would put up with the little pest if it soothed the man he loved. He brushed fingers down Gilgamesh's chest more firmly, his brow furrowing.

Gilgamesh tilted the man's chin up and kissed him softly. "I'm okay. Truly. I'll probably have some bruising. You can inspect it later if it makes you feel better."

Enkidu frowned but dropped his hand and tucked the cub back into its place. Gilgamesh moved around him and pushed onto his toes to peek past the boulder. Another rock sailed in their direction, and he yanked Enkidu down into a crouch beside him as the projectile grazed the boulder and burst into a cascade of pebbles and dust.

Beyond were the peaks of Mount Mashu that Utu had mentioned. It had to be them. Two mountains sat adjacent, their tops reaching for the heavens. There was apparently a doorway at the base that they needed to find to go through the mountain.

A pair of monsters, one male and one female, stood at the bottom. Half their bodies were scorpion-like and ended in massive, curled stingers, the other half appeared human. They had soft brown skin ornamented with gold jewelry and large, perceptive dark eyes. Guards.

They'd make it past, though, Utu already foretold that.

The cub released a squeal of pitiful whines, and Enkidu massaged the creature's head with his massive hand. It was amazing it survived when its siblings had died—it was a pitiful thing if Gilgamesh had ever seen one.

Enkidu stood and slowly looked up over the rock's edge. Gilgamesh reached out and grabbed his calf. He needed to feel the man, to have some connection to him, to have the ability to yank him away from danger if necessary.

Enkidu dropped back, an arm tucked around the cub. His movements were as fluid as water. No stones shot at them so he'd either gone unnoticed or the monsters were only out to attack Gilgamesh. Both possibilities.

Gilgamesh's hand still rested on Enkidu's leg. "You may need to leave the cub—"

"Urmah. His name is Urmah."

A complaint sat in Gilgamesh's mouth, aching on his tongue. With anyone else, he'd growl and say he didn't give a damn about the creature's name. But Enkidu looked up at him with his forest-wild eyes, and Gilgamesh's heart dipped into his stomach.

He loved this man—stupidly. Without pause, he'd give his life to spare Enkidu's. He could budge on a name. After clearing his throat, he continued. "You may need to leave Urmah secured here while we deal with these monsters."

"They look like humans."

Gilgamesh's lips thinned. Enkidu was choosing to be contentious. "What part of giant-scorpion-body makes them look human?"

Enkidu grazed fingers over a horn. "What makes me not a monster, then?"

A sigh rushed from Gilgamesh, and he moved closer, gripped Enkidu's horn, and pulled him until their noses touched. "You're human. Those things out there with bodies of death that are throwing boulders at us, they're not. And I like these damn horns."

Color flushed across Enkidu's cheeks and over his nose. Gilgamesh kissed him. Enkidu tangled fingers into his hair. The cub—Urmah—jerked around at being pressed between the men, and Gilgamesh leaned back to frown at the creature.

Enkidu smiled, though, and readjusted the material. He pulled the sling off and tucked Urmah into the rocks. "You must stay here for now."

The cub yowled, its pink tongue lolling out of its mouth.

"Stay," Enkidu said firmly before tucking his pack in front and turning back to Gilgamesh. "What is your plan?"

"I need to take down at least one of them so we have a chance."

Enkidu frowned. "Then you'll need me to act as a distraction so you can attack without being noticed."

His breath hurt, throbbing his chest, and Gilgamesh clenched his teeth. Enkidu might end up injured or worse. The ache in his breast spread, and Gilgamesh parted his lips to protest, to tell Enkidu to sit with Urmah and wait. But Gilgamesh couldn't do it alone, and this journey was important. It was the only hope they had for saving Enkidu's life. "Yes, but protect yourself primarily."

Enkidu's lips tipped up. "And Urmah? You want me to keep him safe too, right?"

Gilgamesh shot him a look which made the man laugh. It was the most beautiful sound, and Gilgamesh bent down to kiss him. "Fine, and the little beast, too."

Enkidu chuckled against his lips and looked up with twinkling eyes. It made Gilgamesh feel unbreakable. He grabbed a copper shield off the back of his pack and lifted it with a grunt. It had been custom designed for him—large enough to protect him from the shoulder to below the knee. The pain in his chest radiated into his arm until it trembled.

They had to make it through Mount Mashu though.

They had to find their way to Utnapishtim.

Or Enkidu died.

Enkidu, despite being Gilgamesh's size, despite pulling a sword from his pack and his eyes sharpening with intent, appeared elegant and gentle. A tree grown in a shady, quiet part of the forest to Gilgamesh's boulder that crashed through life.

Gilgamesh swallowed, nodded for Enkidu to follow, and threw himself out from their shelter. When Enkidu made it behind him, he ran. A rock pounded into Gilgamesh's shield hard enough to knock him off his feet, tumbling Enkidu down as well, but he jumped up, kept their protection lifted, and plowed forward.

As soon as they reached close enough to make out the face paint the scorpion creatures wore and the rubies studding their jewelry, Gilgamesh slammed the shield into the ground, creating an artificial shelter.

Boulders pounded into it. A spear hit hard enough that the blade sank through. Their breathing echoed back. Already the sun lowered in the sky. Utu seemed to watch them suspiciously, eyes narrowed and a frown forming.

Gilgamesh would prove to any gods watching that he wouldn't give up.

One of them may have cursed Enkidu. The others had become complicit. But he was Gilgamesh, two-thirds god and doer of great deeds. He'd fight the heavens to save Enkidu. If the gods wanted to stop them, they'd have to do so themselves.

Gilgamesh nodded to Enkidu, and they both jumped up. All those afternoons of practicing sparring together was coming to fruition. Enkidu lifted his sword and ran towards the scorpion creatures. A gasp ached through Gilgamesh's chest, but the monsters' focus on Enkidu gave him his chance.

He plowed forward, curving around the side where the

monsters weren't looking, pushing until his muscles strained.

An ache seized his lungs.

His stomach clenched.

The male scorpion flipped towards him, but it was too late for the monster to sidestep him.

He grabbed the beast's tail with one hand, swung himself onto his back without releasing the whipping stinger, then slammed an arm around his neck.

The creature cried out. He thrashed.

Gilgamesh sank his feet against scales and refused to yield.

All he needed to do was jerk his arm hard, and he'd snap the beast's neck.

He tightened his grip on the roaring, fighting creature and—

"Stop!" Enkidu shouted.

Gilgamesh froze but didn't release the beast. The female scorpion had a spear lifted towards Enkidu, but tears streaked her cheeks. Enkidu had his hands raised. He kept his focus on Gilgamesh, as though a sharp, deadly weapon aimed at him in the grip of a killer meant nothing. He didn't even have his sword in hand anymore.

"She loves him," Enkidu whispered. "Don't you see?"

The female scorpion gasped in breaths, her breastplate catching the sun's reflection with her ragged inhales.

"It doesn't matter," Gilgamesh said. The male scorpion had stopped fighting for the moment, his gaze fixed on his partner.

Gilgamesh prepared to end the creature, but Enkidu took a step forward. His voice was breeze-soft and wild in the way a hatchling was, all tender feathers and vulnerability. "She loves him how I love you."

Gilgamesh's lips parted then closed. The scorpion creatures still looked at each other, wet cheeks reflecting the sun's golden glow. If this creature loved his partner with half of how Gilgamesh felt for Enkidu, then he was no monster, and Gilgamesh couldn't bear to kill him.

He released his grip and dropped, rolling off the guard's back before jumping to his feet again. The scorpions hissed, baring pointed teeth. Enkidu and Gilgamesh stood unarmed before them. Their tails rattled menacingly, the pointers on the ends gleaming.

This might be it. If that was the case, he'd throw himself in front of Enkidu.

He could die protecting him.

That would be a life well lived.

The male scorpion's tail rose, Enkidu gasped, and the female scorpion raised her hands to intercept.

But the male swung his tail around, swiping Gilgamesh off his feet with the flat side.

Gilgamesh dropped with a grunt to the ground.

The creature hadn't stabbed him. He slammed a spear towards the dip in Gilgamesh's neck. Gilgamesh swallowed against its point.

"Please." Enkidu stepped towards the female. "I spared your mate. Do the same for me."

The woman shifted her gaze towards Gilgamesh. "Harran, release him."

"He has axes, Disha." He spoke their language clearly, but his words had a hiss to them.

"And you have a spear," the female replied. "Release him."

Harran's eyes flashed. A circle of crimson swirled around their center as he stepped back. Gilgamesh stumbled up and Enkidu rushed to meet him, to put an arm around his back.

His hands lingered in the same way Gilgamesh's had around his leg behind the boulder. Like he wished to remember Gilgamesh was alive. Like he wanted to hold him back from anything foolish.

"Thank you," Enkidu said.

Gilgamesh wanted to growl and complain about him thanking creatures that nearly killed them or snap about how the reason they'd ended up in the defensive position was because Enkidu had lowered his weapon.

"We have no fight with you," Enkidu continued, but his gaze remained fixed on Gilgamesh. It was so intimate it coursed over him like a touch, a lover's appraisal. His frustration left, his shoulders slumping. Enkidu was safe, and that was what mattered.

"That's not how things appear," Harran said.

"You threw boulders at us." Gilgamesh broke his focus away from Enkidu.

Harran's eyes flared with their fiery color again. "And you approached us with weapons."

The creature still held his spear and had it lifted, ready to throw. Gilgamesh had bested him once, but the moment of surprise passed and he wouldn't get another opportunity. They got out of this through speaking or not at all. Gilgamesh leaned towards Enkidu and kept his mouth shut. He knew his strengths—inspiring diplomacy with his words wasn't one of them.

Enkidu shifted. "We're on a quest, and we have Utu's blessing to be here."

Gilgamesh jerked away. Enkidu shrugged as color swept over his nose. Oh great. Enkidu was going to lie, and do so poorly, to massive divine monsters that could kill them both with a swing of their arms. Gilgamesh closed his eyes. He should have talked after all. At least the shed he said would have been honest, if inflammatory.

"Is that right?" Harran asked before dashing his partner a look.

Disha circled them. "Utu does not give mortals permission to come here."

"Mortals couldn't make it this far, could they?" Gilgamesh asked.

Enkidu raised his empty hands. "Listen, we've started poorly but—"

Harran shifted his spear towards the distance. He pulled his arm back and released the weapon. Enkidu turned to see what he aimed at then jumped nearly as high as the guard and grabbed the spear mid-air.

The scorpion-people hissed as Enkidu slammed the spear down, forcing it off its path and into the dirt. He tumbled at the motion, skidding over the dirt.

In the distance, Urmah limped forward, his tail swinging. When he reached Enkidu, he nipped at him as the man recovered his footing then scooped the cub up.

Sand whipped around in an unusual breeze, and Disha's brow furrowed. "He nearly got himself impaled saving that creature."

Enkidu walked back with Urmah tucked in his arms, and Gilgamesh sighed. Enough with the back and forth. Enough handling things diplomatically. He'd be himself, consequences be damned. "Yes, he's a fucking sentimental man for all his size would make it seem impossible. He can't have you killing his pet. He's grown rather attached to the creature."

Harran frowned at Gilgamesh, but the King massaged his temples and continued. "And he's a damn terrible liar, at that. But for all those things he's a good man and I love him." Gilgamesh turned to the woman. "I love him fiercely. A goddess has cursed him, and this journey is my only chance to save him. Utu didn't approve our journey here exactly. But he knows of it, and he's allowed it."

"You're Gilgamesh?" Disha hissed. He nodded, and she scurried forward on her thin legs towards her partner and whispered to him.

Harran huffed a sigh but turned back to Gilgamesh as Enkidu smiled down at a playful Urmah who hung upside down in his arms. Harran frowned. "Has Utu informed you about Mount Mashu?"

"He told me about it."

"What is your plan to get through?"

Gilgamesh turned towards Enkidu, as if the beautiful, tender-hearted man might have answers despite knowing he wouldn't. He looked at him, lion cub in arms, skin scuffed and bleeding from his fall, his brows pushed together, and a frown turning his lips down. Damn if he wasn't a terrible liar, more unprepared than him, too gentle-minded to live, and yet... And yet, Gilgamesh wished he could bind their hearts together, shelter him from the gods, and do anything to enable him to save some other ridiculous creature again.

"Get through?" Gilgamesh asked.

Harran scuttled back before the mountain's door. "When the sun is up, everything within the mountains burns with volcanic fire. Only the divine can move through this path without dying."

Enkidu's hand froze on Urmah's scruff. The cub whined then gave his neck a shake to release him.

"We can travel through the night," Gilgamesh said. "Does the mountain burn when the moon rules the sky?"

"No, but even if you run," Disha said, "you'd never make it in time. Mortals cannot outpace the sun."

Gilgamesh raised his face to the golden ball that tracked down the sky. To Utu, the god who'd given him an omen, but no means to interpret it. Who could fight and help him but wouldn't.

"Mortals may not, but Enkidu and I can."

It was Enkidu's turn to swivel towards him with wide eyes. A smile spread over Gilgamesh's face, though. They could make it. He knew it.

CHAPTER TEN

BY SUNRISE

URMAH NIPPED ENKIDU'S THUMB, and he sucked in a breath but loosened his hold. He'd frozen, gripping the creature's scruff again. The cub lapped its rough tongue over Enkidu's arm as though to apologize. Blood trickled down Enkidu's flesh and onto his palm as he stared at Gilgamesh, then the towering guards, then the peaks behind them.

The mountains were massive, as though gods had scooped up earth with their eternal fingers and created a fortress for the divine.

Running through it in a single night was impossible.

Running through it in multiple nights, even, was impossible.

He blinked and turned his face back towards Gilgamesh who grinned into the sunshine, his hand resting on an ax head.

Damn the beautiful, foolish man for never knowing his limits. Damn him for always wishing to fight first and discuss things second. The two creatures before them didn't inspire trust, and Enkidu wasn't the naïve, foolish man he'd once been. Still, Gilgamesh would have killed them without a thought. He'd do anything along this journey without hesitating all for the purpose to spare Enkidu's life. That didn't ease Enkidu's churning stomach.

Harran ran his hand over his chin and shifted, his scorpion-legs denting the dirt. "Fine. If you say Utu approves your journey and he hasn't ended you yet, I can accept it's within his will." He nodded to his partner who gave a matching bob of her head.

"There's a cave nearby that's not connected to the mountain." Disha thumbed behind her. "You could stay there for now unless you plan to run it tonight?"

"No." Gilgamesh worked his jaw as he lifted his face to the mountain. The sun had dipped below it, casting a shadow like an arrow over them. It slowly bled along and would slice through their group soon. "We'll need a day of sleep first so we can go with our full energy."

"Very well." Disha nodded to her left. "The cave is not much farther down that path. This area is guarded; you can rest easy."

Gilgamesh grunted. Enkidu wanted to poke him the way Shamhat did or grip the man's hand hard enough to draw his attention. The guards had been helpful and kind after they'd barreled in threatening them. Yet, Gilgamesh wouldn't extend gratitude.

"Thank you," Enkidu said right as Urmah popped his head out of the sling, lifting his face to take in Disha's enormous frame. The cub squealed in the same terrified manner he had when they'd found him, then popped his head back within the fabric.

"Mind your pet. The divine realm is a dangerous place for mortal creatures." Harran narrowed his eyes at the sling then flicked his fiery gaze to Gilgamesh. "And if you attempt to harm us again, we will usher your spirits into the Great Below, Utu's will or otherwise."

Gilgamesh scoffed, and Enkidu grabbed his arm. "We understand and thank you."

Gilgamesh's lips parted like he might say something more, but Enkidu tightened his grip and pulled him towards the boulder where they'd stored their bags. The guards watched the entire time.

Once they found the cave and made sure it was empty, Gilgamesh gathered stones and piled them at the entrance. Darkness had swept across the silent valley and with each additional rock added, he blocked more of the moon's silvery light.

"Locking us in?" Enkidu asked.

Gilgamesh dropped another boulder with a groan and looked back over his shoulder. "Creating a barrier between us and everything else. I don't trust those creatures."

Enkidu sat and ran his thumb down Urmah's back. The cub stretched then curled into Enkidu's lap and rubbed his whiskers over the man's leg. It was soothing and Enkidu released a breath that allowed his shoulders to drop, his teeth to unclench. The pitiful bundle of ribs and hunger they'd found had already filled out in a few days' time, curves rounding his once emaciated form. His appetite increased day by day and his eyes often glittered with mischief. Now the cub tucked alongside Enkidu, his body growing warm and heavy.

If Enkidu did nothing else with his life, he'd saved this creature.

With a deep sigh, Urmah fell asleep. Enkidu should have jumped up, maneuvered around the rocks, lifted some and helped Gilgamesh finish his barrier. It didn't matter, though. All this striving accomplished nothing. Enkidu lived on time a goddess dictated. No gods intended to intervene.

They would allow Inanna to kill him.

It wasn't a substantial loss to them, anyway. Another goddess had created him to curtail Gilgamesh's restless striving. He'd achieved that. What more did his life matter? That ached in his bones, burned to the marrow. How desperately he wanted to love and be loved, to have significance. Once he'd scoffed at Gilgamesh's restless striving for legacy. Perhaps he now understood it. He didn't have enough time to unspool it all, though. That's why they took this ridiculous journey into a realm of dangerous divine creatures. To give him time so he could make an impact, so he could stay at Gilgamesh's side and love him until the end as he'd once promised.

He tucked Urmah beside his bag then wrapped the sling over him. The cub yawned but curled back into himself and fell into the heavy breaths of sleep again.

Enkidu was glad to help Gilgamesh, to love him, to share his bed. But that it was the only impact he'd make— that he'd have no impression of his own to leave on the world—ached at him.

Urmah was one exception.

Of course, a lion wouldn't live long. Especially if Gilgamesh released him into the wild where he'd have to fight and hunt and fend for himself. A decade would pass, Urmah would die, and nothing bearing Enkidu's influence would remain in this realm.

If Gilgamesh perished with him on this foolish journey, then nothing would remain of him at all except legends and perhaps a mosaic or statue Shamhat might commission. If Inanna killed Enkidu and Gilgamesh lived, whatever influence his love had on the man might die along with him.

Gilgamesh would likely revert to his previous ways—storming and angry and burning with the need for glory and retribution.

Gilgamesh placed a last stone which sealed the cave in with shadows. Enkidu pulled his knees to his chest as the man dropped beside him. Soft lips brushed his cheek. Enkidu sighed, all his worries and thoughts swirling out with his breath as he leaned against him.

Another kiss pressed over his temple. "What is it, love?"

Enkidu burrowed closer. He wanted to sink into his skin, become some part of him. Remain in Gilgamesh's heart even when his soul left this realm.

"Love?" Gilgamesh's voice had gone hoarse. He rubbed Enkidu's back. "Are you worried about going through the mountain?"

Enkidu shuddered, and Gilgamesh wrapped both arms around him, steadying them both.

"Yes." He couldn't discuss his thoughts about his impending death. Doing so would only unleash Gilgamesh's worry and fears and sadness. Enkidu couldn't bear it that night. "You've seen how large these mountains are. How will we ever pass through them in time?"

Enkidu's eyes adjusted to the shadows. A scrap of light reached through gaps in the rock wall, flowing along Gilgamesh's arm as he ran a hand up and down Enkidu's back.

"We're designed for greatness, Enkidu. Most mortals couldn't achieve this, but we can. Utu told me in the dream that I would see the gods' gardens in person. That cannot happen if we die within the mountain."

Lips parting with another sigh, Enkidu's mouth brushed Gilgamesh's neck. He shivered. Gilgamesh held the flavors of salt and sweat, of dust and earth. Enkidu liked it when his body tasted a little wild, when his oils were a secondary flavor, a sweetness against the sharp bite of his musky flesh.

That's what Enkidu needed: Gilgamesh's touch and the escape it offered. Enough with the spiraling thoughts and questions he couldn't answer. He traced his tongue down Gilgamesh's curving neck.

The man groaned, his hand curling around Enkidu's hip. Enkidu shifted to sit in his lap, grabbed his beard and forced his mouth to his for a kiss.

Gilgamesh pulled back. "Wait."

Enkidu's chest heaved. He had no desire to stop, though he forced his fingers to loosen, to sit up where he could make out Gilgamesh's glittering eyes in the darkness.

"We can't do this here."

"Why not?" Enkidu asked. It wasn't like the gods lacked knowledge of their relationship. They could see any aspect of the mortal realm—surely they'd already espied the two of them in passionate embraces. The gods could watch, for all Enkidu cared. He wanted Gilgamesh's body pressing into him, his strength holding him in place, the release it promised. So little time remained for that.

"Your little beast is here." Gilgamesh jutted his chin towards the bags where Urmah snored quietly.

Enkidu stared at the cub then turned back to his lover. "Urmah?"

"Yes." Gilgamesh's hands gripped Enkidu's hips, but he'd leaned away, resting his head on the cave's wall. "I'm not interested in having an audience."

"A sleeping cub is scarcely an audience."

"We'll wake the damn creature."

Enkidu chuckled. Here was a king who plowed into battle without a drop of hesitation, who made love with vigor and passion, who slashed his axes towards enemies and thought about strategy as blood splattered his clothes. But he worried about a lion cub seeing them together. "Wild creatures do not care. Mating is natural to them."

"Fine for them." Gilgamesh still hadn't released his grip, and Enkidu had to fight to keep from grinding into him. "Bedroom matters are a private event for me."

Shadows flowed over Gilgamesh's lips, swallowing them into the dark. Enkidu grazed fingers along them, earning a shiver as he discovered their shape despite the darkness, and smiled. "We're not in a bed, Gilgamesh."

"Sex, then. You know what I mean."

"The cub will not wake."

"If he does?"

"Then we can stop." Gilgamesh's thumb brushed circles over Enkidu's hip, then along the delicate flesh of his abdomen. Enkidu dipped towards him, pressing the hardness of them together. They both groaned, and Gilgamesh's fingers tightened. He pulled Enkidu's hips forward, beginning a rhythm Enkidu longed to maintain. Forcing himself to pause, though, he kissed Gilgamesh's cheek. "If it makes you truly uncomfortable, however, we don't—"

A pair of strong lips stalled his protests, and a stronger hand slipped beneath his tunic, gliding over skin and finding a nipple, then flipping Enkidu over to lie beneath Gilgamesh.

"You have oil?" Enkidu breathed as Gilgamesh moved over him like the sea lapping onto a shore.

Gilgamesh growled a response and tumbled over to his bag. He uncapped a jar, the sweet scent of cedar sweeping between them. Enkidu's body flamed with desire even before rough hands dripping oil trailed up his thigh.

They met like elements combining, water and sand

joining to become silt. And Enkidu, for a moment, forgot his worries about the future, about the purpose of his life, about surviving the mountain. For a moment nothing mattered aside from Gilgamesh's powerful body, his nipping teeth and gliding hands.

For those hours of the night, he was pleasure in his lover's hands, breath against his neck, a warm mouth and willing body.

He didn't belong to the past and had no future.

His entire existence rested on that glorious moment.

On feeling and experience and love.

If Urmah ever woke, neither of them noticed.

* * *

The problem with using sex as an escape was that the pleasure passed. Then the worries one attempted to drown came roaring back. Enkidu laid his head back on the cave wall and his horns scraped the rock.

Urmah pounced around. Enkidu had tied a feather to a stick and waved it mindlessly to keep the cub entertained.

Beyond, Gilgamesh slept with his hands resting over his bare chest. His dark hair cascaded around him like a waterfall. He'd tucked one leg up, the other was stretched out over the dirt.

He was beautiful in sleep with his lips parted. The glowing orange light that made it through the rocks at the cave entrance danced over them. Enkidu needed to wake him. They'd taken turns resting throughout the day so they didn't risk sleeping too late. The sun had begun to set, draping dramatic gleaming light as it dropped.

Enkidu tucked the feather stick into his bag and Urmah dropped onto his bottom, yowling and licking his nose. He offered the cub's head a scratch, and the creature lay down, but his eyes mourned the end of the game.

That's how life was. One could enjoy a moment and some larger hand of fate could sweep in and take it all away without warning. Enkidu offered the lion another pat born from pity.

He sat beside Gilgamesh and stole a moment from the scrambling spill of time. Gilgamesh's breathing was a rhythm like the forest, the moon's rise and fall, a shush of river water over smooth stones. The man lying before him was majestic. A goddess had created Enkidu for him, but it didn't change the awe he still felt to get to be with the mighty, beautiful, powerful King Gilgamesh. For all the teasing he offered him about his pridefulness and how he loved to boast over his reputation, Gilgamesh wasn't wrong.

Brushing knuckles softly over the man's arm, he whispered, "Gilgamesh."

His eyes fluttered open. They skimmed over Enkidu's face, then a grin slid across his jaw. "Good morning."

"Good evening."

"Ah." Gilgamesh reached out, tracing a thumb along Enkidu's cheek before sliding his hand over a horn. Enkidu shivered but stood and offered a hand. He pulled Gilgamesh to his feet. They stood chest-to-chest, breathing together but not moving. It was like they both felt the weight of fate pressing on them, boulders to wall them into the gods' will.

Gilgamesh curled his fingers around Enkidu's shoulder and pressed a kiss to his neck. "Are you ready?"

No.

"Yes."

"And the beast?"

Enkidu clicked his tongue and stepped away. "He has a name."

Gilgamesh chuckled, his eyes sparkling as he stepped up to his barrier and stretched to remove the highest rock. Damn the man for knowing exactly how to fluster him, to cause him to narrow his eyes, or to make heat flush over his skin.

Enkidu scooped up a flailing Urmah and stuck him into the sling. He'd have to stay there for an entire night while they ran through the mountain. The cub would protest but Enkidu would have to force him to remain in his pouch or they'd never make it, especially with his leg still healing.

An icy finger of fear scraped down Enkidu's spine. He didn't speak, but joined Gilgamesh, removing one stone after another. They walked back to the mountain's door in silence.

Harran and Disha stood dressed in the same gleaming breastplates as the previous day, though their expressions were less hostile. Gilgamesh nodded at them before eyeing the massive copper door they stood before. His mood had tempered with a day's rest, apparently. Heart racing, Enkidu scarcely met the guards' assessing gazes. Gilgamesh didn't doubt, but that was natural to him. He approached the world like it was a creature to fight. And he'd never lost. Enkidu didn't wish to fight, to affect the world like lightning striking. He wanted to fall like rain, to help things grow and replenish drought-empty stream beds.

Rain wasn't useful if it only lasted a season, though.

Gilgamesh shifted towards Enkidu and frowned. Worry swirled in his dark irises. There was a question in his gaze. If Enkidu truly pushed, he'd give up this foolish venture.

But then Gilgamesh would always wonder what would

have happened if they'd attempted it. What if they'd succeeded?

Enkidu would be gone soon. It was Gilgamesh who'd remain with the heartache and questions. Enkidu shook his head and offered a forced smile which only deepened Gilgamesh's frown.

Disha stood in a spill of bronze and pink light. The sun drifted behind the peaks. In a few moments, it would slip away, and they needed to begin their journey.

"Thank you once more for your help," Enkidu said.

Disha bobbed her head, but Harran turned his face into the shadows as he spoke. "May you get what the gods desire for you."

Enkidu's breath caught in his throat. He couldn't find words.

The gods desired his death.

They longed to punish Gilgamesh.

And this journey was foolish.

Gilgamesh strode forward, snatched Enkidu's fingers, and met his gaze. He looked at him as though Harran and Disha had disappeared, like they were the only two remaining in the world.

Gilgamesh's eyes said that if there was strength in his body, breath in his lungs, and a drop of hope in his spirit, he would never give up on Enkidu. His belief filled Enkidu like he breathed it in until it stretched out his sails. He offered a nod, a sincere one that hid nothing.

For you, I'll defy the gods.

Gilgamesh's lips turned up, then he raised his face. The sun slid down behind the mountain. He lowered his chin again, one more question in his expression.

"I'm ready," Enkidu said.

Gilgamesh grazed a thumb along his knuckles, stealing

another moment. The guards moved away from their positions.

Then Gilgamesh opened the door.

Heat washed out of the tunnel before them. Sweat broke over Enkidu's flesh, but he followed Gilgamesh into the mountain. The inside was oppressively muggy. Enkidu already longed for water, and the stone beneath his boots burned through the soft leather.

The door shut, and darkness swept over them.

Gilgamesh swallowed. The sound echoed.

"You're afraid of the dark," Enkidu whispered. During their journey to Humbaba, Gilgamesh had trembled and stumbled when the monster snatched away the light.

"I fear other things far more."

Enkidu shuddered. He grew so tired of them speaking around his impending death. Urmah squirmed, claws raking Enkidu's chest, and he shifted the sling, making sure it was tight. "I'll lead. You trust me, don't you?"

"Yes." Gilgamesh spoke without a breath of hesitation. This man, this glorious, frustrating, beautiful, vindictive, passionate man trusted Enkidu even in the depths of darkness.

"We shouldn't waste more time. Let's go." Enkidu trailed fingers down Gilgamesh's arm. Coarse hair had grown damp in the humid air. Even without sight, Enkidu knew him. Knew the length of his arms, the rhythm of his breaths, the shape of his form. He could reach out to glide fingers over his lips and not miss. He didn't need sight to find the other half of his soul, no matter how dark things became.

Enkidu turned and ran.

Gilgamesh's thunderous steps echoed behind.

That's all they needed to do. Put one foot after another

as fast as they could. Sprint for an entire night—but only one. A single moonrise in a lifetime. They could do it.

The first hours passed quickly. Heat slowly spooled away. A welcome kiss of cool air arrived. Urmah sighed then slept on and off. He seemed to understand the situation's severity. Once they'd begun running, the cub didn't yowl or scratch anymore. Instead, he remained still, his breathing and his warm weight on Enkidu's chest the only sign the lion remained.

More time passed.

The mountain grew cold.

Gilgamesh remained close and he could feel his heat occasionally when their pace slowed and their bodies neared.

But ice crawled over the cave walls, biting Enkidu's fingers when he reached out for guidance, and the tunnel became frigid.

Soon it was cold enough that the heat of Enkidu's breath tingled over his frozen cheeks. His feet ached numbly with each pounding footstep and his lungs burned with every inhale.

They couldn't stop though.

One miserable, long, endless night. He could do that for Gilgamesh's sake. For Shamhat's. For young Usun who wanted nothing more than his father's attention and would never have it if that father didn't return.

Enkidu pushed himself harder. His body felt new, like his spirit might leave his mind and join his blood that tried to race through frozen limbs, sluggishly moving through muscles and past stiff joints.

When he'd reached a point of clenching his teeth to fight the pain, warmth crept back into the edges.

At first, he sighed in relief and slowed.

"The sun rises soon," Gilgamesh said, his voice splintered and raspy.

"Oh." It was the only word Enkidu could form and not just because of his parched throat. The sun rose, Utu drifting back through the sky. The mountain would heat until it became volcanic. Until it burned with such intensity only the smooth stone beneath their feet would remain at the day's end.

Enkidu picked up his pace.

His heart thundered like it would explode.

His legs had gone numb, and every other piece of his body hurt.

Another hour, maybe two. He couldn't stop.

They had to make it out of the mountain.

Warmth spread like honey over bread. Comforting at first, then hot, then burning. It thawed Enkidu's legs and intensified the pain to the other half of his body. Tears pierced his eyes. Urmah whined. Enkidu attempted to pet him but couldn't coordinate his hands to reach for the creature, to comfort him.

The soles of Enkidu's boots baked until he gritted his teeth with every slap upon the dark path.

His skin burned.

They wouldn't make it.

They'd boil alive inside Utu's mountain.

This had all been a trick of cruel gods.

A light sparked in the distance. It surprised Enkidu so much he stopped running. Gilgamesh slammed into his back and his hands swept around him, but they trembled. His strength was sapped.

"That's it," Gilgamesh growled. "We're almost there."

A flame licked in the distance behind, sparking a light down the narrow ebony hall.

"Fuck." Gilgamesh grabbed Enkidu's hand and yanked him forward. The contact stabbed, making every joint in his fingers, his wrist, his elbow ignite. Enkidu whimpered. They'd stopped and now his body didn't have the strength to continue pushing forward. "Run, Enkidu. Don't give up."

Gilgamesh's voice was cinders of a once warming fire. But even for his ashes, Enkidu would fight. He forced his feet forward, forced his body to keep going.

A flame exploded behind them, and Enkidu slammed Gilgamesh down to the burning stone floor to keep it from hitting them. Urmah growled and hissed, jerking around within his sling.

Gilgamesh took hold of Enkidu's hand.

Amid all the misery, he was there.

Steady.

His grip a sanctuary from the world's fears.

Enkidu found a renewed burst of strength and with it, together, they tumbled out the door right as the hall exploded behind them.

They hit soft grass, and Enkidu struggled to not land on Urmah. He fell onto his side, relieved as wind kissed his blistered flesh and water trickled in the distance. Urmah bounded out of his cloth and licked Enkidu's cheek.

He wanted to respond, to touch the cub, to reach for Gilgamesh.

But his eyes were heavy as they drifted closed.

CHAPTER ELEVEN
IN THE GARDEN OF
THE GODS

FINGERS TANGLED in Gilgamesh's beard, tugging, insistent. He wanted to reach out for Enkidu, slide his hands over the coarse hairs on his arm. Another tug and Gilgamesh groaned. The third yank was hard enough to cause him to clink his teeth together.

He opened his eyes to glistening light and a breeze that brought a rich, sweet scent to him. The lion cub whined and bit a chunk of Gilgamesh's beard, pulling at it and taking a few hairs with him.

"Hey," Gilgamesh rasped, "stop that." He shoved the little beast back. The creature had looked like a starved rat when Enkidu first followed his cries into the cave of death. Now he was rapidly turning into a strong, healthy cub with a glossy coat and a patch of wild mahogany hair sprouting from his head.

Saving him should have been impossible—the cub had been hours from death, but Enkidu had nurtured him back to health and—

Gilgamesh shot up.

He looked around, a hundred gleaming emerald plants blurring together.

Gilgamesh winced at the suddenness of his movement. Fear of moving his injured form so rapidly trickled down his spine. His skin had blistered in the mountain. Blood had caked between his toes, and he spread them, feeling the dried stickiness break apart. Yet, it didn't hurt.

His body pulsed with fresh energy. His clothing was ragged and singed, but his skin stretched smooth and tan. Not so much as a scratch marred his flesh.

Stumbling a step forward, Gilgamesh flung hands out to steady himself. Everything swayed, like the world had tilted. Urmah cocked his head and looked up at him but didn't seem disoriented.

Slowly Gilgamesh turned towards the garden.

Enkidu lay a few steps ahead, a single arm stretched towards Gilgamesh, the hand unfolded like he reached for him.

Above him, someone in a dark cloak hunched and hissed scratchy words.

Enkidu lay so still.

He'd been that motionless before. When he nearly died from Humbaba's attack. Death hunted Enkidu like a tracker. And that was Gilgamesh's fault. Someone so beautiful and innocent would lose his life because of Gilgamesh's choices. That was the thing he couldn't face, couldn't discuss with Enkidu or Shamhat. Enkidu was cursed because gods had shackled him with an arrogant king who angered a vindictive goddess. Enkidu didn't deserve his fate.

He lay still and pallid over glimmering, pale grass as some creature attacked him while at his weakest.

Gilgamesh lunged forward, causing the world to blur.

"Ah ah, mortal king." The hunched figure jerked her head back so her hood dropped. The woman had dark, thick curls bound back with a golden strap and searing black eyes. Despite that, her face possessed a softness, her cheeks curving gently, but her mild features didn't undo the predatory glare she aimed at him.

Gilgamesh's body froze like she'd turned his flesh to stone. He fought the forces holding him but couldn't so much as twitch his smallest finger. He only knew she hadn't actually transformed him because his heart still thudded and the swoosh of his thrumming blood echoed in his mind.

The woman returned to Enkidu, and Gilgamesh's heart seized. Urmah gnawed at his tunic, and he longed to shake his leg and discourage the creature. Only breathing and blinking remained under his control, and he exercised both intemperately. *What are you doing to him?* He wanted to cry out the words, but his tongue was frozen, his mouth mortared.

"Healing him," she said without looking up. "As I did for you and the cub."

This divine woman—goddess most likely as she could read his thoughts—had healed them. She could have been lying, though she possessed no reason to do so. She held him in place with no more effort than it took for Gilgamesh to press his cylindrical seal into soft clay.

"You're right to suspect I'm a goddess." Light gleamed over her thick hair as she continued moving along Enkidu's form. Gilgamesh couldn't see her hands, couldn't follow what she did. The static-like bite of magic hovered in the atmosphere, and Enkidu grimaced. Gilgamesh jerked against his invisible chains once more, but his body no longer listened. It obeyed the goddess scarcely paying him mind.

"Would you rather I focus on you or on him?" With a sigh, the light dimmed, and she turned towards Gilgamesh, looking up at him with storm-dark eyes. "I'm Gula."

The midwife goddess. Her domain was a domestic one filled with bloodied infants and mothers who danced the line between this realm and another. Why she bothered with him and Enkidu baffled Gilgamesh.

Gula scoffed. "Oh, yes, look down on midwifery. As though that art isn't the reason you stand here today. Who do you think delivered you, arrogant king?"

Gilgamesh couldn't look away and break her piercing gaze. She stood, and the motion made her appear like a waterfall in reverse, her image blurring then resettling as she reached her full posture.

She'd saved his life, and he'd sneered at her. Enkidu, were he awake, would intervene. He'd have kind words and bring his compassionate view of the world. Gods, the man probably thought midwifery was the peak of importance.

"He's a wise one, then." Gula tossed a grin at Enkidu who still slept, now without a grimace. Were he awake he'd grow wide-eyed at the scenery. Green ensconced them, flushing a hundred shades in leaves and vines. Flowers Gilgamesh couldn't name—pale violet ones with navy and gold centers—peppered around a pathway that dipped over a hill ahead.

Urmah curled onto Enkidu's chest and licked at his cheeks. Lovely that the beast woke Gilgamesh by pulling hair off his face but gently roused Enkidu.

"Well deserved, I'd say." Gula glared over her shoulder, and Gilgamesh tried to shift his thoughts to more positive musings. It was difficult when gods could read one's intentions.

"Yes, rather annoying I imagine." Gula pulled her hood back up.

Enkidu blinked then squinted into the garden's brightness. Gilgamesh longed to shout, to run to him, but he remained statue-still. Enkidu ran his long fingers down Urmah's back then looked around. He stumbled up, and Gula offered him a hand which he accepted.

"Gilgamesh." Enkidu met his eyes and frowned. "What's wrong?"

Gula smiled wickedly as she turned to face the King. "He's under divine punishment currently."

Enkidu's frown deepened, and he walked over to Gilgamesh, grazed fingers over his arm. Gilgamesh couldn't feel it and he longed to cry out. *Kill me, that would be fine. Perhaps I deserve it. Don't allow Enkidu to suffer, though, for his eyes to grow wide and worried.*

"Fine," Gula huffed.

Gilgamesh's muscles unwound, and he tumbled towards Enkidu, all the fight he'd been mentally directing at his body exploding him forward.

Enkidu fell with an oof but kept his arms wrapped around Gilgamesh's back and cushioned the drop.

"Anu and Utu wish for you both to have dinner with them." Gula nodded towards that path that wove up through shrubs. Before Gilgamesh could question her, she disappeared with a burst of pale blue that swept out on the wind.

"You're okay." Enkidu sighed and tangled his fingers into Gilgamesh's beard. Gilgamesh sighed and let their foreheads rest together while he ran fingers back through Enkidu's hair. They were alive and together, healed from injuries sustained within the monstrous mountain. Even Urmah's injured leg appeared fully healed. All Gilgamesh's exhaustion and pain was gone. He hadn't even thanked Gula for sparing Enkidu's suffering. He wished he had. So few gods seemed to care about the man.

Gilgamesh fought a groan at the thought. Enkidu really was bleeding into him, shaping his thinking and grinding down the rougher edges of his soul. He didn't deserve Enkidu who still lay beneath him so their legs tangled together. Gilgamesh kissed him softly, then pulled him up, weaving around a yowling Urmah.

Enkidu scooped the cub up. "Are you hungry, Urmah? I'm sorry we weren't awake when you needed to eat." Enkidu dipped into his bag and pulled out a piece of dried fish, offering it to the lion who snatched it between his teeth then rubbed his head over Enkidu's chest.

A smile lightened Enkidu's countenance, wrinkling the corners of his eyes and coloring his cheeks.

Gilgamesh remained still.

He wanted to hold that moment, that image.

Enkidu standing ankle deep in glittering, divine grasses, holding the creature he'd rescued, warmed with the joy of caring for it.

Enkidu with his broad shoulders and thick muscles nearly humorously large compared to the cub curled in his arms and contrasted with his soft touch, the gentleness of his heart.

"Well, sounds like we have an appointment," Enkidu said as he raised his face. His lips turned up when he met Gilgamesh's gaze as though there was nothing in the world more precious. As though Gilgamesh would ever be worthy of the man. He lowered the cub gently to the path and tucked the sling into his bag. "It will do you good to get some exercise, Urmah. This walk shouldn't be far, do you think?"

He addressed the last part to Gilgamesh who turned towards the path and frowned. "Probably not."

He honestly couldn't say. At least it wasn't running through a mountain that tried to kill them. Enkidu nodded then prodded Urmah to move. The cub pounced along, twining his body through plants then growing mesmerized by a butterfly.

Enkidu grabbed Gilgamesh's hand and pulled them forward. "We made it through the mountain."

He said it as though they'd succeeded at their goal. Enkidu still bore the weight of a curse, they'd nearly died multiple times, and Gula had made Gilgamesh aware of how little control they had.

He wanted to rage, to demand more from the gods, to pull his axes loose and chop down their precious garden.

"We did," he said instead. They were at the gods' behest and angering them in their territory wouldn't help. In Uruk, Gilgamesh had politics as a shield. People may question the gods if too many chaotic things occurred. However, if he died here, no one would find that odd. Mortals shouldn't travel into the divine realm. If a god struck him down in their realm, the people would consider it fair.

He twined his fingers tight with Enkidu's. They traveled through this place where they had no authority for his sake. If they could spare him, Gilgamesh would pay any price. He'd lay down his life in exchange if he could.

The path gleamed in the plants' glow. Everything possessed a light though they were all in different hues.

"This is the garden from my dream."

Enkidu was smiling at Urmah who'd leaped for a butterfly and tumbled into a pile of grass but turned his face towards Gilgamesh. "Utu spoke true, then. He said you'd walk it yourself."

Gilgamesh planned to reply, until they turned a corner and both stopped moving. In a clearing beneath flowering trees with lilac and peach blooms, a table sat ladened with food. Sitting in a chair, Utu gleamed golden, his light spilling over the feast so it became mundane in comparison, the garden drab. Next to him, a god who had to be Anu swirled a glass of wine. He glowed as well, but it was a pale, ivory light that somehow dominated Utu's flashier color.

"Join us." Anu's voice was thunder. It trembled the earth and clattered dishes on the table.

Gilgamesh swallowed but led Enkidu to a seat then took one himself. Enkidu pulled out Urmah's sling, then snatched the cub up and tucked him into it. Probably best that he kept the beast from getting into trouble in the gods' garden.

Fog obscured Anu's face but didn't hide wrinkles across his brow that looked like rock crevices. He cut slices of roast lamb and placed them on Enkidu's and Gilgamesh's plates. Continuing to another dish, he piled on stuffed grape leaves, barley bread, brined olives, and glazed vegetables. A brothy, meat-studded stew was ladled into bowls. He finished by pouring wine into both their goblets, then he leaned back in his chair, wisps of his immensity spilling over the furniture in a mist that crawled around the garden behind him.

Anu ate, his chewing falling into rhythm with the rattling of tree limbs in the wind. Utu didn't serve himself food, nor did he look at Enkidu or Gilgamesh.

They sat, waiting.

"Eat," Anu said.

Gilgamesh lifted his wine and took a small taste. It was

foolish to worry over the food. If they desired him dead, his soul would already haunt the Great Below.

"True. Therefore, eat." Anu ripped a piece of bread. Gilgamesh sighed, lifted an olive, and nodded to Enkidu. He frowned at the rich food but scooped a pile of vegetables, popped them in his mouth, and chewed them slowly.

Twilight settled in the gardens, the sun falling behind trees as Utu's glow dimmed. Utu looked behind him as his light faded into night's shadows. He turned back to the table with a sigh but didn't speak.

Gilgamesh chewed as though he executed a drill with his soldiers. His tunic drifted down his shoulder and he readjusted it only to realize how filthy he was. Gula had healed him, but it didn't change his sweat-stained and burnt fabric, the beaten bag he'd carried on their journey, the grime still clinging to his flesh.

Unlike the gods at the table, who shimmered like they struggled to stay in the human-like form they'd donned, Gilgamesh stank and sweat and was anchored to his body. He'd always lorded his godhood over others, but sitting with the divine, he'd been wrong to believe he belonged among the heavens.

Gilgamesh was mortal.

Enkidu whose fingers trembled as they reached for bread, who swallowed the food loudly, was also mortal.

From his experiences so far, Gilgamesh preferred the mortal world. He stopped mid-drink at that thought and choked over the wine, setting it down and grabbing a napkin to wipe his mouth. He'd always longed to overcome the human realm. But he loved people's passion and how their sense of life's shortness drove them to do great things. The hum and clatter of his city filled with children's laughter and rich, sweet incense and the imperfect rhythm of mortal musicians. He loved Uruk, loved living there, preferred a human life to this glittering, false reality.

If only death wasn't part of human existence. Then he'd have no desire to reach for more.

Anu set his glass down with a clack and turned towards Utu. The sky god's light increased, and Utu sat up then shifted to face Gilgamesh and Enkidu. "As I foretold, you've made it to the gardens of the gods. You've lived to see wonders hidden from all other mortals and have done so under our protection. I hope, at this point in your journey, you will understand it is best for you to return home. I'll take you myself and save you the trouble of traveling through the mountain again."

Enkidu released a breath, his shoulders dropping, but his lips turned up. He actually thought turning around and returning home would be a good thing. Gilgamesh clenched his chalice so hard if it were a human-made material it would break.

He finally resided in a world that could handle his strength and size.

He loathed it.

Loathed the gods fixed on petty jealousies they took out on humans who had no control. Mortals they treated worse than Gilgamesh's roughest children playing with their untreasured toys.

"We cannot return yet."

A peal of thunder echoed across the garden, the sky darkening as clouds swept across the purple twilight. Anu lifted his face, and even with his features blurred, the pale misty light covering them, Gilgamesh could make out the snarl wrinkling a scarcely visible nose. Enkidu gripped Gilgamesh's knee beneath the table, and he set a hand upon it but didn't heed the warning. He would face gods to save Enkidu, face death.

Another echo of thunder. When Anu spoke, his voice hissed along the table, like snakes chasing prey. "After you killed my prized Bull of Heaven, you should be grateful I've spared your life, mortal."

Urmah whined and tucked deeper into his sling, but Enkidu ignored him, his focus fixed on Gilgamesh, his grip almost painful. He wanted them to thank the gods and turn back, accepting Utu's offer to return them home.

No. Not on his life.

"Grant what I desire," Gilgamesh said. "And I'll return."

Anu jumped up, his chair falling with a smack. Moths fluttered out of grass behind him as lightning streaked the sky. "Perhaps I should kill you and be done with this trouble."

Gilgamesh jumped to his feet as well, shaking off Enkidu's hold and pressing his hands on the table. "Perhaps you should."

Anu didn't respond. Maybe it was the acquiescence in Gilgamesh's voice. He'd face his death without hesitation if it would guarantee Enkidu lived. Those with god's blood shouldn't rule mortal cities, anyway. It would be an improvement if he were gone and Inanna was forced to relinquish control over Uruk's ruling family. If the divine could see how much trouble mortals with god's blood were, perhaps they'd put an end to it. Then Usun would also be safe.

Utu rose as well, his light growing and gleaming against the shadows that had overtaken the table. Gold sparkled over bowls and glistened along the sides of olives. "Father," he said gently, "perhaps consider Inanna used the bull as a weapon and—"

"Do you take these mortals' side over your sister's?"

Gilgamesh remained silent. If even a single god would stand on their side, even if it was Utu who had no temple in Uruk and no reason for loyalty, he wouldn't argue with it. Utu's light flickered but brightened once more. "Mortals are mortals, but that doesn't mean my sister is perfect. She is young, as we've discussed. Let me handle this."

Anu didn't respond, but the clouds in the sky thinned, streaks of purple appearing.

Enkidu had sunk into his chair, his eyes fixed on the divine argument. His skin had paled, and Gilgamesh longed to reassure him, to reach for his hand and squeeze it. He couldn't offer any promises though—these were gods they stood before, and with a breath, both of their lives could be gone. They were at the mercy of divine whims, but Gilgamesh had had enough of the games.

"Mortal king," Utu said, "hear me. You've traversed places your feet do not belong. You have stories that will make your name last forever. Return home and accept your fate."

"I'm divine as well," Gilgamesh said with more steadiness than he actually felt. "Explain why I don't belong in this world. Further, it's Inanna who wishes to continue creating mortals with god's blood who walk the earth but can transverse into the divine realm as well. Where is it that I belong?"

He slapped a hand across his chest where his heart thumped into his breastbone. His answer would be next to Enkidu. He'd never fully belonged to the mortal world. Others found him intimidating—even those he wished to commune with as family. Here among the divine he didn't belong either.

But alongside Enkidu, their strengths matched, their

desires equal, and with the man always pushing back against his personality, he'd found a home like he'd never experienced before. These gods wished for him to return to his palace, let the year slip away, allow their relative to sneak in and kill Enkidu for retribution.

They could stop it but wouldn't.

What was one mortal death to a divine?

To Gilgamesh, Enkidu's demise would take his soul with it. He'd far rather the gods end him as well.

"I told you," Utu said in a measured tone, "you have a purpose." He shifted towards Anu. "Remember the prophecies foretold, Father."

Anu sighed—a sound like howling wind. "Fine. Continue your journey, but know you'll no longer stand under our protection. This realm is dangerous for mortal creatures." Anu stopped, his silvery light shifting to land over Urmah who'd wiggled his front paws free from his wrap to reach a piece of lamb. He gnawed on a bone.

Enkidu gasped and pulled the bone free as Urmah yowled his protests. He set it on the table where it contrasted with the gleaming, rich feast. Utu chuckled and reached out tendrils of golden light that formed into a hand, pulled a fresh piece of lamb off the platter, and offered it to the cub who eagerly accepted.

Enkidu smiled as he scratched the lion's head.

"Heed my father's words," Utu said. "This realm isn't safe. I'll offer one more time to return you both to Uruk. You'll have a hero's welcome."

Enkidu parted his lips as though to speak, but Gilgamesh found words first. "And will you spare us your sister's curse? Will you change our fates?"

"Gilgamesh," Enkidu began. "It doesn't matt—"

"It does." Gilgamesh didn't even turn to look at Enkidu,

to meet the sadness in his eyes that would match his tone. "It means everything."

Utu's light fluttered and flowed along the table. "A divine curse is a vow, mortal king. It's not undone without spilling god's blood. You worry about your personal tragedy. Perhaps consider the millions of mortal lives a divine war would cost."

Gilgamesh frowned but didn't retort. He remembered Shamhat's grief at her parents' death, her howl of sadness and the way she'd clung to him. How sometimes she still looked at Usun with tears illuminating her eyes, and he knew she was thinking about how her parents didn't get to see him grow up, didn't get to watch their legacy unfurl. The way their loss made him feel mortal for the first time in his life, helpless to control anything.

He wouldn't wish that on his people.

Gilgamesh ground his teeth together. He knew the decision he made would define him. With Enkidu's warmth reaching his side, he could choose nothing else. "Fine, but I cannot give up my task. If it damns me, I'll accept that."

Utu dimmed but nodded. "You may stay in the garden for one night. Eat your fill." He waved an indistinct hand over the table. "Wash and rest. Then you must leave. This place is for immortals."

Gilgamesh offered a nod. Before he or Enkidu could speak again, both gods disappeared in bursts of light and shadows. The table drifted into darkness. Crickets chirped. Stars gleamed beyond tree boughs.

Gilgamesh sighed and dropped back into his seat. They might as well eat as much as they could. Some of it might even keep for a few days and they could pack it to ease the burden of gathering food. Enkidu's brows pulled together, but he seemed to share the same thought as he ripped more meat for Urmah then resumed dinner himself.

Warmth flooded Gilgamesh's body. His muscles had grown heavy, and his eyelids drifted closed. He reached for a grape leaf but missed, his hand landing heavily on the table.

He was so very tired.

Tired to the bone, to the core.

Tired enough to sleep a lifetime.

His head fell back on the chair.

His last sight was Urmah turning away from his dinner, leaning towards Gilgamesh with a worried yowl.

Then he drifted into a sleep that felt like resting among his ancestors' bones. He didn't fight it. Instead, he curled down and flowed into the peacefulness.

CHAPTER TWELVE
WITH GREAT EFFORT

Enkidu's body was a stone dropping into a lake. The lake where he'd lived before meeting Gilgamesh. Soon the Wolf would arrive and take him hunting. They'd chase after antelope and catch fish. Beneath the pale face of a full moon, the Wolf would howl songs of his history and—

Something sliced through Enkidu's finger. His eyes snapped open. Urmah had his teeth clamped down hard upon his hand, blood coursing around his teeth and dampening his muzzle.

A breath caught in Enkidu's chest.

Urmah attacked him.

The cub released his grip and emitted a pitiful cry. Enkidu couldn't make sense of it, but his eyes drifted closed again.

Another searing pain. Urmah released his fingers as soon as he woke. Wait. Enkidu forced himself up in his chair where he'd reclined. The garden was deep in night's shadows and the clearing they sat in had gone quiet like everything abandoned it.

Urmah yowled again and butted his head into Enkidu's chest.

"Oh, you're keeping m-me… awake." Enkidu yawned before he got the words all the way out. He was so exhausted…

Urmah butted into Enkidu's chest again. He sat up, gave his head a shake, and brought the bleeding fingers up to his mouth to suck on them. Gilgamesh lounged on his chair, his neck at a strange angle, his body deathly still.

Enkidu jumped up, dropping Urmah gently to the table and stumbling closer to his love. "Gilgamesh."

His words were as slurred as if he'd drank wine the entire day. His body wouldn't follow directions, and even standing he longed to curl down into the soft grasses beneath his feet, let his eyes drift for just a moment.

Urmah swiped claws over his leg, and he winced. He'd knelt in the grass and didn't remember doing so.

"Good boy," he murmured to the cub while giving him a pat.

Somehow the animal knew things weren't right. They needed to escape the garden, but Gilgamesh lay statue-still. Enkidu staggered to his feet, tripped over a branch, and caught himself on Gilgamesh's chair.

The man's lips were parted, but no breath rushed from them.

"Oh gods, no." Enkidu pressed his bleeding hand over Gilgamesh's chest. Nothing. Then a slow, lazy thud. A whimper pealed past his lips, and he kissed Gilgamesh's forehead.

"Love, wake up, please."

Gilgamesh didn't move, didn't seem to breathe.

Enkidu grabbed his tunic and gave him a shake. Gilgamesh's head lolled then dropped, his chin hitting his chest. Enkidu stretched fingers over his neck and didn't move them until another lazy thump beat against them. Gilgamesh was alive, and Enkidu had to find some way to wake him.

Perhaps after he rested for just a moment. Urmah bit Enkidu's leg, snapping him out of the drowsiness once more. He hadn't broken skin, but the cub possessed sharp teeth. Urmah turned his focus towards Gilgamesh and sank those razor incisors into his leg.

Gilgamesh didn't move, didn't even gasp at the pain or shift his leg. Perhaps Urmah had woken Enkidu in time, before the spell drew him too far down.

Oh, shed. Enkidu staggered to his feet and looked around. The garden was unnaturally dark, ebonies blending in with each other. In a far corner, though, a golden glimmer sparkled.

Utu. Enkidu had to make it to him.

He lurched towards the light, but fell, scraping a knee. The pain scarcely radiated to his consciousness before it drifted beneath the warmth and heaviness again. He stumbled. Struggled to his feet. Attempted to pat a whining Urmah and missed.

It took great effort to make it down the smooth path and through the gods' garden. When he finally reached Utu—a dim golden glow that floated beneath the boughs of a pine—he could have wept. Instead, he dropped on his knees before the god, prostrated himself, and struggled to stay awake despite Urmah's claws, teeth, and insistent nipping and growling.

"Please," Enkidu begged, "r-release Gilgamesh from w-whatever curse this is."

Utu shimmered, and the outline of a face appeared within the light. A sharp nose formed, then bright eyes and a thick jaw. "You know Gilgamesh will never be satisfied with the lot given to him."

"W-what you s-say"—Enkidu struggled to get the words out past his clumsy, awkward mouth—"isn't untrue."

He remembered a moment in Gilgamesh's tent from months before. *You're demanding and capricious,* he'd shouted at the King as smugness slid from his face and anger sharpened his features.

You're obnoxious and speak when you shouldn't, Gilgamesh had snapped back. Enkidu certainly proved that. Here he was begging a god who'd already decided their fate.

Gilgamesh was demanding, relentless, striving.

Yet was he not created to be so? How could a creature with god's blood not have those attributes?

"You have a point," Utu said. "I often think Gilgamesh and my sister are two sides of the same plant."

Enkidu wanted to argue. Gilgamesh would never curse a being out of retribution. But he would—he had even. The gods had sent him to King Zage-Si to enact their justice, and he didn't hesitate to act. Ultimately, he wasn't selfish like Inanna, though.

"I'd be careful before assuming you understand a goddess' motivations, mortal one."

"I-I'm sorry." He supposed he didn't know Inanna's intentions. It had felt so personal that she'd damned him, but perhaps there was some deeper reasoning behind her actions.

"It's endearing"—Utu tilted his head and his features all rearranged until they formed the shape of a face again—"how earnest you are. Aruru certainly poured some of her attributes in when she formed you."

Urmah rubbed Enkidu's leg. He longed to reach for the

creature but didn't think he had the coordination to achieve it. Utu said he was like Aruru, the goddess who'd created him. He hoped that meant she was kind, though he wasn't likely to meet her.

"You say Gilgamesh is l-like your sister." Enkidu forced his body upright against the weight pushing him down. "Y-yet, the gods grant Inanna grace to grow and learn, but curse Gilgamesh to die in this garden."

"He won't die. He'll only sleep until the time has passed and Inanna's curse has played out."

Enkidu's heart leapt forward, tumbling over its drowsy beat. Gilgamesh would sleep until Enkidu died. They wouldn't even get a goodbye or the last months promised to them. The gods were cruel. In order to punish Gilgamesh, they'd take the last months of joy from Enkidu's brief life.

"It's not malicious." Utu's form expanded as though he'd stood. Urmah tucked behind Enkidu's legs and crouched to the earth as the god moved. "Surely you under-stand, Enkidu, that this journey is fruitless. Gilgamesh will not come to terms with it and he's willing to provoke the gods to achieve his ends."

Enkidu straightened again, fighting the overwhelming exhaustion. "How can one mortal man—even a king with god's blood—provoke the divine? If we go on this journey and fail, how does that harm y-you?" His words slurred again, and he gritted his teeth. "If failure is inherent, then let us experience it by our own hands. Don't steal our last months together for anger. I b-beg you. Please."

Utu sighed and lifted his face to the heavens. A cloud drifted across the moon's face as though Nanna hid. As if the god looked away to allow Utu whatever decision he'd make.

Enkidu bit the inside of his cheek until coppery blood

flooded his mouth, and he used the pain to fuel his words. "G-give me the opportunity, and I will remove Gilgamesh from the garden and keep him away from any part of this realm you desire. If you already know nothing will come of our trip, there's no harm to be found in it."

Utu didn't answer but sat pulsing with light. Waves of warmth flushed over Enkidu. He waited. He had no control over the gods' will. Somehow, he trusted Utu to be kind, perhaps to even have a soft spot for mortals. He'd saved them after Humbaba had nearly torn both of them apart, after all.

"I can remove the mist that's clouding your minds," Utu said softly, a whisper like he wanted to keep the words beneath the sky. "I cannot quell my father's anger. Gilgamesh has offended him by killing his prize bull and upsetting his favorite child."

The last words came brittle, a crackle of fallen leaves.

Enkidu lifted his face to meet Utu's gaze. He knew somewhat what it was like to have a divine parent who didn't favor him. Aruru had never even shown herself to him. Perhaps he and Utu shared that.

"As soon as Gilgamesh wakes, you must both run east of here. Don't stop until you've reached a lake. That is outside the gods' gardens. Beyond that, seek out the Alewife. She'll have answers you desire. I can't say how my father will react or if he'll allow you to continue your journey that far."

It was a chance, though. A chance for Gilgamesh to not lie here and wake to Enkidu's dead body months from then. To the grief that would cause. "Thank you."

"I offer this not for Gilgamesh's sake, but for yours. Your heart is full of light."

Lips pinching, Enkidu bowed deeply to Utu, then

jumped up. The fog lifted from his mind until he could run with Urmah tumbling along behind.

Gilgamesh blinked awake as Enkidu made it into the clearing. He grabbed Gilgamesh's hands with his sore fingers and pulled him to his feet. "We must run."

"But we haven't—"

"Please." Tears spilled from Enkidu's eyes and trailed warm streaks over his cheeks before landing in his beard. "Will you just trust me?"

Gilgamesh frowned. He reached out and cupped Enkidu's neck then nodded. "I will."

"Then we run. We run like the mountain will soon burn us and we start now."

Gilgamesh studied him for a moment, looked back over his shoulder, then turned and gave another bob of his head.

They gathered their few items and ran out of the garden's manicured plantings, beyond it and into a wild territory where vines tangled over the path, and finally to where the path gave out altogether. Enkidu lifted Urmah back into the sling. The creature was getting bigger but not strong enough to make an entire night of exertion yet.

When they finally reached the lake, Enkidu stopped, his chest heaving, sweat trickling along his brow. Utu's sun reflected in the lake and seemed to watch from his perch in the sky, like a shield holding back Anu's anger. At least Enkidu hoped that was the case.

Urmah had grown restless and tumbled around within the fabric, pulling Enkidu's shoulder. He unwound the material and released the cub who dashed towards the water, wading up to his chest then greedily drinking.

"I'm going to wash up as well," Enkidu said, his voice still breathy.

Gilgamesh grabbed his arm, holding him back. "What aren't you telling me, Enkidu?"

He stopped, felt the weight of his lover's fingers gripping his flesh. Closed his eyes. Then turned to face the man. "Anu placed a curse on us in the garden. We nearly lost everything."

"Of course." Gilgamesh stepped closer. "Something was awry. I'd be a fool not to know the gods had some malicious force upon us. But that isn't what I mean." He raised his free hand and spread it over Enkidu's chest. "I mean what is burdening your heart that you aren't sharing with me."

Enkidu turned towards the lake where Urmah leapt after a frog, but Gilgamesh gently turned his chin back. Gilgamesh's warm brown eyes reflected the lake and sparkled like the water. "You came on this trip for my sake, and—" Enkidu tried to speak but Gilgamesh shook his head. "If you truly wish to turn back, we can."

The way he said it, like it was really as simple as that, had Enkidu releasing a breath. "You'd leave?"

"Yes. I've nearly got us both killed twice now." He leaned over and pressed a kiss to Enkidu's forehead. "You are precious to me, but I've acted arrogantly and foolishly. If you want to return home, we will go."

Home.

The only home Enkidu had ever known was the arms of this man. The palace was just a physical location where they lived. He'd been at home standing at Gilgamesh's side in the cedar forest, making love in a strange house, or even here, running from gods in the divine realm just as much.

Enkidu longed for some location that felt like home, some place he could settle into and know its nuances. How the tile felt underfoot at different times of the year and the rain's rhythm as it danced upon the roof.

He wasn't likely to get that.

Gilgamesh would be his only earthly home. With the man staring at him as if he'd trade everything to see his face forever, it wasn't such a bad compromise.

They could return to Uruk.

Live out the remainder of the year.

Gilgamesh didn't rush him for an answer. A breeze blew his beard back along his neck, and Urmah splashed through the lake, breaking the quiet.

If they returned to the palace and Inanna enacted her retribution, it would break something in Gilgamesh. Perhaps he'd revert to the vindictive, arrogant man Enkidu had initially met.

If that happened, everything Enkidu had done in his life would be gone. He'd leave no mark, no change, no compassion or love or joy.

Just a broken man and a ruined life would remain of his brief journey through the world.

His heart dipped. No. They had to keep going so Gilgamesh could feel like he did everything he could. Shamhat had been right. Gilgamesh was a physical man—he had to step into the forest himself or he wouldn't believe in the trees' existence.

Enkidu released a breath and ran his fingers through Gilgamesh's tangled beard. "I want to continue, but I wish to add a condition."

Gilgamesh raised an eyebrow.

"Should I die in the end,"—the man stiffened under his hand, his jaw clenching—"I want you to promise me you won't revert to living out of fear and focusing on conquering the world. That you'll remember the love we shared."

His eyes went as dark as Mount Mashu's tunnel. "You won't die, so it doesn't matter."

Enkidu shoved away from him and turned towards the water. "I am tired of us pretending that isn't a reality. I'm sick of us not discussing it as though if we don't speak about it, we'll avoid it. There's a strong possibility I will no longer live this time next year, and I can't bear to keep avoiding the topic no matter how unfair it is."

"It is unfair," Gilgamesh roared, the water carrying his voice, making it louder.

Enkidu dropped his words to a whisper, unwilling to match his shouting, to meet him in his fury. "It is, but none-theless it's true. A goddess has cursed me and no other divine will intercept. It's unlikely we will find someone else to break the curse."

"You think we're searching for a way to break the curse?"

Enkidu's lips snapped apart, but he struggled to form words. Of course that's what they were doing. Why in Enlil's name did they tromp through divine territory and anger gods other than to break his damned curse?

They'd clearly done a poor job communicating with each other. Here they were, filthy, hearts still pounding from yet another run from divine wrath, standing ragged and tired before a lake's lilac water, speaking words the other didn't understand.

This miscommunication was probably Enkidu's fault. He'd asked limited questions and often shifted the conver-sation when the topic arose. Despite agreeing to go on the journey, he still felt it was foolish especially after experi-encing the dangers they'd come across already.

Gilgamesh frowned. "We're not trying to break your curse;

we're trying to break the terms. A mortal curse can't affect an immortal. I need to locate Utnapishtim because he has the divine touch, the ability to grant immortality. Don't you see? If you're immortal, Inanna's wretchedness can't touch you."

Enkidu stumbled back a step. *Immortal.* Gilgamesh intended to deify him and remove him from mortal existence. Then again, neither of them had ever belonged to it. They'd crashed through it like boulders.

"Do you intend to become immortal as well?" He didn't wish for eternal life if Gilgamesh wasn't a part of it.

"Of course." Gilgamesh closed the space between them again, grabbing his hand. "When I said I wanted forever with you, I meant it. And I promise you—if I can manage it, that's what I intend to do."

Enkidu's head grew light. He fought against swaying. He shifted his attention to planting his feet on the bank's soft sand.

If they could remain alive together forever, that changed everything Enkidu believed they fought for. Adding a few more decades to his life hadn't felt worth the risk they'd been taking. But if they became gods.

"What of your..."

"Family," Gilgamesh finished for him. His eyes darkened as his gaze drifted towards a clump of trees in the distance. "I've thought about that, but consider my logic. If something were to happen to us—to me—and our journey and actions convince the gods not to put anyone else with god's blood on mortal thrones, then Usun would inherit mine. You know he's good and strong. He'd make a fine ruler for Uruk. I've already put in place everything Shamhat needs to guide the city until he's aged. Shamhat..." His voice broke, and he swallowed, blinking hard. "She is a strong woman. Uruk will be safe in her hands."

Enkidu nodded. "Utu said this journey would bring about a change."

"This must be it." Wrinkles swept across Gilgamesh's brow. "Losing my family would hurt. I would visit them, of course, as my mother does. I don't deny there would be grief involved. But it's to protect them, protect my city. Enough of the gods meddling in mortal affairs."

He snatched Enkidu's wrist and ran a thumb along the vein. "Neither of us belong in the mortal world. We've both always known it. I didn't understand until I met you just how hungry I'd been to have someone who could handle me. Physically, yes, but also my ambition and spirit. No one else questions me as you do." He brushed his nose along Enkidu's. "No one else calls me arrogant. And sure as fuck no one else throws figs at me."

Enkidu chuckled. A damp Urmah plopped down at his feet and licked his paws. "You deserved to have that fig thrown at you."

Gilgamesh scowled then pressed a kiss to Enkidu's forehead. "I know. Don't expect me to admit to it ever again, however." A gentle smile swept up his lips that reminded Enkidu of Usun. The boy waiting at home for a father who didn't intend to return. His heart burned. If it was for Usun's ultimate benefit, it might be worth the pain. Perhaps they could protect him from Inanna's predation as well.

"I should have discussed this plan more with you. I've been afraid of speaking or even thinking about the plans specifically. Afraid gods would overhear my intentions and intervene." Gilgamesh dipped his face away, towards shrubs that curled around the lake. His lips thinned, shifting his expression into an array of sharp edges, like a statue carved and fixed permanently for time. "But I do not wish to return to Uruk and allow Inanna to harm my family and take you. I intend to defeat her, to bind up my city and save the people there, and to protect my family." He pressed his forehead to Enkidu's and breathed over his lips.

"Then I want to spend eternity finding honeycombs and catching fish and naming the stars with you. However, if you wish to return to Uruk, we will. I'll find some other way to deal with Inanna—I always have." He leaned back and opened his eyes so the sun kissed them with a touch of amber. "If you want, we can continue this journey together and see if we might defy the gods. Perhaps the two of us will become more than fools in love or men navigating the world. Maybe we'll become legends who changed humanity's fate."

Enkidu's heart had warmed with each passing word until his chest burned with it. Even his face had flushed. Gilgamesh was right. He should have shared the plan with Enkidu, because hearing it, listening to the words spill from his lips like honey, he was ready to face anything. Gods included. He'd lift a sword, brandish a shield, fight a monster.

"Yes," he said. "Let's defy the gods and change history. Utu even offered some help. We need to seek out the Alewife."

Eyes sparkling, Gilgamesh nodded. "I've heard legends of her. I know where we should search."

"But there's one issue with your plan."

Gilgamesh's smile faltered. "That is?"

"I doubt you'll make any divine friends for our immortal life between this plan and your ability to offend everyone with a look."

Gilgamesh rolled his eyes, but his grin returned. "I'll get you all to myself, then."

"I said I doubted *you* would make immortal friends. I've already found a few."

A fish jumped in the distance. The sun glimmered peach and draped over the valley. Gilgamesh grunted. "Fine with me. I don't need a large group of friends."

"And that"—Enkidu yanked his beard and pulled him in for a kiss—"is why you end up with fruit on your face."

Gilgamesh laughed, wrapped his arms around him, and stumbled them backwards until they reached the water. They fell in with a tremendous splash that reached Urmah, spraying his drying fur. He yowled then gave his body a shake. Enkidu floated alongside Gilgamesh as their legs tangled together.

Some new feeling had sprouted in his heart during their conversation.

It tasted suspiciously of hope.

He'd get more than a lifetime with Gilgamesh if they achieved this. And he'd have found some purpose—a way to improve other's lives. They'd even protect their family and help Usun.

It was the perfect plan.

That burned in him like kindling, catching and crackling through his bones.

It was enough of a flame to drive him through whatever else the journey might bring.

CHAPTER THIRTEEN
ALEWIFE

Lightness had entered Enkidu's steps after they left the gods' garden, an ease that reminded Gilgamesh of their first journey into the cedar forest together. There, Enkidu had known each bend of the river and hunting path. As they walked among another wood, far more fantastical with trees painted in streaking colors and a lilac sky overhead, Enkidu had regained his surety once more.

Gilgamesh should have spoken more clearly sooner. He'd feared the gods intervening and stalling their journey. They'd done so but Enkidu had petitioned Utu and saved them once more. Gilgamesh had a tendency to thrash through life, expecting others to track along with him.

But Enkidu wasn't just anyone.

He was *the* one.

The man looked back, light dancing over his hazel eyes making the gold circle in them as bright as treasure. Gilgamesh's stomach warmed as he returned a smile.

He loved him.

Loved him fiercely.

Enough to anger gods and risk his life and destroy his legacy over it.

The plan, however, was perfect. All they needed was Utnapishtim's touch. Then they'd have forever. They sought out Gilgamesh's ancestor. The man would grant him his wish if, for no other reason then because of their shared blood.

Urmah loped alongside Enkidu, keeping pace. He'd become too large for the sling. Luckily his stamina had increased with his size. When they paused for meals, the cub ate quickly then napped, but he scarcely lagged anymore as they moved through the divine realm.

"Your little beast," Gilgamesh said, "is turning into a proper lion."

Enkidu sighed as he reached down to scratch the creature's tuft of brown hair that had grown to spread down the back of his head. "His name is Urmah."

Gilgamesh's mouth split into a smile, and he grabbed Enkidu's tunic to pull the man towards him before grasping a horn and kissing him hard enough to bruise the man's lips.

Enkidu sighed happily and leaned against him.

There was no greater warmth than Enkidu's flesh against his. Enkidu tilted his chin so he could meet Gilgamesh's gaze. "One day you'll call him by his name."

"And one day I'll make love to you beneath stars that are named for us."

Color spilled over Enkidu's nose, and Gilgamesh smiled until his teeth grazed Enkidu's skin. The man remained so innocent, so easy to blush and so easy to pleasure. That's what Gilgamesh wanted eternity for—to love this man into forever's grand expanse.

Urmah pounced ahead, catching a mouse and ending its squeals with a crunch.

"Already getting his own food." Gilgamesh pressed a kiss to Enkidu's forehead. "Maybe the beast isn't such a burden after all."

Enkidu growled his disapproval at Gilgamesh refusing to use Urmah's name, and Gilgamesh grinned back. He released the man, letting his fingers slide away from his horn.

Pale yellow clouds had trailed into the sky above the tree boughs, and Gilgamesh lifted his face then took a deep breath.

"What is it?" Enkidu asked.

"Do you smell that?"

"You mean the tanginess? I believe we're near the sea."

Gilgamesh nodded. "Siduri, the Alewife and goddess of wine lives on the shore. We're getting close."

Enkidu's playful twisted lips and sparkling eyes left along with his relaxed posture. Tension strung his muscles tight and rolled his shoulders back. "The Alewife is a god? We're going to deal with more divine beings?"

Gilgamesh walked alongside him and took his hand. Shed, he needed to get better at sharing things with his partner. His entire life he'd practiced keeping things hidden and it was strange changing habits.

Anu had ignored them so far as they'd continued their journey. Utu must have found some way to defer his father's anger. Gilgamesh didn't spend long thinking about or questioning it. Better to accept the gods' grace and not draw their ire with impertinent thoughts.

"Don't worry," Gilgamesh whispered gently. "According to folklore, the Alewife despises the other gods and lives on the shore of Death's Sea to avoid them."

"Death's Sea." A strain entered Enkidu's voice. Urmah abandoned the soft spot in the moss he'd curled into and pounced over before thudding his head into Enkidu's leg. The man reached down to pet the creature. "All's fine, boy. We're all right."

"As long as we stay out of the water."

Enkidu snapped a twig then twisted it, staring down at it with a bunched brow. "We'll have to keep a good eye on Urmah."

"Legends say animals avoid it naturally. I don't think you'll need to worry about the little beast."

Enkidu clicked his tongue. "Fine. Lead the way to the next divine we have to face."

The worry clinging to Enkidu didn't spread to Gilgamesh. They'd already angered Anu and escaped thanks to Enkidu's intervention. Together they could face anything.

They walked towards the tangy breeze. Followed it until the echoing crash of waves reached them. Breaking free from the forest, they stepped onto a shore. The sand was familiar in texture—small grains that formed a soft mass. But they were the color of emeralds, lapis lazuli, and rubies. They glistened under the pale sky and crunched with a musical pitch when the men stepped on them.

Enkidu frowned out at the beach's expanse and the rich, black water that lapped over the shore. It was as dark as bitumen, and clawed its way along the earth, longing to grab something to pull into its depth.

A shiver coursed over Enkidu, and Gilgamesh moved closer.

They'd be fine. They weren't foolish enough to get near the waters.

And the Alewife could help them. She understood how

to navigate the ends of the world—the realm that not even deities traveled.

Gilgamesh turned to look out across the sea.

Beyond the dark water that could kill even gods, Utnapishtim and his wife had fled. When Hirin had first shared the tablet with that information, Gilgamesh had wondered about the sea and how they might cross it. His ancestors had gone to some island at the world's end where the divine wouldn't travel, where mortals couldn't judge them. Despite always disrespecting Utnapishtim for his choices, Gilgamesh was beginning to understand. If he could find an island to escape with Enkidu to, he'd start building a boat at once.

A breeze blew, brushing sweat-dampened hair off Gilgamesh's neck. He took a deep breath of brackish air and smiled.

They'd made it.

Every step had led them towards their destinies.

Enkidu turned back to the forest's edge where Urmah lay flat on his stomach, ears pressed to his head. Enkidu walked back and crouched before the creature. "Come, Urmah. It's all right."

The lion gave a moaning growl and shrank farther against the earth.

"I'll keep you safe, dumu." He murmured a string of soft endearments. The gentle words coaxed the cub free from the forest, but his ears remained pasted to his head, and he prowled along the shrubs' edge, staying as far from the lapping water as possible.

Enkidu's skin shimmered with sweat that trailed along the furrows in his brow as he stood. Gilgamesh knocked his shoulder into Enkidu's. "Is the little beast your child now? Dumu, hmm?"

Enkidu rolled his eyes but looked at the cub, worry fluttering over his expression like a moth seeking light. "I guess you were right that he'd avoid the water." A grin slid his cheeks wide, and Gilgamesh's heart expanded, warming his entire chest. He wanted to see him happy forever. "He's clearly not an idiot like his fathers."

"Do not include me in this lion-as-a-child concept. I'm not attached to the thing."

"Mhmm." Enkidu hummed his reply, but his eyes sparkled. Gilgamesh switched between watching the horizon for any evidence of the Alewife and looking at Urmah. The creature crawled belly-to-sand along the beach and kept his focus on Enkidu. He'd follow the man anywhere. A flutter of something unexpected sparked in Gilgamesh's chest. The little beast had moments of being endearing.

In the distance, a dark splotch broke up the expanse of sand. As they kept walking its form came into view—a half oval that crested the land. A hut built from driftwood and stones with a mud-thatched roof took shape.

It appeared so mortal, humble even. Gilgamesh hesitated a step and frowned.

This couldn't be what they were looking for. Despite the unremarkable construction, it stood with thick vines growing over the doorway but trimmed back. Someone lived in it.

Gilgamesh slowed, and Enkidu moved closer to him so their shoulders brushed. The breeze became a whisper in darkness, a screech before death's killing blow. Hair rose on Gilgamesh's arms, and he slowed. According to legend, the Alewife had once received visitors gladly, then she changed, avoiding others. Perhaps there was some reason she hid away. Gilgamesh wished he knew more about her story so they could understand what they faced.

A woman stepped from behind the hut, dark curls flowing out on the breeze. Her tunic trailed with it, a smear of cream over the ebony sea. She crouched on the beach beside large, flat stones and brushed something from them into a basket.

Gilgamesh picked up his pace again as she moved to the next stone.

Kernels of dried grain were scattered over them, drying in the sun. Grains that made beer and ale.

They'd found her.

If Utu sent them this direction after being so generous with them multiple times, then this had to be the path they sought. Utu had told Enkidu the Alewife had information. And Gilgamesh was hungry for answers.

The woman jerked up, her basket pressed to her hip. Her eyes widened, glistening and reflecting the sun even from a distance. She turned and ran into the hut, slamming the door behind her.

"Shed," Gilgamesh cursed.

Enkidu tilted his head, revealing an expanse of his neck. "Well, we're off to a good start with her."

"You're the one who said you'd befriend all the gods," Gilgamesh said with less of a disgruntled tease than he'd intended. He'd remained fixed on Enkidu's stretch of neck, remembering running fingers across it, lips, teeth. He snapped himself out of the distraction. "Now's a wonderful opportunity to start."

Enkidu scoffed but called Urmah to him who reluctantly crept towards the man as he approached the hut and knocked. "Excuse me, we're sorry to bother you. We're only looking for Siduri, the Alewife. Utu sent us here."

Trees rustled together, dancing in the ocean breeze as the slick, black water lapped over the shore.

No one answered.

Gilgamesh walked up to the house's side and kicked his heel back against a stone. "There's always my way of handling things."

"We don't need that. She seemed frightened. Do you really think scaring her would help?"

Gilgamesh twisted his lips but kept his mouth shut. It obviously wasn't a question that desired an answer. And his answer wouldn't please Enkidu, anyway.

"My name is Enkidu," he said to the closed door. "I wonder if I could have a moment of your time to speak with you."

"Go away. The being you seek isn't here."

Gilgamesh rolled his eyes. Gods, this was a waste of time. He could pound upon the door, demand answers or, if her words proved true, instructions to reach the Alewife's residence. This hut with its flowering vines twisting over the walls' uneven planks had seemed suspect since they came across it. What divine would live in squalor like this?

"Do you know where the Alewife resides, then?" Enkidu asked.

Silence again.

Gilgamesh worked his jaw back and forth before turning to Enkidu. "We could break the door down."

Enkidu sputtered a sigh as he turned to face him. "No, we cannot break her door down."

"It wouldn't take much effort." He eyed the shack again.

"We can't break her door because it's a bad thing to do, not because it's physically impossible." Enkidu ran his fingers back through his hair, sliding them across his horns. He used to touch them with hesitance, disgust. Now he glided hands over them as smoothly as he touched his curls. Gilgamesh loved the horns, the way he could grasp them, pull the man's mouth to his with them.

The same man who currently turned narrowed eyes on him.

"Right, of course not." Gilgamesh offered a thin smile. Then he tacked on, "I was joking."

The notch that formed between Enkidu's brow made it clear he didn't believe a word of the last remark. "We should explain to her why we're here and tell her the truth."

"I certainly don't recommend you try lying again. You're not very good at it," Gilgamesh grumbled.

Enkidu scowled but stepped forward, grabbed Gilgamesh's cheeks, and kissed him. Soft at first. Then deeper, his teeth scraping Gilgamesh's lips as he pulled away. Gilgamesh's body loosened at the touch as he stared into forest-wild eyes, his hands curling around Enkidu's hips like wolves returning to their den.

Enkidu brushed knuckles over his cheekbones once more before turning to the door. "I'm searching for Siduri because a goddess has cursed me to die. My lover and I travel this dangerous realm looking for a way to escape our fate."

He looked back at Gilgamesh who'd frozen. He didn't even breathe.

Enkidu had been right. This was a topic he avoided because the idea of Enkidu truly gone from his world clenched his soul, stalled his heart. He didn't know how he'd breathe without the man. How he could stand for the sun to rise or the moon to fall.

This trip was a gamble—a handful of hucklebone dice tossed onto the ground with a whispered prayer.

But the potential winnings if they could achieve it were worth more than his entire palace.

Death was the one curse he couldn't fight. If Enkidu suffered some other malady, he could find a solution, beg the gods, spend a king's fortune to solve the issue. But death would remove Enkidu's gentle, precious soul from Gilgamesh's reach.

The door cracked open. A pale face with large brown eyes capped with wild, wind-blown hair peeked out. "Who are you?"

"I'm Enkidu," he whispered, "and this is King Gilgamesh."

Her eyes darted in his direction. "Truly? Mortals wandering through the divine realm?" Her gaze pierced through Gilgamesh like a thrusted spear. "I've heard rumors about you, King."

"And I you. But I've often found that stories have embellishments." For example, legend said the Alewife lived in a fine residence near the sea and once hosted majestic parties. The pitiful shack this woman crouched in didn't come close to matching the lore's grandeur if they'd arrived at the right destination.

She bit her lip, a dimple forming between her brows. Her skin was as smooth as the sky, her hair dark and lustrous. But she was divine. She could be thousands of years old despite appearances.

"Do you truly love this man?" She gestured to Enkidu who stood in stark contrast to her. He'd bent down to help untangle Urmah from a vine, but he raised his face at the question. Wrinkles marred his tanned skin and even crouching he was far larger than the goddess. His tunic had grown tattered, his beard untamed.

He was beautiful.

Like a forest growing wild. Thick, sturdy trees and star-glittering nights. The cool wash of lake water. The sweetness of honey on the tongue.

"Yes," Gilgamesh said, still staring at Enkidu. "With my entire heart and soul."

Enkidu raised his chin, and the corner of his lip lifted. The love they shared flowed between them like an element. Another thing to drift on the wind and skim across the crashing waters of Death's Sea. Something worth defying fate for.

The goddess opened the door farther. She skimmed her eyes over both of them then nodded. "Come in."

CHAPTER FOURTEEN
WINE SO SWEET

ENKIDU DUCKED his head to enter the house then paused. "Do you mind if Urmah joins us as well?"

The cub waited at the door, watching Enkidu but not moving forward without his permission. Gilgamesh was right. Urmah was growing into a proper young lion. He'd more than doubled in size, his head reaching Enkidu's knee.

The goddess smiled down at the creature and knelt before him. "Urmah, is it?" She offered a hand and Urmah pressed his head into it, twisting so her fingers ran down his neck. He had no fear of humans or human-like beings. That would cause him trouble in the future if Enkidu didn't survive to see after his welfare and Gilgamesh didn't keep him.

A smile parted the goddess' lips. Something about it made her seem older, a woman who'd faced hundreds of years rather than the two decades her appearance suggested.

She rose and gestured for them to enter.

Urmah loped alongside Enkidu then accepted a bone the woman offered him as Gilgamesh crouched to enter.

The hut was small and rough-hewn. A shelf across the back wall held hundreds of crocks in different sizes. Half a dozen large pots sat stacked in a corner. Above them, twirling like temple dancers, dried herbs tangled together.

"Have a seat, Enkidu and Gilgamesh." The woman watched them like a hawk. Whether it was with the bird's curiosity or its predatory focus, he was unsure. His mouth went dry. The last thing Enkidu desired was to anger another god in their territory. He didn't wish to interact with the divine again at all. Yet, he'd committed to this journey.

He accepted a chair that shoved his knees up towards his chest. Gilgamesh frowned before he sat as well. He spread his legs so they covered the furniture making it seem like he floated in the air rather than sitting on something.

The woman crossed her arms and appraised them both before speaking. "I'm Siduri."

"I thought you said the person we sought wasn't here?" Enkidu asked.

Gilgamesh huffed and crossed his arms to match. This wouldn't help his faith in others, though Enkidu had begun to believe that might be a lost cause.

"That's true." She turned to lift her face to a high, thin window that allowed a trickle of sunlight to spill in alongside the briny wind. "You asked for the Alewife. She's been gone for a century." Shifting back to them, her almond-round eyes glistened. "I'm called the Wine Maker now."

"A wine maker who makes beer?" Gilgamesh nodded to the dried grains she'd gathered.

Siduri stared at the kernels. Dark hair tangled in the breeze, but she didn't move. Stillness filled the space. Urmah's bone clattered over the wood wall as he gnawed at it. Gilgamesh readjusted, the chair groaning with his movement.

Grabbing a basket, Siduri then plopped it into Gilgamesh's lap before he could raise his hands to block it. "Yes, that's true. And if you want to ask me questions, you'll make yourselves useful while I talk."

Gilgamesh wrapped thick fingers around the basket's straps and frowned down at the contents. Siduri grabbed a mortar and pestle and thrust it at Enkidu, releasing it before he had a good grip.

He'd been right to compare her to a bird. Her movements had the same anxious, flightiness of the creatures. Prepared for an attack. Ready to dash away.

He readjusted the tools which fit within his palm and raised his eyebrows in question. Gilgamesh shrugged, and Enkidu gestured to the basket. He'd gladly work if it helped them get answers. Utu had sent them here, claimed this woman had the information they needed, and he trusted the sun god. Really, he'd help solely because the Wine Maker had asked. She seemed so alone in this house by deadly waters, so nervous and uncertain. He wished he could do something to soothe her.

"Fine," Gilgamesh said and grabbed the mortar and pestle free from Enkidu. Apparently if one of them was working, it would be Gilgamesh. He added grains and began mashing them, holding the small tool between his finger and thumb.

Siduri settled into her seat and nodded at Gilgamesh's work, her long ebony hair piling in her lap.

Gilgamesh didn't half-heartedly work at the grains. Despite the tools being too small, he ground them diligently and poured the fine flour into a bowl on the table.

For all his gruffness, impatience, and boastfulness, he kept his word when given and did things well.

He wasn't afraid to work, either. To hunt or gather or grind if need be. Sometimes Enkidu would get frustrated with his relentlessness and the way he barreled into life before thinking through things. Then he'd see him like this, working away humbly at something, taking a task he'd likely label as unpleasant from Enkidu so he wouldn't have to endure it. Heart warming, Enkidu shifted so their legs touched.

Enkidu wished Akkiru could see Gilgamesh crouched in that hut, dirty and unpolished, grinding away at some labor. Akkiru would either laugh or be too stunned to do so.

Siduri frowned at Gilgamesh. "You seek immortality? Another king desperate to hold on to life beyond his allotment."

Instead of replying to her, Gilgamesh turned towards Enkidu. Pleading welled in his eyes. He didn't know how to speak to Siduri without arrogance tinging his words, without angering yet another divine. Individually they both had their struggles, but together they complemented each other like the gods had created them as a matched set. Enkidu kept his gaze on his lover, the brash and tender king who always managed to contradict himself.

He poured more grains into Gilgamesh's mortar and snuffed out a smile. Gilgamesh was hopeless and masterful, clever and foolish. The way he hunched into the small house expressed his entire life. He didn't quite fit in the world. Perhaps if they succeeded though, he might.

"Inanna has cursed me," Enkidu said softly over the crunching of grains. It felt strange saying the words aloud. A few syllables, scarcely a breath, and they meant everything.

"I've heard about this curse." Siduri slid down her chair and turned her attention back to Gilgamesh. "You've angered a rather fierce and popular goddess, mortal king."

Gilgamesh swallowed then poured more ground grain into the bowl. "I have." There was no arrogance left in his voice, none of the victor who made pretty speeches to Uruk's citizens. Only fear remained. Only heartbreak. He lifted his face and nodded at Enkidu. He was trying honesty and vulnerability. Pride's warmth surged through Enkidu, overtaking the hopelessness the conversation had imbued. "If I could go back and do things differently, I would. I'd prostrate myself before Inanna and even accept her demands if it would spare Enkidu."

If they were alone, Enkidu would interject. Inanna's demands had been ridiculous. She wanted to use Gilgamesh to produce a child who would take his throne. The idea of the cruel goddess' body against Gilgamesh's, using him, sent bile surging up Enkidu's throat. Usun had once shared how much he detested the goddess. His assessment had been right. Only her self interests mattered and she'd harm and destroy anyone to achieve her aim.

Siduri uncrossed her arms then crossed her legs then switched them. "Inanna is stubborn."

Gilgamesh's lips thinned and he bobbed his head in agreement. Enkidu longed to hold him. He wanted to bury his face into his neck and whisper words of comfort, even if they'd be false. At the moment, his hatred of Inanna possibly burned hotter than Gilgamesh's.

"I've heard rumors of a rather stubborn mortal king as well."

Gilgamesh lifted his chin. The vulnerability slid away, a gleam sliding across his eyes like a shield. "I doubt either of us shall ever change."

Fighting a frown, Enkidu looked away. Perhaps Gilgamesh wouldn't change. Inanna would win, killing Enkidu. Then Gilgamesh would return to that stubborn, arrogant man he'd met. It seemed cruel that he wouldn't get to live his life and what impact he made, Inanna would erase.

Siduri tutted and jumped to her feet in her jittery manner then grabbed a wine vessel. She poured some into goblets then passed them around. Gilgamesh scarcely had time to set the tools and grain on the table before accepting the drink.

She swallowed some of hers then nodded at the men who stared at her. "Go on. Drink."

Gilgamesh's jaw worked, but he lifted his goblet and took a sip. Enkidu followed his lead. The wine washed across his tongue, bold and dry with a hint of sweetness in its wake. Never had he tasted anything so complex before. It reminded him of when Shamhat had found him in the woods and offered him a first taste of beer. He'd never wanted to drink anything else again.

Siduri finished her portion and poured another. "I loved once, the way you do now."

Taking a deep breath of herb-scented air, Enkidu met her gaze. Pain seemed to weep from her, filling the room with its intensity.

Gilgamesh set his drink on the table and leaned forward on his knees. It was amazing he wasn't demanding and prying. Perhaps he'd learned some temperance along their journey, or maybe the Wine Maker's odd behavior intrigued him as much as it did Enkidu.

She looked up at the window again. "For a human, he was a beautiful man. He had these curls that always tangled in the wind…" She laughed, but it wasn't for them. She scarcely seemed to notice they still sat in the room. "He always wanted to cut them, and I always begged him to let them grow long."

"I imagine he kept a head of curls, then," Enkidu said. If he guessed correctly, their love was no small thing.

She startled as she turned her attention back to him but nodded. "He did. He was a fisherman in a time long before even your stories reach. At that time, there wasn't the division between our worlds and brave mortals and foolish mortals would travel into the divine realm." Another smile graced her lips, one as wispy as a spiderweb. "He was a bit of both."

"You met him fishing?" Enkidu asked. Gilgamesh seemed to hold his breath, his eyes tracking between the two of them, but he remained quiet.

"Yes, and I told him he was an idiot. I was different then." She tangled her pale fingers into her hair. "Younger, believing myself infallible."

Gilgamesh cleared his throat. "Did he answer you?"

Siduri swiveled to face him. "He said I wasn't telling him any new information."

"Did he catch anything worth sharing in the mortal world?"

"He caught more than he intended." She tucked hair behind her ear and dashed her face away. "He never returned to the human realm. He stayed here with me. I donned this form permanently, and we built this house together. For fifty years,"—her voice went soft—"we laughed and made love and built great fires on the beach and crushed grapes with our feet and hosted lesser divinity. But one morning…"

She swallowed. Fiddled with her tunic's hem.

"One morning he didn't wake." A hush had entered her voice, a quiet that belonged to tombs. "Part of my heart didn't wake either."

Gilgamesh's color drained, leaving his skin grayish. "So, you remain here to remember him?"

"No." Her eyes narrowed into hawk-like sharpness again, and Enkidu fought the urge to shift in his seat. "I remained here to avoid the gods who refused to save him. No matter how much I pleaded and wept before them, they dismissed me. They said death is a mortal man's plight. I've learned this curse—this inevitability—spares no one in the human realm. How do so many survive this misery? I don't understand it, but somehow, they do."

Her eyelashes batted her cheeks. "I've learned something else as well. May I share it with you, mortal king?"

Gilgamesh pursed his lips like he debated it but offered a nod.

"Living is painful. You came into this world awash in blood to the sound of your mother's cries. If you're lucky, you'll leave this world to the music of those who love you weeping. You cannot control that. However, all the hours between those events rest in your hands. You desire my advice, let me offer it.

"Stop seeking after that which you can't control. Death is unavoidable. Go home. Enjoy the life you have." She lifted her goblet. "Drink good wine. Eat fine food. Listen to music that brings tears to your eyes and watch the colors Utu paints across the sky at sunset. Most of all, treasure those you love. Hold their hands and kiss their lips and share their laughter. And grief, when that comes,"—she ran her fingers down the table's edge—"feel all of it. All the pain and heartache and desperation. There's meaning in it, purpose. It makes you better and enables you to connect with others. It's one of the most universal experiences for humans—loss. All endure it at one time or another."

Gilgamesh's eyes darkened. His voice shifted to a blade, an ax head. Something designed to damage. "I've experienced grief before. It did not make me a better person."

Siduri leapt forward, the hawk diving from her perch. She leaned across the table. "Truly? You don't think losing your father made you more cautious? More able to manage politics and the gods? You don't believe your in-laws' deaths didn't make you consider your legacy and the future? Enkidu wouldn't even exist if you hadn't gone through that ordeal."

Gilgamesh released a breath like it was his final one and sank against the creaking chair. Enkidu turned the goblet around in his hands.

Had Gilgamesh not suffered before, not hungered for legacy, then Shamhat never would have interceded on his behalf. Ninsun never would have sought a goddess to create him.

He wouldn't exist.

As painful as the idea of dying was, worse was the idea of not existing. Of never running with the Wolf, hearing music, tasting bread.

Never challenging Usun, laughing with Akkiru.

Never loving Gilgamesh.

His heart seized.

He could accept death if it was the cost of living.

Siduri slid her eyes to him and smiled before returning her attention to Gilgamesh who brushed grains from his tunic. "Thank you for sharing your wisdom, Wine Maker."

The King's tone was flat, his gaze distant. "We came here seeking different answers, though."

"And Utu sent you my way hoping I'd discourage your quest. However, I didn't understand the love you shared." She ducked her chin so shadows entombed her eyes. "What you're looking for is the Ferryman and the Stone Ones."

"Is that who can cross the waters?"

Enkidu jerked towards Gilgamesh, and the chair wobbled, groaning precariously before it settled again.

Gilgamesh planned for them to cross Death's Sea.

He'd been desperate, foolish, and unrelenting.

This was something else, though. They couldn't survive traversing a sea whose water swallowed souls. He started to wonder if Gilgamesh had lost all reservations since Enkidu's curse. There seemed to be nothing Gilgamesh wouldn't do to save him. He wanted to live, but not if it came at the cost of Gilgamesh's life.

A crash had all three of them turning towards the doorway. Urmah sat surrounded by shards of a broken pot. Enkidu jumped up and crouched down beside him to gather up pieces. "No, no, Urmah."

The cub appeared uninjured and swished his tail back and forth as he watched Enkidu tidy.

Siduri walked over and knelt beside him, helping.

"I'm so sorry. I'll replace it and—"

"Don't worry about it." Her voice went soft, a feather drifting to the earth. "That is one lesson grief teaches. Things do not matter in the end. Clay pots can be replaced. Love cannot."

Enkidu's hands froze, and he met her gaze, the sadness in it.

She reached out and draped fingers over his hand. "Love cannot be broken or stolen either. Not even death can take it away. Once you've touched someone's heart, you stay with them forever."

Enkidu's breath came shaky. Death was a curse. Death was natural. Perhaps both were true. When it ripped him from those he loved, he could only hope he'd made some impression that remained.

"It's been hundreds of years." Siduri stared at him with a summer sun's beating intensity. "Love from one brief mortal life still thuds in my heart every day."

Enkidu blinked as a tear slipped down his cheek. He rushed to wipe it away.

Siduri studied him, like she dove into his soul, twisted through it. Then she rose and turned towards Gilgamesh. "I shall tell you what you want to know, mortal king, though your hopes are an impossibility. The only humans the gods ever granted immortality to are Utnapishtim and his wife. It was supposed to be a reward for their obedience. But when you meet them, you'll understand why the gods have never done so again. And you'll understand why your ancestors wouldn't wish you the same fate."

She set the broken slivers of the pot on a table as Enkidu stood next to her. "Follow the sea south until the forest ends. Continue three weeks at a steady pace, then you'll come to an older wood, darker and full of magic and monsters. There, you shall find the Stone Ones and their master."

Gilgamesh stood and pushed the chair under the table. "I've never heard of the Stone Ones before."

Enkidu swallowed as the uneasiness from moments before shivered down his spine. They'd already traversed divine territory, but so far Gilgamesh had known the legends and even had some sense of direction. Now they would head for some lore he'd never heard of before.

"Oh, that's an old tale," Siduri whispered. "Far older than your civilization, mortal king. There was a time when the divine rewarded great mortals after death. The Ferryman would have the Stone Ones escort them across the sea to the island where Utnapishtim now lives."

A cruel grin slid up her face, making her seem as ancient as she'd said, as damaged as she'd implied. "They shoved wicked mortals into the water. The sea here contains the waters of true death—death of the spirit. If you fall into those waters, not a memory remains. You become nothing."

Hair stood on Enkidu's neck, and his heart pounded so he could feel it thudding in his lips, the tips of his fingers. All Gilgamesh had once wanted was to become something —to have a legacy that outlived him. With Inanna's curse rapidly approaching, Enkidu understood that inclination more than he once had. If something happened to them during the crossing they'd become nothing. Was it possible that not even stories would remain of the great god-king of Uruk, of the city he'd fought for, of the love he'd shared with Enkidu?

"But for the cruelest humans of all, the gods sentenced them to become the Stone Ones. You want to know what those pitiful beings are?" She gave her head a shake, and her expression was wild, her eyes holding a storm. "They're tormented souls that have lived in agony for a thousand years. They were once human. The gods changed them into monsters and with every step they take, the pain of boulders crushing their bones shoots through them."

"That's horrible," Enkidu whispered.

Siduri turned her back to Gilgamesh so she could face Enkidu. "Surely you know by now that we live in a brutal world?"

Enkidu's stomach clenched. He wanted to believe in a

beautiful reality, where good happened and forgiveness existed. Love was more powerful than cruelty. Even if he and Gilgamesh both died, even if Death's Sea swallowed them and their memory, some spark of the love they shared would remain. It had to. Enkidu refused to believe otherwise. Moments before he might not have believed it, but now he was certain. Love was eternal, regardless of life's shortness or the world's heartlessness.

"Why not push them in the waters and let them cease to exist?" Urmah had tangled between Enkidu's legs, and he scratched the cub's chin. "That seems a grim enough punishment."

"Hmm. They killed the old Stone Ones every century when they replaced them. Only beheading kills them and frees their souls." She ran a slim finger across her neck. "The gods decided at some point that mortal lives weren't worth the trouble of ferrying. The present Stone Ones are those that are forgotten. They've suffered for so long your ancestors wouldn't remember their era. The gods have now created the Great Below for dead humans instead. The Stone Ones and the Ferryman are leftovers that the divine have abandoned."

Gilgamesh stepped forward. He frowned, but his eyes stayed fixed on Enkidu. If Siduri didn't stand between them, he'd have an arm around his waist, a thumb brushing a comforting rhythm.

"An even crueler fate to become forgotten," Gilgamesh said.

"Spoken like someone who hasn't suffered for a long time," Siduri answered.

"I thought you said pain improves you."

"I said pain alters you. You get to decide what the alterations are."

Gilgamesh's jaw shifted back and forth. "Thank you." He shuffled around her, grabbed Enkidu's hand and Urmah by the scruff, and pulled them out the door.

Enkidu looked back, though.

At those sharp and watching eyes.

At the pain within them.

CHAPTER FIFTEEN
THE STONE ONES

THE WOODS WERE alive with noise—leave rattling in the wind, birds crying, and predators howling into the lavender quiet of twilight. It seemed where the gods wouldn't tread, so close to Death's Sea, the animals returned.

Among them and the tangling wild plants, Enkidu had lost his fears and hesitations.

Gilgamesh couldn't stop watching him.

He bounded over rocks with the strength and ease of a panther but gathered eggs and reeds with a scribe's finesse. He belonged out there among the wild things. Keeping him trapped in Uruk had been a cruelty.

Time passed. Gilgamesh wasn't rushing them along anymore. He wished they could get lost among the trees, disappear in a grove. If they could evade Inanna's curse there, he'd ask Enkidu to stay.

Even without that luxury, they had some time to spare. They'd gotten so close to Utnapishtim. All they had to do was cross Death's Sea and they'd find him. They could discover the path to immortality. And the curse, like the Wine Maker, would remain behind them.

Something about the odd woman's remarks hung around Gilgamesh like an itchy shawl that brushed his arms.

He tried to forget her words and the way her eyes seemed like endless pools, full of sorrow.

That level of grief terrified Gilgamesh.

That's why he took this journey. He didn't wish to live the next fifty years mourning Enkidu. She'd said to enjoy the days he had, and something about it stuck into Gilgamesh like a burr. He found himself dragging, urging Enkidu to slow, spending lazy afternoons searching for food or resting on his chest as he grazed fingers along his horns' curves.

One day, he discovered a clutch of berries and dangled them above Enkidu who'd stretched out over a mossy boulder. He opened his forest-colored eyes, the browns and greens and golds blending in with the surroundings, and smiled. "You found dessert."

Gilgamesh popped one in his mouth then dragged his lips down his finger. Enkidu's eyes followed the motion then flicked back up. Gilgamesh grinned. "If you want them, ask me nicely."

Enkidu rolled onto his side where he was closer and twisted a section of Gilgamesh's beard around his fingers. "Fine, then. Oh, great and mighty King Gilgamesh, he who surpasses all—"

Gilgamesh shoved a handful of berries into his mouth.

Enkidu sputtered and laughed, chewing through them. "You nearly choked me."

Gilgamesh smirked at him. "No, you can handle a mouthful. You've proven that much." He pecked a kiss on Enkidu's warming cheek.

Enkidu lay back and dappled sunlight shimmered

across his exposed chest, making the hair gleam. "Wouldn't that be ironic, though? For me to choke to death in the divine realm, evading the curse?"

Gilgamesh frowned. "It would be nonsensical."

"Oh, more nonsensical than shoving an entire bunch of berries into my mouth to stop me from—"

"Being impertinent? Yes."

"You're ridiculous." Enkidu's eyes glimmered, his lips tipping up. Gilgamesh leaned over him and traced a horn, causing Enkidu to catch his breath. Something simmered between them. Even as Gilgamesh's lips crushed Enkidu's, he knew what it was. They'd talked about his death—joked about it, even. He'd finally stopped growing angry and disconnected when Enkidu brought it up.

Enkidu clutched him like he wanted their souls to merge.

Gilgamesh yearned to make it happen.

In the distance, Urmah yawned and curled up for a nap. Gilgamesh had stopped caring what the lion thought. Siduri's words came back to his mind again. *Treasure those you love. Hold their hands and kiss their lips and share their laughter.*

His mind pushed and pulled at the idea.

He wanted to drown their time with Siduri and forget it happened.

He wanted to clutch it to his chest and heed her words.

They sounded eerily like truth.

Unlike the Wine Maker, though, Gilgamesh wouldn't flail in grief and loss, spilling out wise platitudes to uninterested strangers. He wouldn't sit around and passively accept what life tried to thrust at him. He'd change their fate, defy the gods, become immortal, and never lose that man who tasted like earth's sweetness.

Enkidu rolled them over, banging Gilgamesh's shoulders into the rock. He grunted at the impact and Enkidu smirked. Gilgamesh grabbed his face and pulled him back towards him. Forget Siduri and her strange words. He'd treasure the time with the man because he loved him, not because some brokenhearted goddess implored him.

Days passed slowly with Gilgamesh regularly dragging them off path to find a cool lake to bathe in, a mouse's nest for Urmah to hunt, a view at the top of a tree to enjoy.

If Enkidu knew why Gilgamesh had slowed, he didn't comment on it.

He watched birds burst over lilac morning skies, stretched his head back into rushing waterfalls, and fell asleep tracing his fingers across Gilgamesh's chest as if he'd also be content to remain in the forest together forever.

Weeks swept by before a chopping sound echoed ahead, breaking their wandering rhythm.

The atmosphere had changed, a sourness entering the realm. Fewer animals appeared, and Urmah had grown cautious, flicking his gaze around the massive trees every few minutes.

Waves from Death's Sea rushed up to the wood line, pushing them deeper into the brush.

They crested a hill where they could see a stretch of naked valley. Tree stumps littered it. A dozen beings hoisted axes and chopped the wood. Massive trees fell with thuds that echoed up to them, but Gilgamesh couldn't tear his eyes from the creatures that downed them. Even Urmah watched as he pressed against Enkidu's legs.

The creatures were taller and wider than Gilgamesh and Enkidu. Their bodies were crafted of stone, a gritty gray mass like the weather had beat upon it for centuries, leaving pores and cracks. They cut the trees down and dragged them towards a central spot.

There, a bald-headed man with a tangled graying beard stood with a whip in hand. Despite the age evident in his coloring and the deep wrinkles on his face visible from even a distance, the man stood tall and broad shouldered, lashing out the whip at the stone creatures every few minutes with cracking, precise strikes.

"Faster, damn the gods. You bunch of lazy beasts." He stormed over to one and shoved it. The being fell with a thud into the earth, wincing, but didn't retaliate. Instead, it rose back to its feet and began its work beneath the whip's slashing.

Enkidu's breathing picked up, his eyes widening. Gilgamesh grabbed for his hand but found a tight fist instead.

The Ferryman kicked a stone beast who'd fallen to his knees. Dust puffed from its body, and it moaned but stood again and began hauling a tree forward.

Enkidu jerked forward, and Gilgamesh snagged his shoulders to hold him back. "There are a dozen of those creatures, Enkidu."

"He's tormenting them." Tears had formed over his eyes, and Gilgamesh wanted to kiss them away, press their bodies together until he absorbed Enkidu's pain.

From everything Siduri had said, it seemed fair that these Stone Ones faced punishment. But Enkidu had never met a suffering creature he didn't feel compassion for. The man trembled beneath his grip, and a tear broke free, sliding down his face until it nestled into his beard.

Gilgamesh kissed his forehead. "If you run down there, you could get yourself killed by these beasts you're feeling so much tenderness for."

"Perhaps my life would finally serve some purpose if I helped them, at least."

Gilgamesh's breath caught in his chest. Enkidu remained focused on the creatures working below them, unaware of what he'd said or the impact it made. Enkidu thought he had no purpose, and Gilgamesh had dragged him on this journey, trying to save him but also using what little time he had left. He didn't understand how Enkidu couldn't see the reality of himself. How wise and compassionate and powerful he was. One day, when Enkidu's legacy was inscribed in the stars, then he'd understand. Then he'd see himself as Gilgamesh always had.

All of Enkidu's hesitations, the sadness in his eyes, the way he'd looked back the entire journey sank deep into Gilgamesh's gut.

He stepped away.

Pulled the axes off his side.

Enkidu turned towards him. "What are you doing?"

"Well, you heard Siduri. The only escape for them is beheading. It frees their souls from this suffering."

"I thought you said there were too many."

Gilgamesh moved closer so he could breathe in Enkidu's earthy scent. Urmah wound between them, the creature's warmth drifting into Gilgamesh's legs.

"You have helped so many with your compassion, Enkidu," Gilgamesh whispered over the smacking sound of axes hitting trees. "You are a good man. And if you feel called to release these pitiful creatures from their suffering, then I'll help you."

"You said we'd get ourselves killed."

Gilgamesh smiled as he twirled his axes. "We've defied death at every turn in our journey. Why should today be different?" His voice dropped again. "Besides, if I perish helping you do something that matters, I will not regret it."

Enkidu's nose flared, and he stared at Gilgamesh. Then he pulled his sword free. "I'm ready."

Gilgamesh grinned even as his heart pounded. They could die, but he couldn't let Enkidu continue feeling like he was worthless, that he'd not achieved important feats. Besides, Enkidu might not have much time left. Every night the stars reminded Gilgamesh of just how much time had passed, how quickly the New Year and Inanna's curse approached. He'd attempted to ignore it and enjoy their time together, but stumbling across the Stone Ones reminded him of everything weighing on their actions. Enkidu needed this.

No. Gilgamesh clenched his teeth. Enkidu would live, and this would be one of many victories he'd claim. Lives he helped.

Gilgamesh dreamed of a future where they disappeared together, but needy beings would always draw Enkidu. If they became divine, he'd likely become the god of broken hearts. Gilgamesh almost sighed. How had fate paired him with someone so tender?

"Stay here," Enkidu said to Urmah. The young lion whined but tucked into a bush. Enkidu turned to Gilgamesh and nodded.

"We take them by surprise. Let's hope our weapons are sufficient." He hefted an ax. The weight was more than most human swords, but it was still mortal-crafted. He'd throw all his strength into the swings and pray they landed true. "If we can fell two a piece before they're aware of us, we'll have a third of the group down."

Enkidu licked his lips.

Bobbed his head.

They climbed down the slope together, taking steps when the thud of a falling tree might cover the sound. Gilgamesh considered reaching for Enkidu, touching his skin once more, finding his lips for a stolen kiss. But he couldn't act as though they'd die in this. He needed to focus on the task, pray his axes were sharp enough and his aim perfect.

When they moved closer, Gilgamesh pointed then touched his neck. Enkidu frowned but looked in the direction he'd indicated and nodded. He'd seen it too. There was a spot on the Stone One's necks that looked like clay rather than rock.

That was where they needed to hit.

"Now?" Enkidu asked.

"Go."

They jumped from the bush together, and Gilgamesh slammed an ax forward. It sank through the soft neck of the first Stone One like he'd smashed the weapon into sand. He'd overestimated the thrust and stumbled forward, trying to catch his balance as the creature's head hit thudded into the ground. With a shriek, the beast burst into rubble, and a silvery mist flew up into the sky before disappearing.

The next closest Stone One turned towards him.

He looked down upon Gilgamesh, his eyes dark slits of granite.

He didn't move, didn't fight even as Gilgamesh hoisted the weapon once more.

Swung.

Removed another head.

Enkidu had already felled three and strode forward without hesitating, his muscles flexing as he gripped the sword.

Gilgamesh ran to catch up with him.

The Ferryman turned and lashed a whip then screamed, "Stop them!"

The Stone Ones all moved away from their work and faced Gilgamesh and Enkidu. Their footsteps shook the ground as they moved in unison.

"Kill them!" the Ferryman shouted.

Gilgamesh readjusted his axes in his grip. Enkidu scarcely moved. He only raised his chin. Gilgamesh could hear the certainty in his words, *I'm ready,* echoing through his mind.

Five down, seven to go.

The beasts attacked as a unit. Gilgamesh growled through his teeth as he dodged axes. How fucking ridiculous it would be to die at the blade of an ax after he'd ended so many lives with his.

A Stone One slammed his weapon forward, and Gilgamesh dropped and rolled, scarcely avoiding the impact. He thudded into a tree stump and groaned but dragged himself back to his feet.

Enkidu weaved through them, his arms swinging fierce blows with his sword.

Another head fell from a creature.

Then a Stone One backhanded him, and Enkidu landed with a bang. Gilgamesh got to his feet and roared, drawing the other beasts' attention. All six thundered towards him.

Enkidu rose slowly and lifted his sword.

He met Gilgamesh's gaze and nodded.

He was okay.

Gilgamesh could face anything as long as he was okay.

He ran towards a rock-studded cliff with a narrow, steep path, opposite the direction they'd left Urmah in, and climbed. The Stone Ones marched behind them. They could maintain their balance without having to hold on to the rocks, unlike Gilgamesh. He found a flat place and got to his feet with a weapon back in his grip.

The creatures favored their right sides. When they placed their left feet down, it took them an extra beat of time to shift back.

Enkidu chased after them in his silent manner. A wolf hunting.

Gilgamesh needed to get them to circle around where they put their weight on their left as he arrived. It might give Enkidu an advantage. Perhaps he could fell several before they attacked again.

Not far beyond, a rock jutted from the cliff's side. It was a massive jump. Gilgamesh placed his axes back in their holsters and swallowed. He crouched low. The Stone Ones had almost made it to him.

Enkidu remained on their heels, his footsteps silent as he maneuvered.

He needed to give him time and the benefit of surprise.

A Stone One leapt forward, and Gilgamesh stumbled, grasping a vine to catch himself. The creature slammed his ax forward, and Gilgamesh leaned back so the weapon clanked into the rock.

Fuck.

Gilgamesh withdrew a weapon and sliced at the creature's chest. The strike ricocheted back into Gilgamesh's arm, leaving his ears ringing and his vision doubling.

"Fucking kill them already," the Ferryman shouted from the valley.

Oh, if Gilgamesh lived through this, the man was going to regret ever drawing breath.

Enkidu had arrived.

The creatures took another step. One more and they'd return to their left side and that beat of hesitation.

Gilgamesh wove around another ax swing and jumped. He hadn't had time to focus or estimate, he just threw his body out into the open air.

The ground stretched beneath him, far enough that a fall would break bones.

Pebbles dropped.

He landed on the rock's edge and clawed his fingers into it. Fingernails lifted, despite the pain he didn't release his grip. His muscles trembled, but he dragged himself back up the cliff side as Enkidu dropped several Stone Ones.

Two turned on Enkidu as the remaining one leapt after Gilgamesh.

He made it onto the rock and up on his feet by the time the creature landed with a crash that shook the stone. Gilgamesh's hands were raw, his fingers aching. He removed an ax and trembled as the Stone One pounded towards him.

Oh, godsdamned Enkidu and his fucking bleeding heart and his—

Gilgamesh dodged a hit.

Jumped back to his feet.

Damn Enkidu for caring so much all the fucking time, and for the shed-eating gods for cursing him, and this whole godsdamned ridiculous journey and—

Gilgamesh swung and missed.

Beyond them, Enkidu finished one of the Stone Ones pursuing him.

Two more left.

The Stone One swung, and Gilgamesh, heart in his throat, remained still until the last moment when he jerked away.

The ax crashed into the crumbling cliff wall behind him.

It stuck, and the Stone One grunted then jerked to pull it free.

Gilgamesh lifted his ax and jumped like he reached into his blood and called on his god's inheritance. He soared then swung.

The blade sliced through the Stone One's neck; its head landed with a thump and cracked on the stone.

Enkidu roared as the final Stone One fell.

The Stone Ones' bodies crumbled into rock and tumbled across the dirt. In the distance, their young lion cried. Enkidu didn't turn back though. He stared down at the pile of pebbles, at the broken remains of a freed soul.

Gilgamesh climbed down the cliff, avoiding his more injured hand. He reached the valley faster than he'd scaled the climb.

Enkidu lifted his face with an expression that held the vengeance of an angry god.

He stormed towards the Ferryman then yanked him up by the tunic. The man screamed and kicked, clawing at Enkidu's hands.

Enkidu didn't even blink.

"You cruel bastard," he growled.

Gilgamesh's stomach warmed. Damn, Enkidu was attractive when he gave in to his strength and fury. Like this, anyone could witness the gods' mark on him even without the horns.

"I had no choice," the Ferryman cried. "The gods assigned me to manage them."

"That's no excuse," Enkidu growled through his teeth, "for abusing them."

"They have to work. It's their curse. Have you ever tried to motivate people who've given up all hope?"

Enkidu's grip tightened.

Gilgamesh sighed and stepped forward. They couldn't kill the Ferryman. Enkidu would regret it. He'd lie awake at night thinking over his cruelty. If anyone would kill the man, it would be Gilgamesh. He'd sleep just fine with blood splashed over his hands. He had plenty of nights before.

More importantly, though, the Ferryman was their only passage across Death's Sea. Their only path to Utnapishtim. To their future.

He placed a hand on Enkidu's back and whispered his name.

Enkidu trembled, his fingers clawing into the Ferryman's tunic. At Gilgamesh's touch, his grip loosened, and he released a breath then the man.

Urmah tumbled down from the hill, and Gilgamesh snatched him up and shoved him into Enkidu's arms. The man couldn't harbor battle fury that still lingered on him with his lion-child in hand. Enkidu buried his nose into Urmah's fur and took a step back.

With a lazy swing of an ax, Gilgamesh stepped towards the Ferryman. He was a pitiful excuse for someone who'd lived so long in divine lands. His beard was matted, his skin haggard and pulling down his cheeks. He took a stumbling step back and cowered, his shoulders hunching to his ears.

Gilgamesh brought the blade to the man's throat and stalled just short of breaking flesh. "You appear like a man who wishes to live."

The Ferryman's face twitched, his nose wrinkling, his eyes wincing. "The gods promised me if I paid my time, endured my punishment for crossing them, I'd get a chance at a second life. A life of riches and privilege. You two feel bad for these bastards?" He gestured to the rubble piles. "If you'd known them, you wouldn't."

Enkidu's jaw clenched, and Gilgamesh smiled wickedly at the man. It had been too long since he could exercise his role as the god-born king. "We're getting to know you now, and we're not pleased with what we're discovering."

"Haven't I proven my loyalty?" He swept his hands out. "Hmm? I've been promised a reward that I've suffered for. Now it's time for me to get what's mine."

"Perhaps I'll remove your head as well." Gilgamesh swung an ax around again and the man stumbled back. "End your suffering for you."

"No, please. What do you want of me? Who told you to come punish me? Ask Enlil. I've kept my vow."

Gilgamesh leaned in so he towered over the man. "You think a god as great as Enlil sent us here? The gods have forgotten about you, Ferryman. No one even remembers your name."

The man stared at him, eyes widening, and slowly shook his head. "He told me, he said—"

"Did he vow it?"

"No, but—"

Gilgamesh tsked. "I'm afraid the gods have taken you for a fool. But perhaps we can help."

"Who are you?"

"Someone who doesn't have to answer questions," Gilgamesh growled. This man was more impertinent than a wicked king. "What role did Enlil put your hand to here?"

"Utnapishtim and his wife require supplies. I ferry them across Death's Sea."

"Good. You'll take us there. Then we'll see what we can do to sort out promises made to you."

Enkidu frowned. Gilgamesh could guess why without

him needing to voice his thoughts. He debated whether Gilgamesh lied to the man or if he spoke true. Either way, Enkidu didn't approve. He disagreed with lying but he also didn't believe the Ferryman deserved a reward. Gilgamesh smiled at Enkidu which deepened his frown.

"You want to go to Utnapishtim?" The Ferryman snorted then shook his head. "You've damned your own soul."

Gilgamesh strode forward and slapped him, knocking the man into the earth. Blood gushed from the Ferryman's nose, trailing over his lips, but he smiled through it. Gilgamesh shouldn't have stopped Enkidu from tearing into the man. It would have been satisfying to watch him rip the bastard apart.

"Tell me why you smile, fool."

The Ferryman gave his head a shake. "Because the only creatures capable of crossing Death's Sea all just had their heads removed from their bodies."

CHAPTER SIXTEEN
ACROSS WATERS OF DEATH

GILGAMESH STORMED CLOSER to the Ferryman and glided an ax blade along his neck close enough to cut. The man sucked in air over his teeth as his eyes widened. "We must get across these waters, and you're going to help us, or instead of a reward you shall receive all the torment you've put these beasts through. Am I understood?"

Enkidu didn't move. He clutched Urmah to his chest and buried his face into his fur. He'd been an idiot. Looking down at the Stone Ones, the agony in their eyes, had broken him. They only fought because the Ferryman forced them too. Watching their oppressor lash out at them, curse and kick and demand, made his body warm more than the run through the mountain.

Now they couldn't make it to Utnapishtim. They'd have to return home with nothing to show for their journey. With no comfort for Gilgamesh to believe he'd done every-thing he could to prevent Enkidu's death. With no hope that Enkidu might defy a goddess' cruel curse and have a chance to live.

Enkidu swallowed, and Urmah licked his cheek, his rough tongue catching on his beard.

"I don't know what you expect me to do," the Ferryman spat, but he trembled, his fingers clutching tree roots. "It was the Stone Ones who rowed the boat. I remained in the center, covered so the waters didn't touch me."

Gilgamesh's shoulders rolled back until he appeared as enormous as the stone creatures. His knuckles had gone pale where they clutched the ax handle. "Well, it seems you've found an opportunity to prove yourself worthy for once, Ferryman."

Gilgamesh looked back at Enkidu, and the hardness of his expression softened as he met his gaze, but Enkidu looked away. Heat burned across his cheeks that he'd damaged their chances. Even if Gilgamesh didn't give up the aim, he'd endangered them—endangered Gilgamesh.

Whether or not Enkidu survived the year, he wanted Gilgamesh to live so he could enjoy his family and the good things the world offered.

He didn't want to cause his downfall.

At times, Enkidu worried that's what the gods actually crafted him for.

Gilgamesh stepped away from the Ferryman and rested his foot on a massive tree the Stone Ones had felled. "It's only our bodies that can't touch the water, is that right?"

The Ferryman sat up and rubbed the blood on his neck. "True, but if even a drop touches your fingernail, you're dead. Worse than death. You're gone forever."

Urmah wriggled, and Enkidu lowered him to the ground with clenched teeth.

Gone.

Forever.

Gilgamesh placed his hands on his hips and grinned at

the logs. There was nothing he liked more than an impossible obstacle. Gilgamesh would rush forward solely to prove he could.

Enkidu would argue and push back, except it was his fault they had no other options. *He'd* wanted to storm down into the valley, punish the Ferryman, and release the Stone Ones from their misery.

Gilgamesh slid his fingers over an ax and turned to Enkidu. "It looks like we need to cut down a few trees. How do you think you'd do with an ax, love?"

Hours later, Enkidu held one of Gilgamesh's axes, slamming it into logs he split. Urmah paced around the Ferryman. If he stood or attempted to run, the cub would grab his tunic and tear at it. A flash of anger would enter the Ferryman's eyes every so often. Once he raised a hand like he'd hit the lion.

If he'd done so, Enkidu would have killed him.

He caught Enkidu's expression and dropped his hand. Enkidu lifted his face in the man's direction every few minutes after that. The Ferryman stopped attempting to leave the clearing or interacting with Urmah and sat with his chin in hand, his eyes narrowed as he stared out into the forest.

Enkidu swung the ax again, splitting the wood.

It was physically intense work. His arms and core and legs were warm, the muscles tensed as the wood cracked beneath his blows.

Gilgamesh dragged another downed tree into the clearing. Enkidu had bandaged his fingers and winced at the dirtied scraps of linen around them. Gilgamesh had brushed his concern off, but Enkidu felt the weight of it. He suffered because of Enkidu's choices. Gilgamesh shot a glare at the Ferryman then walked over to Enkidu. "You're doing well."

Enkidu followed his gaze to the poles he'd cut from the trees. He'd stacked dozens of them into a growing pile.

The plan was ridiculous.

Impossible.

Dangerous.

It was everything they'd ever done together. Their entire relationship.

Gilgamesh reached out and grazed knuckles down his arm. Enkidu turned towards him like a sail catching wind. Gilgamesh was his center, the force that pushed him along.

Leaning closer, Gilgamesh whispered to keep his voice from carrying to the Ferryman who kicked pebbles away from the stump he sat on. "What's wrong, love?"

Sweat trickled down Enkidu's spine. "It's nothing."

Gilgamesh grabbed his arm, keeping him from turning away. "It's something, and I'd like you to tell me. I thought we'd committed to speaking honestly with each other."

Sweat glimmered across Gilgamesh's brow, and a healthy flush of color warmed his skin.

"You already know what I would say about this idea of crossing Death's Sea."

"I do." Gilgamesh ran his fingers down the wild mass his beard had become. Enkidu untangled and combed through it every night. During the day, though, it knotted in the wind. "Which is why I'm confused you aren't protesting with every breath."

Enkidu lifted his gaze to meet Gilgamesh's perceptive brown eyes. "We've already angered gods, walked into the divine realm, fought monsters, and stood at Death's Sea. What's one more foolish adventure between us?"

Gilgamesh grinned, but it wasn't the arrogant smile he donned when facing a challenge. Instead, it was as soft as fluff in a bird's nest. Something to curl down into, and Enkidu's heart warmed at the sight of it.

"We make it across the sea, then we'll have our answers." His voice was as gentle as the smile. "We're almost there. Then we'll have forever."

"Forever," Enkidu whispered. It felt impossible but perhaps Gilgamesh was right. They'd done many impossible things. If someone told their story, he didn't doubt Gilgamesh would achieve his original hopes. His name would go down in history.

But not for cruelty or expanding his rule.

He would be remembered for his bravery, his devotion, his love.

Something untethered within Enkidu, sending him emotionally off balance. The gods sent him to cure Gilgamesh of his ceaseless hunger for legacy. If Gilgamesh lived to tell his stories, then Enkidu had enabled him to achieve the thing that burned through him when they'd met.

He'd made his dreams come alive.

Gilgamesh still stared at him. Enkidu stumbled over words. He wanted to explain the thoughts tumbling through his mind but couldn't form them into anything solid. Instead, he nodded. "At your side, I'm no longer afraid. Let's finish our task and see where it leads us."

A chuckle rumbled Gilgamesh's chest, and he clapped Enkidu's arm before heading back to the forest.

Enkidu hoisted the ax and chopped like he shaped their destiny instead of wood.

* * *

Ebony water splashed against fallen trees that lay on the gravelly shore. A large boat bobbed on the waves, tugging the ropes that held it in place and kept the sea from swallowing it.

Enkidu fidgeted with his bag. Chopping wood and loading the boat with it had blistered his hands. They weren't as swollen and red as Gilgamesh's so he shouldn't complain. Gods knew Gilgamesh continued working without so much as a complaint over damage he'd taken. Loaded, the boat sat low in the water, closer to the soul-stealing sea.

Enkidu wasn't the only one having doubts. The Ferryman frowned and crossed his arms. Even Gilgamesh hesitated. Then he set his jaw. "Best to not waste any more daylight."

The sun glistened on the sea, gold over black. The ocean dashed the reflection apart as though it could strangle Utu.

"Come on, Urmah." Enkidu pushed the cub forward, but he pressed his feet into gravel and refused to move along. Gilgamesh directed the Ferryman onto the boat, demanding he ready the vessel for the journey.

Crouching before the lion, Enkidu pulled dried meat from his bag and waved it before him. Urmah pressed his ears back and didn't snatch the treat and eat it. He had no intention of moving a whisker closer to the deadly waters.

Beyond, the forest cried and called. Birds flew between branches.

In their time in that wood, far from the gods, Urmah had caught most of his food. He could manage on his own. He'd probably remain safer if he stayed behind.

Enkidu's lip quivered, and he tangled fingers into Urmah's growing mane. This creature had given him hope when he'd desperately needed it. Had loved him through various trials. Enkidu's heart had grown with the cub.

He didn't know how to say goodbye.

Gilgamesh strode up behind him. "Are you ready?"

"I don't think Urmah will go. He's nervous, and he'd probably,"—Enkidu's voice broke—"be fine in the forest here. I already did everything I could for him. It's best to let him go."

Gilgamesh looked between Enkidu and the lion cub several times, then he leapt forward and wrapped his arms around the animal.

Urmah thrashed and yowled and slashed sharp claws into flesh until blood trailed Gilgamesh's muscled arms. On the ground, Enkidu had frozen. He should have interceded but didn't know how. He didn't understand what Gilgamesh was doing.

With a huff, Gilgamesh rose to his feet, scratched and sweating with an unhappy Urmah clenched in his grip. "Come on, then," he said. Enkidu rose and followed him to the boat where he dumped the lion.

Enkidu swallowed as he stepped onto the vessel. The dark water knocked into it, swaying them. Soon they'd float over death, be surrounded by it.

"Let's go, Ferryman," Gilgamesh commanded.

As the man unmoored the boat and Urmah growled and curled into a grumpy ball on the boat's floor, Enkidu stepped over to Gilgamesh and examined the cuts Urmah had given him. The boat hitting the sea caused them both to stumble, but Enkidu grabbed his bag and pulled out a salve to rub on the injuries.

"Why did you do that?" he asked.

Gilgamesh allowed him to fuss over the injuries. They weren't serious. Urmah had grown large enough that he could damage muscle and flesh. They'd seen him drag kills back with deep bites and gouges on them. Gilgamesh's cuts were surface level in comparison.

Urmah had not wanted him to pick him up or drag him onto the boat. But he didn't mean to actually hurt him.

Warm fingers tilted Enkidu's chin up, and Gilgamesh grinned at him. "We weren't leaving your son behind in the forest. And look at him, he's fine now."

Urmah lay curled into a tight ball looking decidedly not fine. Selfishly, Enkidu was happy to have the cub still at their side.

The boat glided through the black sea, spray rising but not reaching inside. As long as the weather remained calm, it would be fine.

"I don't see Urmah as a child," Enkidu said. "Dumu can be a word of endearment and not just mean 'son', can't it?"

"It can." Gilgamesh leaned against him so their hips brushed. He curled his fingers around Enkidu's waist. "But I don't think that's how you meant it. Besides, he's wild and beautiful like you, is he not?" Gilgamesh looked down at Urmah and frowned. "Well, in his better moments."

Enkidu laughed and kissed him. "I love you."

Gilgamesh tucked hair behind his ear. "You love every pitiful creature you run across, so that makes sense."

"You were not pitiful when I met you."

"Not physically, perhaps." His voice had dropped to a hush that snaked beneath the waves' rushing thunder. "My soul was. Then I met you and came alive truly for the first time."

Enkidu gave his head a shake and ducked it to hide a smile. He loved Gilgamesh too, fiercely. Foolishly. Enough to go on this outrageous journey, face death, and dare it to touch them.

"Go, see after your son," Gilgamesh teased. But his expression was soft again, belying his tone.

Enkidu brushed his nose over his neck, pressed a kiss there, then walked over to sit next to Urmah who whined pitifully for an hour but allowed Enkidu to scratch his head and pull him into his lap.

Gilgamesh grabbed the poles they'd crafted to push through the water. He used one, his muscles straining as he attempted to get as far with the row as possible, before releasing it for the water to swallow. Risking water splashing back if they used them like traditional paddles wasn't something he wanted to chance. Hundreds of poles were at the ready and soon Enkidu would trade him, helping pull the boat forward.

Avoid the water. And make it across the sea. That's all they had to do. According to the Ferryman, the journey was less than a day. Soon they'd stand on a shore only a few other living mortals had ever trod on.

Soon they'd find the answer to immortality.

Maybe in the future Enkidu and Gilgamesh would be deified. They'd keep Urmah, love him into his old age and make whatever impact on humanity Utu foresaw. Perhaps the future was bright.

Clouds bunched in the sky as if they argued with Enkidu's thoughts.

They swept in like Enlil scattered them. Like dice clattering over a game board.

Wind picked up, and Gilgamesh strained against the poles as the boat veered off course. Waves rose, crashing into the hull.

"Stay here," Enkidu whispered to Urmah, and he jumped up and gripped the oar with Gilgamesh, fighting the sea's angry thrashing.

The Ferryman dropped and pulled a wine container free, removing the cap to take a drink.

"What are you doing?" Gilgamesh cried. "Get your ass back on your feet and tell us what direction to steer through this storm."

The Ferryman took a long drink then lazily raised his eyes to Gilgamesh. "It doesn't matter which direction you turn us."

Enkidu lifted another pole, pushed it into the water, and fought the storm. Rain fell, peppering his skin. Urmah yowled, but he couldn't turn towards him.

Gilgamesh snarled. "You know how to navigate these waters. Get up and do so or we will throw you overboard."

"Do it." The Ferryman took another swallow and laid back on the wood. "I don't know what god you've angered, but this storm isn't natural. We won't live to see land."

CHAPTER SEVENTEEN
WHEN HOPE IS GONE

RAIN THRASHED GILGAMESH'S BODY, pattering alongside his pounding heart. So far, they'd evaded water from Death's Sea touching them, but only because of the boat's deep interior paired with sheer fucking luck which did not appear to favor them any longer.

Enkidu strained against the makeshift oars, pushing with each pole as far as he could. He dropped one at the last moment, and water splashed. As he jumped back, Gilgamesh's body went cold.

If one drop of that water touched his flesh, this entire journey would be a waste.

Gilgamesh rounded on the Ferryman, yanked the wine jar from his hand, and chucked it into the churning, black waves.

"Hey! Why would you do that?" The Ferryman curled his fingers into fists before he met Gilgamesh's gaze, the inferno that had to blaze in it. He stumbled back.

Gilgamesh grabbed him by the tunic, yanking him off his feet. Rain spat down upon them, sliding over the man's sun-burnt flesh. Any inebriation he'd managed with the drink fled, and his eyes went large and bright.

Throwing him off the boat would be deeply satisfying and almost worth the loss of information he possessed.

A wave rocked the vessel, and Gilgamesh stumbled to regain his footing. Urmah cried behind him, and Enkidu turned towards the creature for a moment before returning to his task of keeping them afloat.

No, Gilgamesh couldn't shove the damned Ferryman into his deserved fate because only he knew how to navigate these damn waters.

"Listen carefully to me, maggot, you will stay fucking sober and explain to us how to find our way to Utnapishtim's island, or I will rip your beard out hair-by-hair and peel skin from your body. Am I clear?"

His mouth flopped like a fish's for a moment before he thrust his hands out into the deluge. "If a god wants us dead, how should we plan to stop it? Besides, what am I supposed to navigate by? Mist and clouds?"

Gilgamesh tightened his grip until he pinched flesh. The Ferryman cried out, but Gilgamesh snarled. "I see why the gods abandoned you with the Stone Ones. You don't know when to shut your fucking mouth and follow instructions."

"We're going to die."

Gilgamesh leaned closer to him so he could whisper and the words would still reach past the howling wind. "You think I fear death? No, I'm here to defy death."

"Then you're a fool." The Ferryman blinked against the elements but didn't break Gilgamesh's gaze.

"Yes, well, one wolf recognizes another. Which way do we need to steer?"

The Ferryman looked around at the gray and ebony

world, the thrashing water, the roiling fog that crept over everything. "I don't know. If you've kept her steady on so far then—"

"We aren't drunkards lying around and giving up. We've kept the damn boat steady."

He kicked his feet a few times then gave up on fighting Gilgamesh's grip. "Then we should continue straight ahead. If the clouds break, I can use the sun to navigate better."

"Excellent. Then busy yourself by praying to Utu for relief, hmm?"

"Utu." The Ferryman grumbled but stopped rolling his eyes when Gilgamesh gave him another shake that caused his teeth to clack. He set the worthless man down and walked towards Enkidu.

The storm wailed and writhed. Death's Sea had turned into a dragon eager to pull them down. Only Enkidu's shaking muscles and diligent devotion kept them afloat.

Gilgamesh grabbed a pole then nodded towards Urmah. "I'll take over for a few minutes."

Enkidu blinked away rain. "We need both of us."

"We need to preserve the material." The pile of wood that had seemed so abundant as they left shore suddenly appeared meager as it sat beneath a lightning-streaked sky. "Go, see to your son."

Enkidu scoffed. "He has a name."

"Yes, but saying it wouldn't let me see your beautiful eyes flash."

Enkidu's lips twisted in a frown that suppressed a blooming smile. With a lurch, the boat tilted and water splashed the side. Gilgamesh clenched his jaw and drove his pole into the water.

Hours passed with them pushing through the storm's

brutality. He and Enkidu swapped turns fighting the sea, fighting death's promise.

Gilgamesh wouldn't accept defeat. He wouldn't accept death. He'd gone on this journey, left his soldiers and family and everything he'd loved to look death in the face and laugh at its cruelty. To save the one that he loved the most.

They'd make it through the damn storm, then they'd become divine and live forever with sneers on their faces for death's curse.

The poles disappeared rapidly. The waters bobbed them about, and thunder boomed. As the Ferryman offered uncertain and unhelpful directions, they grabbed pole after pole shoving them into the sea.

Gilgamesh's heart stuttered when he lifted the last one.

Enkidu looked up from where he held Urmah, a hand methodically grazing through the cub's growing mane. His eyes held sorrow, defeat.

Where Gilgamesh had physically yanked the Ferryman off his feet over his doubt, he wanted to do the opposite with Enkidu. He longed to pull him into his arms, whisper promises into his hair. As he hefted the last log and thrust it into the water, he wasn't sure anymore if he could keep his vows.

The sea swallowed the pole as he released it.

He stood at the edge and watched it sink beneath the violent water.

With no poles to fight the current, to direct them beyond its thrashing, they would lose their course and drown. When their bodies hit the water, it would swallow not just their physical selves but their souls.

The Ferryman clutched the railing and wept. Gilgamesh wanted to throw something at him. Nothing remained though but the four of them and a few tattered bags with their precious supplies.

Gilgamesh sat beside his love. Enkidu burrowed close to him, clutched his arms.

"We tried," he whispered.

The boat teetered, twisting to the side before landing with a thump that ached through Gilgamesh.

They had minutes left.

He wanted to demand Enkidu not give up, beg him to seek another solution. But none came to him. They bobbed along with no control in a ceaseless storm with nothing but their battered changes of clothes and some preserved food.

All would soon sink to the bottom of the sea.

He clutched Enkidu to his chest, kissed his neck.

If he had to go, at Enkidu's side amid a journey they'd fought and scraped their way through would be the way to do it. The story would be lost, but it didn't matter. Enkidu mattered.

Shamhat and Uruk and Usun and their futures mattered.

If only he'd had time to make a plea to the gods, to beg them to stop making semi-divine beings to rule mortal cities.

Usun would face Inanna now—her wrath and manipulation.

Gilgamesh shuddered.

The only god who'd cared to intervene was Utu. But where was he now? Hidden behind Enlil's dark clouds in his father's angry sky.

"We should pray," Enkidu said.

"Pray?" Gilgamesh hated prayers. Hated begging callous immortals for pinches of grace. He'd rather make his own way. Find some path even if he struggled against its brutality than turn to the gods.

"I'm praying to Utu. He's helped us once."

A retort sat on Gilgamesh's tongue, but he kept it swallowed down. If it made Enkidu feel better, then a prayer harmed nothing. Enkidu lowered his head and leaned into Gilgamesh. His horns brushed Gilgamesh's cheek as Urmah's warmth grew between them.

The boat tumbled like a hucklebone die, soon to flip over and doom them.

Gilgamesh pulled Enkidu closer, pressed a kiss to his hair, and felt the weight of him. He didn't wish for death, but he could accept it at this man's side. He could accept anything with him.

Perhaps it wasn't death he was fighting but loss.

Grief.

Heartache.

Clutching the man he loved as they sank into nothingness together wouldn't be so bad.

Warmth pooled over Gilgamesh's shoulders. He looked up to where the sun broke through the clouds and draped over Enkidu's form.

It made him golden, a statue carved by divine hands.

Enkidu raised his face, and the hazel and greens in his eyes gleamed. He smiled up at the sunshine. Clouds swept across it, then the light spilled forth again.

A fight happened above them.

A war between family.

Utu, Gilgamesh prayed. *Thank you. I'm not gracious enough, but even if all you offer is hope for Enkidu before our end, I appreciate it.*

Why have you stopped fighting, mortal king? Am I to fight

for you as you give up? The voice came violently, like a command he'd shout at his men before they ran into battle.

We've run out of hope. If this is what the gods wish for us to learn, that we are not divine, we understand it.

You are too clever to quit now. You've lived next to the Id-Ugina River your entire life, yet you have no other ideas?

Gilgamesh thought of the Id-Ugina, the slick blue water that tucked around his city. Early in their marriage, he and Shamhat often stood on a rooftop looking out at the river as boats sailed down it. As they dreamed of what all they could build together. Wind would ruffle through their hair, clatter their jewels, then kiss the boat's sails and—

Gilgamesh jumped to his feet.

Enkidu startled and looked up, clutching Urmah tighter.

"Give me your clothes."

Enkidu rose as well, slowly and uncertainly. The boat pitched like it meant to toss them, but the sun still gleamed through dark clouds and hope had filled Gilgamesh's chest.

"My clothes?" Enkidu spread his hand over his rain-soaked tunic. Their journey had soiled the fine material. What was once crisp burgundy and purple had faded to a grayish color. Enkidu's body was so beautiful though, so strong and graceful, that clothing didn't matter.

"No. I need clothes from your bag. Mine too. We're going to make a sail."

Enkidu's furrowed brow washed away. "Is this wind in the right direction?"

Gilgamesh turned towards it, felt the breeze lift damp locks of hair off his neck. "It is."

His heart pounded. This was an answer, a sunrise after an endlessly long night. Utu fought for them. Gods knew why, but Gilgamesh would take it.

Enkidu settled Urmah down, pulled open their bags, and handed him their spare tunics. Gilgamesh ripped the edges then quickly knotted them together. Enkidu grasped one end, Gilgamesh the other, and they raised the ragged sail above them.

Wind battered into it, and the boat soared like an eagle.

Urmah tumbled and yowled.

The Ferryman cried out prayers to gods Gilgamesh didn't know.

But Gilgamesh and Enkidu stood fast, their feet planted on the deck, the wind pounding into them.

The boat rushed forward until it raced past the storm then into calmer seas and finally towards a stretch of ivory sand.

"We've almost made it," Gilgamesh cried.

Enkidu's arms shook but he didn't release the sail.

The boat hit the shore with a thump that knocked them both off their feet. Ebony water creeped over the pale sand.

Gilgamesh yanked Urmah by the scruff and, with Enkidu at his side, landed gratefully on the island. Even if it wasn't Utnapishtim's he'd have been happy to see it. He wasn't sure he could ever be compelled to step onto a boat again.

The Ferryman crawled off the boat and landed with a thunk.

Ahead the sun shimmered over a calm, pale blue sky.

Trees and shrubs swayed together in the remaining eddies of the storm. Among them, a man stood, leaning on a cane. He frowned, his bushy silver-streaked eyebrows pulling together. "Who in Enlil's name are you?"

CHAPTER EIGHTEEN

A MAN AND A MYTH

THE MAN STANDING on the island had wiry silver eyebrows and gnarled fingers he curled around a walking stick. That didn't change the likeness he shared with Gilgamesh, though.

They both had the same thick nose, the same sharp, assessing eyes, and the same way they clenched their jaws.

Enkidu leaned closer to Gilgamesh and whispered over his rain-drenched flesh. "Your bloodline is a strong one."

Gilgamesh grunted and didn't look back at him, but he slid a hand to the small of his back. Enkidu leaned into the touch. That they both survived the boat had Enkidu unsteady on his feet even as they stared at the stranger—Gilgamesh's ancestor and one of two humans in the world to experience immortality.

Utnapishtim.

The man leaned on his cane as he stepped down the slope then growled at the Ferryman. "Where are your stone freaks at, eh?"

"These two killed them." The Ferryman waved frantically at Enkidu and Gilgamesh. Urmah growled, and

Enkidu combed his tuft of a mane back and willed the cub to calm. He sat, but his hackles remained raised.

The Ferryman continued speaking even as he rose to his feet and stumbled several times, sliding in the sand, his soaked tunic clinging to his bony form. "They're lunatics. Related to you so that makes sense."

Utnapishtim ignored the Ferryman who seemed keen on getting as far from Death's Sea as possible. He moved past the man and wandered up the slope before sitting on a rock beneath a palm. Several fronds were scattered around the island. The storm winds must have reached it.

Utnapishtim walked up to Gilgamesh and used his cane to lift his chin. Gilgamesh stiffened, his muscles tensing and eye twitching. Enkidu almost wanted to smile at his reaction. It was rare to see him hold his temper back. Only the potential of finding the secret to immortality was tempting enough to keep his tongue still.

"So, you're from my seed, huh? Don't turn out like they used to. Blood gets watered down with generations." Utnapishtim dropped the staff and squinted at Gilgamesh as he looked up at him. "In my days, men were twice your height."

Gilgamesh stared down at him and frowned, his jaw ticking.

"This is Gilgamesh, King of Uruk." Enkidu could feel the crackling disapproval coming off Gilgamesh in waves. Perhaps he could smooth things over before his stormy personality took over. "And I'm—"

"His whore." Utnapishtim turned towards Enkidu and skimmed his eyes slowly down his form.

Heat rushed across Enkidu's cheeks, down his neck, and over his chest. He'd never considered his status as Gilgamesh's lover as something demeaning. Shamhat had accepted him so fully that it felt natural. And their love was so pure—something greater than sex or labels. It was soul deep.

Gilgamesh lunged.

He knocked Utnapishtim off his feet with a thud and a huffed breath. "Fucking speak about him like that again."

Urmah yowled, lifting his face from the beetles he'd been harassing in a patch of grass. Enkidu gripped him by the scruff to stop him from joining, but he otherwise remained frozen.

Gilgamesh wrestled with his ancient relative.

A man who'd lived long before Gilgamesh's great-grandfather had died.

Utnapishtim rolled Gilgamesh, and the King growled then plowed a fist into his stomach.

"Stop," Enkidu said but didn't move. His body felt cemented to the beach. The Ferryman rested against his knees and leaned forward. His lips parted like he might cheer for a favorite, then he caught Enkidu's gaze and snapped his mouth shut.

Gilgamesh and Utnapishtim continued fighting until the latter tucked his arms and rolled away then jumped to his feet with a laugh, his cheeks crimson, his thick beard tangled. "Ha ha, boy you gave me a good tussle there."

Gilgamesh plowed towards him, but Utnapishtim jabbed his cane towards his stomach and chuckled. Enkidu stepped forward and stood at Gilgamesh's side.

"Apologize," Gilgamesh spoke through his teeth.

He had the same wild-eyed look he'd had when Inanna cursed Enkidu. His nose flared and his fists bunched until his knuckles bled their color.

It was his relentless look.

Utnapishtim laughed and slapped his leg. "I'm sorry,

boy. You'll forgive me for poking at this one's temper." He gave Gilgamesh's stomach another jab with the cane that caused his lip to curl. "Had to see if it still existed. Nice to know time didn't steal some things."

Enkidu nodded but didn't reply. Somehow this part of the journey that didn't involve flaming lava or deathly waters was proving to be his least favorite. He pulled Urmah closer to him. The lion was getting large enough that it required effort.

Utnapishtim bent down to look Urmah in the eyes, placing his cane across his knees. "Now, what do we have here?"

"His name is Urmah," Gilgamesh said.

Enkidu turned towards him, his lips parting. He'd called the cub by his name. Gilgamesh rolled his eyes and turned to frown at his relative.

"Urmah, eh?" Utnapishtim reached a hand out for the lion to sniff. Urmah did so then looked up at Enkidu as if he sought permission. All three of them were already on edge with Gilgamesh's strange ancestor, but Enkidu nudged him towards the man. Perhaps he could act as a bridge.

Urmah rubbed his head into Utnapishtim's hand, and the man scratched him. The wrinkles on his face, the curling of his nose, and twist of his lips smoothed out. "Haven't seen a beast like this since my actual lifetime."

Several minutes passed where he petted and praised Urmah. Then he stood again. "So, you two killed the Stone Ones, did ya'?"

"They were tortured souls," Enkidu said. He'd finally found his voice again, though it wobbled. He didn't trust whatever Utnapishtim might respond with. At least Gilgamesh was logical and predictable unlike this chaotic man who stood before them.

A fiery obstinacy filled his chest. He'd never back down from advocating for what was right. Doing so had nearly got them killed, yet he didn't regret it. They'd found a way without abusing the Stone Ones who'd remained trapped for so long.

"Yeah, poor bastards." Utnapishtim turned back to the Ferryman then scowled. "The only ones with a more wicked fate are Kizzura and me."

"The gods blessed you with immortality." Gilgamesh straightened. Even in his sopping, faded tunic and tattered sash, he appeared as noble as the sun that stretched in the sky behind him.

Utu—who'd saved them.

Thank you, Enkidu whispered in his mind. He hoped his gratitude seeped through his pores and pounded in his heart. He hoped the god knew it.

Utnapishtim laughed so his teeth glinted. "Gifted us with it, eh? Cursed us with it more like." Gilgamesh parted his lips to speak, but Utnapishtim cut him off. "Well, come on, then. You'll want to clean up. You look like Enlil shit ya' straight outta his asshole. Kizzura and I'll find something for you to eat while you two bathe. Then you can tell us your story. And as for you"— he glared at the Ferryman— "go wherever you want, but don't come near our home."

"How am I supposed to return?" the Ferryman asked.

"Not my problem." Utnapishtim scratched over his beard. "Perhaps pray about it. Boys?"

He turned back to Gilgamesh and Enkidu. With a sigh, Gilgamesh nodded, and they followed.

* * *

The cave's water was warm, and it gleamed in sunlight that filtered through the entrance. Gilgamesh scrubbed at his hair, running soap through his locks. His muscles flexed with the motion; the hair on his chest had pasted against the swell of his body.

Enkidu moved closer to him, grazed fingers along his arm.

They couldn't do more in this cave. Not with Utnapishtim and his wife liable to walk in at any moment. But he needed to touch the man, to know with certainty they'd survived the sea.

Gilgamesh dropped the soap and kissed Enkidu's forehead, resting his hand against Enkidu's back as though he could read the anxieties spinning through his mind. "We're alive, love."

"Your ancestor is—"

"An asshole. Maybe he's right and some things keep through the blood."

Enkidu chuckled and moved closer to Gilgamesh. Their legs tangled beneath the water and the scrape of his hair, the feel of his firm thigh grazing his, caused Enkidu's gut to clench and warmth to burn through him.

"You're not an asshole. You're—" A splash stole Enkidu's attention. Urmah had tumbled into the water after getting too close and dragged himself sulkily out of the pool. He shook his fur until it stood up like a dandelion. Enkidu laughed again.

Gilgamesh pulled him close and kissed him, parting his lips. Enkidu melted into him. It had been weeks since they'd been truly clean and free from fear. Here on this strange island, the gods felt gloriously distant.

Their fate felt beautifully far off.

What was another few weeks when they had this

moment where Gilgamesh ran rough fingers over his damp skin, where he pressed kisses onto his neck, gripped a horn?

Gilgamesh stopped and sighed. "We should go deal with my relatives."

"I'd really rather not." Enkidu's voice had gone husky.

He'd give up the entire adventure if Gilgamesh would allow it. Spend the next weeks cocooned in the island's sanctuary. Avoid Utnapishtim and his wife and make love to Gilgamesh until his heart ceased to pound.

It might be enough.

"The old bastard has answers."

Gilgamesh's reply stilled Enkidu's wandering hands. He pulled back and dipped beneath the water. The soap needed rinsing off, but more than that he had to hide his response from Gilgamesh.

Where Enkidu tried to forget the curse, Gilgamesh burned with Inanna's venom. He lay awake at night, studying the skies.

Not with the fascination of a young boy.

Nor solely for explaining them to Enkidu, which he often did.

He watched them to mark the passing of time. The constellations that appeared noted another season passing. More time drifting away.

I'm right here, Enkidu longed to say. *I'm alive now. Stop focusing on my death.*

It wasn't a fair thing to ask. If the curse were reversed, he wasn't sure he could honor that same request.

When he pushed up above the water, Gilgamesh had already exited the pool and wrapped a towel around his waist. Their battered tunics, which they'd washed, hung over rocks. Gilgamesh scraped his fingers over his, then pulled it down.

Enkidu dressed beside him and refused to meet his gaze, the questions in it.

He didn't have answers.

Didn't have responses that would please him.

They followed Utnapishtim's directions and walked up a hill together. A fluffy and still-damp Urmah followed alongside them. He pounced after every butterfly and tangled through the grasses.

"Your beast will be filthy before we make it to the house."

Enkidu sighed and shook his head. "You seemed to know his name earlier."

"I'm allowed to pick on him, but no one else had better fucking look at him the wrong way."

"Oh, is that right?"

Gilgamesh only cocked an eyebrow in response, and Enkidu smothered a smile. This impossible damn man and his giant heart he always kept hidden and his ridiculous jokes.

Enkidu didn't want eternity without them.

When they reached the hill's crest, Gilgamesh frowned at the door set crookedly in the side of another rise of land. Grass swayed around it. Gilgamesh sighed. "So, he lives in a hole in the fucking ground and he's judging me."

"He really bothered you, didn't he?"

Gilgamesh's eyes flashed the way they had before he charged to battle Humbaba, to seize Zage-Si's city, to destroy the Stone Ones. "You're surprised I won't let others speak poorly of Urmah, but I hope you aren't fucking perplexed that I'll destroy anyone who calls you vile names. If I wasn't so desperate for his answers, I already would have."

"I think he was just trying to provoke you."

"He achieved his goal, then." Gilgamesh took a deep breath and rolled his shoulders back. "Let's go have dinner with the asshole and see if we can get away from here soon."

The island's peacefulness cocooned Enkidu. The lure to find another section of it, to die here honorably without fighting to the last breath dangled before him.

Sunset's orange draped across the land. Bugs chirped. Water rushed in the distance.

It was peaceful.

It reminded him of home.

Of running wild with the Wolf.

Urmah loped forward after Gilgamesh, and Enkidu turned away from the island, from its allure, and followed his lover instead.

CHAPTER NINETEEN

A CHALLENGE

THEY HAD to hunch to enter the foolish little house. Gilgamesh pressed a hand to Enkidu's lower back as they ducked beneath the doorway.

He wanted to hold Enkidu close, protect him from his ridiculous relatives.

All they needed was Utnapishtim to grant them anything that would allow them to evade Inanna's curse then they could leave.

Gilgamesh could tamp down his temper for one evening if it meant saving Enkidu.

Utnapishtim scowled at them as they stepped into the cave-like room where roots grew through the ceiling and candles sent wisps of smoke trailing along the packed-dirt floors. Some smoke traveled out through thin, high windows, but a great deal hovered in the room making it foggy. It irritated Gilgamesh's eyes which perfectly matched his frustrated energy.

Urmah, who'd reached the size of a small wolf, lumbered after them, but Enkidu stretched his arm out, stopping the cub.

A woman in an oversized tunic with a tumble of gray-streaked curls whirled around from the fire she cooked over and clapped her hands. "Oh, our guest has arrived!"

Gilgamesh cleared his throat. He'd make a better impression on the woman than he'd done with her husband. With Enkidu's warmth and steady personality at his side, he'd remember why they'd come.

"Sorry about Urmah," Enkidu said, pushing the lion back from the threshold. He yowled and stretched his mouth wide in an unhappy yawn.

The woman bustled forward, but before Gilgamesh could speak she bowed before the lion. "Oh, I've been waiting to meet you. Urmah, is it? Well, come in. Come in."

Enkidu released the creature who tumbled forward into the smoke and warmth, his clawed paws leaving marks in the dirt-packed floor. She patted a stool by a low, wide table and Urmah leapt up.

"Are you hungry?" She placed a plate of roasted meat before Urmah who swiped his tongue across his whiskers but turned towards Enkidu who looked at Gilgamesh. He shrugged. He didn't know what the fuck to make of these people, but if she wanted a wild creature to eat at her table, then there seemed no harm.

With a nod from Enkidu, Urmah plowed into the food.

"Oh, are you starved, little one? Were your travels long?" The woman jumped up and pulled more meat to the table. She seemed oblivious that Gilgamesh and Enkidu stood nearly scraping her ceiling. Enkidu hunched slightly to keep his horns from grazing the roots.

"Well, quit your gawking and take a seat." Utnapishtim nudged another set of stools beside the table.

Gilgamesh hesitated a moment before pulling the door shut and directing Enkidu towards the table.

They sat.

Utnapishtim growled at his wife. "Only going to feed the lion, Kizzura?"

She frowned at him but rose and dished up some food for him, then plopped the mystery roasted meat and olives onto Enkidu and Gilgamesh's plates.

Enkidu cleared his throat and shifted in his seat. Utnapishtim and Kizzura bowed over their plates, sucking meat off bones and popping olives into their mouths with their fingers.

Gilgamesh sighed and reached for the food. He and Enkidu had eaten similarly around a fire in the woods many nights. But a dinner at a proper table with guests being treated so coarsely felt like petting Urmah from tail to scruff. It was unnatural and uncomfortable. When he started eating, Enkidu did as well.

Their knees pressed together beneath the table. Gilgamesh shifted his leg a little closer, letting their thighs touch as well.

The meat was rich in flavor, making his mouth water. He couldn't place the flavor or smooth texture of it. He vowed not to ask what it was.

Utnapishtim licked his hands then leaned back, resting his head on interlaced fingers still gleaming with grease. Enkidu swallowed loudly and shifted again. Gilgamesh had to fight a smile. For being a wild man, he had more refined manners than many who lived in the palace.

"So, what is it you're here for?" Utnapishtim rocked his stool, so it thudded on the dirt floor.

Gilgamesh decided against trying to twist and polish his words. "We want you to grant us immortality."

Kizzura, who'd been watching Urmah with her chin propped on her hand, snapped her face up. Awareness seemed to dawn over her features, drawing her into the conversation truly for the first time. "Why would you want that? And who are you anyway?"

Gilgamesh ground his teeth together which gave Utnapishtim the chance to speak first. "One of your foolish descendants."

She frowned at her husband before turning back to Gilgamesh. "Are you really related to us?"

He wanted to deny it. He'd rather not claim them, especially with Enkidu at his side. His stomach twisted at the reminder that Enkidu had never met his father who'd been a good man for the little Gilgamesh knew of him. But he needed a tremendous favor from these people, and the way Kizzura looked at him with wide eyes that appeared gray in the low light, it might prove helpful to agree.

"I'm the grandson of Euechoros."

She blinked rapidly. "Have you heard of him, Ut?"

"Not in my life. Listen, boy, we walked the earth long before your grandfather. Name someone older."

"Utnapishtim," Gilgamesh deadpanned. "The art in my palace has immortalized your stories."

The old man grinned then shook his head. "Immortality ain't something to be seeking after. Be wiser than your forefathers. Go home."

"No," Gilgamesh growled. Enkidu slid his hand over his thigh, calluses grazing across his exposed knee. His eyes were honey in the candlelight, and they gleamed with a warning, and with that lingering thing always dancing in them—love.

They were here because of love. "It's our only chance," Gilgamesh said, shifting back to face his ancestor. "We're under a curse."

"Oh, is Urmah under one as well?" Kizzura flung a hand across her chest.

Enkidu smiled at the cub who'd stretched out over his bench and lazily pawed at a loose thread on Kizzura's tunic. "No," he said. "Urmah is fine."

"Oh, what a relief." Kizzura patted the lion's head. Gilgamesh was ready to flip the table. She found more value in a lion's life than Enkidu's. She didn't know him, but she didn't know the damn lion either. He wanted to gather the little beast, shove him into Enkidu's arms, and exit the damned house.

Kizzura's face wrinkled like a crushed leaf, her voice going soft. "We lost all our children. Some when we were human, others after." She lifted her storm-gray eyes, and a tear tracked down her cheek. "Parents shouldn't bury their children."

Gilgamesh fidgeted in his seat, his lips parting but words not coming. He didn't know what to say to that.

He'd never imagined burying Usun. Placing his youthful body in a tomb.

He was the image of health and vigor.

If something happened though, his wife wearing mourning goatskins for her child and wailing his name as it echoed around a cold tomb where they'd leave him... He released a breath.

"There aren't words for some experiences," Enkidu offered gently. Urmah turned around at his voice, watching him as intently as the people in the room did. "I'm sorry for your loss."

She dusted off the table and turned her face away. "It was a long time ago."

"I do not think it hurts less because of time."

She shifted back. With the way her lips pinched, it emphasized her chin's sharp angle. "It does not."

Enkidu reached towards her. She startled before accepting his grasp, curling her smaller fingers within his palm. Gilgamesh's heart warmed until it could spill over and heat his entire body. He loved this man so damn much.

"We're fighting a premature grief as well," Gilgamesh said to Kizzura. "Inanna has cursed Enkidu to die after the New Year."

Kizzura sucked in a breath and looked down at the hand she held. Urmah pounced up and licked Enkidu's arm. He grinned down at the lion, seeming unbothered but what Gilgamesh had said.

Gilgamesh, however, was bothered. It pricked at him all over. Time sailed by, stealing hope with it. They needed a solution.

"Ut," Kizzura said in a scolding voice.

He snorted and sat back up. At her glare he sighed but turned to Gilgamesh. "Fine. You want me to grant you immortality?" He nodded. He wanted nothing more. Not a legacy or success or money or sex. To save Enkidu burned in him like a sun. "I'll tell ya' the secret to it if you stay awake seven days and seven nights."

"That's a great deal of time," Gilgamesh replied. Their time had drifted from a year, to months, to mere weeks remaining now. They couldn't waste that much of it for some ridiculous challenge. Every corner they turned some ridiculous obstacle stood in their way. Could not one thing come easily?

"Well, if you can't do it, then that's your answer."

"I can do it." He was pretty sure he could. Though he'd remained awake over three days at once before and he could still remember the achy fogginess of that. He didn't have god's blood for nothing. "But we're limited in time before Enkidu's curse is enacted."

"Then you'd better get started, hmm?" Utnapishtim raised an eyebrow, snatched his cane, and jumped to his feet. "Me and Kizzura don't need sleep, so we'll stay up with ya'."

Gilgamesh hissed a breath between his teeth but gave a curt nod before turning to Enkidu. The man frowned at him but didn't speak. Gilgamesh understood the lines of his face, the angle of his lips, the slight flaring of his nose. He disagreed with Gilgamesh's choice.

They could fight about it once he'd secured his salvation.

In fact, Gilgamesh would welcome the fight. Their passionate outbursts often turned physical, and he wanted to hold the man beneath him and know he was safe.

A day passed in the smoky house. Enkidu took Urmah out for a walk across the meadows alongside Kizzura to pass several hours and came back windswept and smiling. He held a bundle of wildflowers and cloth-wrapped honeycombs in his arms.

Gilgamesh accepted food, tasted the sweetness of his lover's find, and enjoyed his laughter and conversation.

But whenever he disappeared from the house's confines, he'd sit at the table and stare at Utnapishtim. Gods, he'd always been right about the man. There was nothing notable about him, nothing worthy of the stories and legends his name inspired. The man stared back at him as though he thought the same of his distant descendant.

Gilgamesh would show him.

He was the fucking King of Uruk, defeater of monsters, two-thirds god and a man who'd had stories worthy of infamy.

Sleep wouldn't take him.

Enkidu lay down next to Urmah on the second night and drifted off quickly, his chest rising and falling, his fingers grazing the cub's mane until they stilled.

Gilgamesh watched him sleep for a long time.

Utnapishtim and Kizzura moved quietly around the house.

He whittled.

She dried flowers.

Gilgamesh planted his feet and refused to yield.

The third day passed similarly, but by that evening his body throbbed, his mind had turned into a swirling fog, and he struggled not to snap at even Enkidu who brought him mugs of cool beer and honeycomb to chew on to help him stay awake.

Enkidu didn't say what he thought—that this was a foolish exercise.

That they should quit.

Instead, he told stories, grabbed Gilgamesh's fingers, kissed his cheeks.

On the fourth morning, Gilgamesh's body hunched over the table. His eyes drooped, but he gritted his teeth. This was the halfway point. He wasn't a quitter. Gilgamesh was a champion. A fighter. A godsdamned beast.

He'd defeat the gods at their games then redefine them.

That evening the house became dark and warm.

Gilgamesh's arms trembled, and Enkidu sat beside him, his brow furrowed. "Love?" He whispered, though the house was so small it had to carry across the room to where Utnapishtim sat creaking a stool back and forth and Kizzura scratched Urmah's neck.

"I won't quit," Gilgamesh said. The words slurred. He ran his fingers through his beard methodically.

Enkidu grabbed his hands, stilling the motion, and lifted his fingers to kiss them. "I'll stay awake with you tonight."

He wanted to deny the offer, say he didn't need it. But he did.

"Thank you."

The fourth night passed. On the fifth, Enkidu offered to stay up again after napping during the day. Gilgamesh accepted with a nod. He trembled with exhaustion, his body aching with every slight movement.

Enkidu rested his chin on his shoulder, brushed his lips over his neck. Gilgamesh sighed and tucked an arm around him. They needed to get up, to pace. But Enkidu was so warm and having him in his arms was better than holding eternity or legends.

"Stay awake," Enkidu whispered.

"I am. I won't stop. For... for your sake, Enkidu."

Kizzura blew out the candles. The sweet smoke filled the room, the space darkening. Gilgamesh's body had grown so heavy.

"Stay awake, love."

Enkidu's voice was distant, a cry from another shore. Gilgamesh hummed in reply and forced his eyes back open. They'd adjusted to the smoke and dim lighting. They no longer ached. His body felt like separate pieces. A puzzle disassembled. For the first time in his life, he understood that his soul was something different from his physical form.

All of that could fade—the strength and muscles and stature.

As long as he had Enkidu.

He rested against him, so happy to be there beside him he didn't even care about the circumstance and the damned house and his stubborn relatives or even the gods.

He'd travel alongside Enkidu into the world's core and be happy if he remained at his side.

Gilgamesh blinked his eyes open.

His body jerked upright, startling a sleeping Enkidu.

Sunlight slipped in through the windows, painting a pale blue rectangle over the table.

Utnapishtim's cane thunked into the dirt floor as he walked to him. "I'm sorry." He frowned, his long eyebrow hairs meeting as they pressed together. "Ya' didn't stay awake, so I cannot tell you the secret to immortality."

CHAPTER TWENTY

THE WAY OF THINGS

Enkidu rubbed his eyes. In his lap, Urmah stretched then rolled onto his belly, before cocking his head to the side and letting his tongue loll out of his mouth. He nuzzled Enkidu's leg then jumped up and walked towards Kizzura. She'd fed him relentlessly. If they didn't get out of this house soon, he was going to become as lazy as a palace dog.

Enkidu jerked upright.

If Urmah had woken him, then that meant—

Gilgamesh glowered at his forefather, his eyes bloodshot and muscles trembling. They'd fallen asleep. Enkidu should have worked harder to stay awake, to help Gilgamesh. Instead, he'd failed him. His stomach sank. He'd had so few tasks in life, and this one that was so important, he'd failed. Utnapishtim sucked air over his teeth as he watched them rouse. "It's a shame, but you gave an honest effort to it."

Gilgamesh pounced to his feet and glared at his ancestor. "You will give me the damn answers. We've played your fucking games."

"Mhmm," the man answered. "And you lost them.

You're welcome to stay as long as you like, however. Been nice to have a bit of company."

Gilgamesh trembled, his hands fisting. Enkidu stood beside him and grabbed his arm, but Gilgamesh shook him off.

"Love," Enkidu whispered, trying to infuse comfort into his tone. But even Enkidu found himself short of words—tired, and struggling to dig up compassion. He wanted to pull Gilgamesh from the room, tell him to leave this behind.

"He tricked us," Gilgamesh roared. Utnapishtim and Kizzura watched him but weren't defending themselves. Gilgamesh slipped axes off his hips. "I'm eager to see how immortal he actually is."

"Stop." Enkidu spoke in the same voice Gilgamesh used to direct his army. With authority. With finality. Angry though he may be, Enkidu couldn't condone senseless violence. Gilgamesh froze, breathing through his teeth and keeping his glare fixed on the man leaning on his cane.

Enkidu fumbled for something to say. "We can search for other answers."

"There isn't time. And we've done nothing but waste it here."

"You're right," Utnapishtim said. "You've wasted time. That is part of the human condition. Congratulations, you're mortal."

"I didn't come here for your philosophical lessons, old man." Gilgamesh had transformed into the seething, growling beast Enkidu had found so deplorable before. Now, he couldn't feel the same frustration with him as he once had. He understood his reasoning, his frustrations. Knew how deeply he loved. How fiercely he'd fight for those he did. But a flutter of worry danced in Enkidu's stomach. If he died, would Gilgamesh turn into the man he'd once been? Would Enkidu's life have no purpose in the end?

Utnapishtim snorted and laughed. "And I didn't invite you into our home to get a lecture from ya, boy. Ya got a damned good fighting spirit, I'll give that much."

"Tell us the answers we came here seeking." Gilgamesh's voice boomed around the small room. His divinity rumbled off him, his eyes flashing, his posture expanding. He held his legacy in his body—the arrogance of Utnapishtim and the fierceness of Anu and every person in between.

Enkidu loved all of it, all of him.

He hadn't always. Now he did.

Enkidu didn't need to live forever, but he didn't want to abandon Gilgamesh, leaving him to less noble pursuits. The gods created Enkidu to balance Gilgamesh, and he couldn't do that if fate thrusted his soul into the Great Below and left Gilgamesh alone to rant and rave and demand.

"I'll tell you." Utnapishtim dropped to a stool and rocked it back and forth as though a man double his size didn't tremble with fury before him. He pulled a knife free and sliced away at another stick. "The secret to immortality is"—he cocked one silvery eyebrow—"that there is no secret. You weren't created to carry on forever. It ain't natural. Yer supposed to die. Look at Kizzura and me. You know the words I speak to you are true."

Kizzura had crouched beside Urmah and scratched under his chin while she watched the exchange. There was something off about these immortal humans and their interactions. Like birds in the wild that didn't dash away when a wolf pounced into a clearing, but stood with cocked, curious heads instead.

There was something unnatural about it all.

Something unhappy.

Gilgamesh shook his head, though. The red streaks around his irises and his curled lip gave him a wild, untethered look. This journey had changed him and not for the better. "How you choose to spend your immortality—running away to this godsforsaken island—isn't my concern. We plan to make different choices. I am your blood and I ask for one thing. Use your divine gifting to spare us this curse or share the secret of immortality with us or give us some hope!"

Utnapishtim rested his chin on his cane. "I s'pose telling you our becoming immortal was magic—magic the gods vowed never to use again—wouldn't satisfy ya', would it? Telling you we live here to avoid the gods' and mortals' harassment wouldn't change your mind either, would it? Nah. You're arrogant. Ya think you'll somehow do differently than your foolish ancestors. Anyway, it doesn't matter because me and Kizzura abdicated the divine powers gifted to us." Gilgamesh's form deflated and he placed a hand against the wall as if to steady himself. Utnapishtim ran a booted foot across the floor, leaving a trail. "It caused nothing but trouble and had mortals coming to us beggin' for one thing or another. Often what we granted caused more issues than it solved. So we gave 'em up, destroyed tablets of our stories, and left mortal lands. I'm sorry to tell ya, but your lover is gonna die. You're gonna die. It's the way of things, boy. There ain't no getting around it."

Breath huffed from Gilgamesh, then his body sank, shoulders crumpling, like a smashed leaf. He turned to face Enkidu. His lips had puckered, his eyes shimmered like the water in his mother's temple.

He believed Utnapishtim.

This was the end of their journey, the end of the adventures, the beginning of the end of Enkidu's life.

Enkidu stepped forward. He paused, afraid that a single touch might shatter Gilgamesh. He appeared so delicate in a way Enkidu had never seen. His soul was on display, a fragile vase normally buried in a tomb strong enough to endure millennia.

"Fine," Gilgamesh said quietly. He turned towards the door. "Come along, Urmah."

The lion whined but walked up beside Enkidu and rubbed his head against his legs. Enkidu couldn't move, couldn't reach for the creature or to comfort Gilgamesh.

Grief crashed through him.

Hotter than the mountain's flames, deeper than Death Sea's waters, more perilous than any adventure they'd gone on so far.

Watching Gilgamesh's heart crack, his soul trembling like it might break, stole Enkidu's breath.

The gods created him to help Gilgamesh, not break his heart.

"Wait." Kizzura pounced up and turned towards her husband. "Tell them what you know."

"Kizzura," he scolded. "Don't."

"Look at them, Ut. Don't you see how they suffer?" Her gaze trailed away, and her voice went quiet. "Don't you remember our daughter? How her heart broke when her companion died young?"

"That was a very long time ago." Utnapishtim spoke to his wife like no one else stood in the room. His voice had dropped low, and was full of unspoken things, hurts he'd shoved into a back room of his heart he kept locked.

"Do you not love her anymore?" Kizzura became shrill. Tears streaked her cheeks.

With a shake of his head, her husband replied, "Of course I do. If I could change anything—if the gods would ever listen to me, ya know I would have traded our lot for hers a thousand times."

Kizzura flung her hands towards Gilgamesh, who'd turned back around. Enkidu slipped his hand into Gilgamesh's and felt the weight of his grip, the warmth. To have him, to have loved him, was his legacy. It might be enough if he could know Gilgamesh would survive his loss.

"How can you not share the one bit of hope they might have, then? This is a son of our daughter. Does time change family ties? Do we not care anymore?"

Utnapishtim rose slowly. His body seemed to have aged a century within the conversation. He cleared his throat before speaking to Gilgamesh, and his voice trembled. "Death's Sea is to the west. To the east is another sea, unnamed as no one visits. In the center, at the deepest point, there grows the Plant of Life. You'll see it for an hour before ya reach it; it glows until the water changes to an unnatural color."

Gilgamesh gasped and stepped forward, pulling Enkidu with him by their linked hands. "What does this plant do?"

"It's not what ya think. It won't give ya eternal life but —" He dragged gnarled knuckles across his thick hair. The same hair Gilgamesh had inherited across the years from his daughter—a woman who'd lived and lost and died. "If your lover here takes it, he should gain some time. It expands your hours, ya see. If he eats a bit, he might gain a few years beyond this curse."

"If he ate the whole plant?"

Utnapishtim scoffed. "It don't work like that. But if ya preserved it, maybe if he took some every couple years." He waved his hands around like he tried to wrestle his words into meaning. "Well, it might stretch the curse out. I'm not sayin' it will work, mind." He looked at his wife, meeting her tear-glistened eyes. "But maybe it's a chance. If it expands his days, maybe it will push the curse's deadline off. It ain't a guarantee, though."

"Thank you." Gilgamesh said the words so earnestly and with so little contempt it startled Enkidu. He nodded to them both and turned to exit the house. Enkidu lingered for a moment, Urmah tangling between his legs. Utnapishtim walked over to his wife and pulled her into his arms. She released a sob.

Enkidu nudged Urmah forward and closed the door quietly behind himself.

Getting Urmah into another boat that Utnapishtim apparently kept docked on the island's east side required bribing. Then, that failing, physically hauling him into the vessel which resulted in scratches on both men that wept blood.

"Fuck the little bastard," Gilgamesh had cried when Urmah ripped his tunic in the struggle to avoid the boat. But he'd said so quietly, affection lacing around the pain.

When they finally had a very unhappy young lion aboard a small boat, they sailed east. Wind whipped through Enkidu's hair, billowing out the sails and making the journey easy.

Enkidu sat with a hand outstretched, feeling the cool spray over his fingers.

Sun warmed his skin. Pain from Urmah's claws radiated across his arm. Hunger rumbled his stomach.

He was alive and relishing it. Perhaps they'd succeed, but maybe not. All he wanted anymore was to live every second he had. He tossed his head back. The wind kissed his brow and ruffled through his beard.

Gilgamesh dropped beside him and wrapped arms around his waist. Enkidu leaned back on his chest.

They were both exhausted and adventure worn. Their tunics were little more than grayish rags and their beards unshaped. Nearly a year had passed since tongs had styled Gilgamesh's hair into neat curls, since lotion had softened his hands, or a copper razor had smoothed his neck.

Now he was rough-edged and wild, his tangled locks flowing out behind him.

"I like you like this," Enkidu said, leaning back to see his face. "Out in the wild."

Gilgamesh's lips turned up in the soft smile he only ever offered to Enkidu. "Once we succeed at getting this plant, I can forsake my throne if you like. We could spend our lives fighting monsters and seeing impossible places."

Enkidu snorted. "I think I've seen enough of the impossible. Shamhat would hunt us down and end you if you did that, anyway." They both laughed. "Besides, I like you in your palace as well. It's been too long since I've seen someone quiver beneath the King's command."

Gilgamesh nuzzled his neck, sucked an earlobe between his teeth. "Is that what you like, hmm?"

With a laugh, Enkidu pulled away from the man's mouth. "I like it when you're authentic." He swallowed. Wind flapped the sail. Urmah lay curled into an unhappy ball in the boat's center, ears pressed flat over his head. There was one conversation Enkidu continued to avoid, but it gurgled up, a stream that had flushed with rain until it poured over.

When they'd watched the sky the previous night, Enkidu had recognized stars. The same constellations that danced across the heavens the night of their vow, the night of Inanna's curse, appeared again. The time had nearly passed.

"There's something that worries me, though."

Gilgamesh readjusted, pulling Enkidu closer to him, back-to-chest. His breath brushed Enkidu's ear. He didn't reply, but waited, listening, his thumb sliding back and forth across Enkidu's wrist.

"If something happens to me—"

"It won't." The stubborn fury crackled through his voice again.

"Please, let me talk about this." Desperation spilled out. Enkidu was exhausted by them pretending the curse might not play out. He needed to share his heart, his worries. Needed Gilgamesh to see them fully. Accept him just as he was, doubts and all.

Gilgamesh tightened his grip, took a deep breath, then rested his chin on Enkidu's shoulder. "I'm sorry. I'm listening."

"I worry if something happens to me you'll get lost again. That you might become driven by the wrong things."

Gilgamesh didn't speak. His beard scratched Enkidu's cheek. Their breaths moved in rhythm. Enkidu could stay there forever, lying beneath the sunshine with the man he loved, the future terrifyingly hopeful.

"I vow it to you, Enkidu." Gilgamesh's chest rumbled and his words came slow and serious. "No matter what happens—even if it breaks me—I'll honor your name in my actions. I swear it. Do you think your spirit could ever leave mine? That you're some leaf that would fall and be forgotten? You have carved yourself into my heart, love. It cannot beat without remembering you."

Enkidu sank back against Gilgamesh with a shaky

breath. His muscles loosened as if he'd finally surrendered something he'd held for too long.

"Wait." Gilgamesh sat up enough to shift them both. "Do you see that?"

Enkidu turned towards where he pointed. In the distance the ocean gleamed a pale, eerie aqua. It glowed so brightly, it overtook the sun's light, fighting Utu for glory.

"We've found it." Gilgamesh kissed his cheek and jumped back to his feet.

Enkidu rose as well, but he couldn't tear his eyes away from the surf's pale gleam. From their only hope. How it glowed like Inanna's eyes had when she cursed him with death.

CHAPTER TWENTY-ONE

A TASTE BEFORE IT'S GONE

As the boat sailed closer to the glowing water's source, the light gleamed until it encompassed them. Even Urmah had grown curious enough to crawl across the boat and peek out at the water. The sage glow shimmered across his eyes. The sail reflected the light. It flashed along Enkidu's form, highlighting his strong brow and puckered lips and thick muscles. It splashed over his beauty like it encompassed him.

This plant was made for him.

It would save him.

Gilgamesh would do anything to save him.

His body zipped with energy. He fisted and uncurled his fingers as they reached the brightest point.

The lights rippled like silk, blocking out the ocean in the distance.

It was only them and the illumination.

Two men who loved each other beyond their destinies draped in divine light.

Enkidu leaned over the boats' edge and frowned. "How do you intend to get it?"

"Swim."

Enkidu's lips pulled down farther. "It's deep, isn't it? You can't swim down that deep."

"I can if I tie bricks to my feet."

Enkidu flipped around with a gasp. He eyed the bricks in the corner and scowled at them as though they were to blame for the curse. Or perhaps he wondered if they had already been in the boat or if Gilgamesh had brought them when he wasn't paying attention. It was the latter. Gilgamesh wasn't taking any chances. He would get that plant, regardless of the cost.

"You'll drown," Enkidu whispered before lifting his face again. "Gilgamesh, this is foolish. Your family needs you. Think of Shamhat. Think of Usun."

Gilgamesh sighed but stepped over to the man and clasped his hand. He smirked. "No mention of Urmah?"

Enkidu's eyelashes batted his cheeks. He'd been right to describe the two of them as wild. Enkidu's beard whipped around in the breeze and his unshaved cheeks gleamed in the light.

He was a mountain range, a running river, a shrub, glossy and vibrant at the peak of its season.

"Would mentioning Urmah dissuade you from doing something stupid?" Enkidu huffed.

A laugh rumbled Gilgamesh's chest, and he brushed his lips over Enkidu's rough cheek with a kiss. The scratch of Enkidu's prickly skin along his flesh had desire sparking in Gilgamesh's stomach. He had no intention of drowning. He planned to retrieve this plant, give some to Enkidu, then make love to him like time meant nothing. Like death was a joke.

"No, because I have a plan. I'll tie rope around my waist and when I tug it, you pull me up."

Enkidu's lips thinned. Urmah butted up beside him and whined. The creature, always aware of Enkidu's moods, accepted the mindless scratches Enkidu offered. "Gilgamesh this seems—"

"Would you drop me?" Enkidu clicked his tongue and sighed, but before he could speak, Gilgamesh grinned. "Would you let me go, Enkidu?"

"Never."

Gilgamesh nodded. He'd known the answer before he asked. It was a truth as ancient as death. Love like they shared was more than just the words. More than the passion, the scraping of bodies and twining of fingers. It was a binding of souls.

Enkidu wouldn't drop him. He wouldn't release him, couldn't even if he desired it. They were no longer individuals, but trees that had grown so close they meshed, their bark imprinting onto the other. Should one be cut down, the other would remain marked for life.

"Let me go, then." Enkidu's forest-bright eyes flashed. "You can tie the rope around me."

"Absolutely not. If you drown, then this entire trip has been for nothing."

"And if you drown?"

Gilgamesh shook his head. He wouldn't die here in the unnamed sea. He could feel it bone deep. It wasn't his destiny. It wasn't Enkidu's, either, but Gilgamesh couldn't risk him. He cradled the man's jaw with his hand and met his gaze—the fear and love in it. "Then return home and tell my son I love him."

"He doesn't want to hear that from me. He wishes for you to tell him."

"I will, when we have this plant and return together. I'll

even let him know you spent our entire adventure harassing me for his sake."

"Harass is overstating things." Enkidu's lips thinned, his eyes flickering away.

Gilgamesh chuckled and tilted his face back. "I love you. I love how easy it is to pull a reaction from you."

He kissed him, their lips peeling apart. Enkidu softened beneath Gilgamesh's touch. But as soon as they parted, he grumbled. "And you say I'm the one harassing."

"You're the better of us." Gilgamesh kissed his forehead before turning to grab rope and bricks and sliding an extra dagger into his belt. "I've never denied that."

"I don't think that's true."

Gilgamesh stopped his work to look up at him. He gleamed in divine light, this man bearing a curse, this being so full of goodness it seeped from him.

"You're good, Gilgamesh. I've never seen another love as you do. If you care about someone, what would stop you from protecting them?"

"Nothing." Not Inanna and her damn curses or any other gods or monsters or the damned world's end. He'd keep Usun safe, protect Shamhat, and save Enkidu. He'd do so if he managed by the fingernails, ripping them off and bleeding as he went.

Potentially drowning didn't scare him.

A world where he couldn't control the fate of those he loved was the true terror.

He could decimate dragons, fight wicked gods, have his body scourged and beaten and burned. That meant nothing.

Manipulating fate to ensure the safety of his family, snatching this damned curse off his lover, and protecting the citizens of Uruk who served the gods with little reciprocation—that's what mattered.

Maybe he couldn't become a god, but perhaps he could defy a few.

He bent down and tied the bricks around his feet. They pressed heavily on his bones. He stretched his toes to balance the weight. A few minutes beneath the sea and he'd have a prize worth the risk.

Hefting the rope up he slipped it around his waist, but Enkidu grabbed his hands. "Let me."

Gilgamesh released it to him and remained still as Enkidu pulled it tight. He knotted the rope carefully multiple times, tugging at with his full strength, then adding another knot. When he finally finished, he smoothed his hand over the rope several times, as if imbuing it with prayers for protection.

"See," Gilgamesh said, "how will I drown with you securing me so well?"

Enkidu groaned. "You'll pull on this rope when you want to come up? Don't push yourself. You can dive a second time if need be."

"Of course." He wouldn't be diving a second time, though. After his first drop into the sea, he planned to return with that damned plant in hand. With Enkidu's salvation firmly clutched in his grasp. He grabbed the man, curling fingers around his rough beard, and kissed him hard. Enkidu clasped his hips, fingers tangling with the rope.

Gilgamesh stepped closer, ignoring Urmah's irritated growl as he forced the lion to stumble back. He pressed every piece of their body together, firmly enough that their souls might meld. His fingers tangled into Enkidu's hair, grazed his horn, then grabbed it to angle his face closer.

When they pulled apart, Enkidu's lips were swollen, his cheeks flushed with color. "That had better not have been a kiss goodbye."

Gilgamesh grinned. "I'll see you in a few minutes."

He leaned over the edge. The boat wobbled, creating ripples on the glowing water. With one last look to make certain Enkidu had the rope secured, he took a breath as deep as his lungs would allow and jumped.

He crashed through the water, the bricks dragging him down. The sea glowed, so even as he fell deeper, he could make out hectares of space.

It was quiet.

Too quiet.

Not a single fish swam by, not one eel or monster wriggled past or blinked at him.

Beyond the rushing water and the few bubbles he released of his limited breath, all remained quiet.

Gilgamesh clenched his teeth to keep from sighing away his breath. As he fell, the light brightened until he squinted his eyes and shielded them with a hand over his brow.

He hit the seafloor with a soft thump. The plant, a small three-leafed thing that outshone Utu, swayed gently in the ocean's current. Gilgamesh dropped beside it and tugged it up.

The light flickered.

When he yanked it free from the sand, it dimmed to a soft glow in his palm.

The ocean went as dark as Humbaba's forest. As dark as the mountain. In both situations, he'd had Enkidu at his side. Enkidu's rough hand in his. Enkidu's soothing voice offering comfort.

Gilgamesh's heart thundered, and he released a trail of

bubbles. Clasping the plant firmly in his grip, he untied the bricks with his free hand then gave the rope two firm jerks.

All around him was dark.

Loneliness.

Death.

He could feel it creeping in, whispering his name. He'd snatched life from the sea and now it would swallow him for doing so.

Something shrieked in the distance. Goosebumps broke out across his neck. His lungs had grown tight with holding air in. His eyes stung but he could see nothing beyond the dim glimmers of light piercing between his fingers.

Another cry sounded. This one sharper, closer.

Gilgamesh clung to the rope.

He rose upward, but much slower than he'd sank into the depths. Water rushed across him and through his fingers. He held the plant like it was Enkidu's soul in his grasp.

The darkness didn't ease.

Had he snatched the sun from the sky by uprooting one small plant?

Had he damned the world with his choice?

A flutter twisted through his stomach.

The last whispers of his breath trailed past his lips when the sea finally lightened in increments.

He crashed through the surface, gasping for air, the first lungful burning in his chest. Enkidu hauled him into the boat, falling, and Gilgamesh landed on top of him. Water dripped onto Enkidu's tawny skin, as his eyes, wild and worried, skimmed over him.

"You scared me."

Gilgamesh laughed. Once he started it grew until he trembled with it. Until laughter took him over, his lips stretching around his lips. Tears formed in his eyes and trailed his cheeks. Enkidu righted himself and crouched beside him as Urmah swept between them both, cocking his head.

"What's wrong, love?"

Gilgamesh shook his head and attempted to say something, but the words came out garbled. Instead, he lifted the plant.

Above the sea it was a pitifully small thing, scarcely bigger than Gilgamesh's palm. Out of the water, it had lost its grace and clung to his skin like a dirty rag. But it still gleamed with light. With hope.

"I got it," Gilgamesh gasped.

Enkidu's eyes widened as he bent closer to inspect the plant.

They'd done it. They'd defied the gods.

Enkidu was saved and—

Urmah snatched at the plant, ripping a bit off and swallowing it.

"No." Gilgamesh clutched what remained to his chest.

A chuckle spilled past Enkidu's lips though, and he swiped tears away.

"Why are you laughing? Discipline your son."

A tongue click broke Enkidu's laughter. "Ah, he meant nothing." He scratched Urmah's head firmly. "Perhaps he'll live a good long time now. The three of us might all live longer than we believed."

Gilgamesh's shoulders dropped, but he let his voice turn sarcastic. "You're going to drag that little beast into our room at the palace, aren't you?"

"You love him too. Say you do."

Gilgamesh scoffed but their gazes didn't break. They could both feel it, the victory, the weight of a curse shifting, falling farther in the future. The gift of time curling around them. Gilgamesh ripped one of the two remaining leaves, the more ragged of the pair, then pressed it into Enkidu's hand. "Eat this one now. The other we'll attempt to plant the roots and see if we can grow it. If not, we'll preserve it."

"You did it, Gilgamesh." Enkidu grinned at the leaf, then flicked his forest-colored eyes up. "You've changed history, as Utu said you would."

He brought the plant to his lips.

A crash sounded.

The world turned.

The boat flipped.

Hitting the water, they all yelped, and Urmah paddled fiercely and whimpered. Enkidu swam to him, and Gilgamesh clutched the single piece of plant remaining in his hand.

The boat bobbed upside-down in the waves.

They could right it and—

Something crashed into him with the force of the Bull of Heaven, dragging him into the dark waters. Enkidu might have cried for him, Gilgamesh thought he heard his voice, but water rushed past his ears, drowning sound.

Beneath him, a monster writhed, attacking, teeth tearing into his tunic.

Gilgamesh freed an ax only for the beast to jerk around again, causing him to lose the weapon. He cried out, losing his breath.

The monster's body was slick and scaled.

A water serpent.

Gilgamesh shuddered and attempted to fight.

It swiped around, towards the fist holding the plant, and Gilgamesh yanked and tried to free himself.

Someone dove, grabbed Gilgamesh, pulled him up.

He'd know those hands in Death's Sea, would recognize them were his soul wiped out. He'd understand the love in the gesture had he grown ancient and separated from him for hundreds of years.

Enkidu kicked, pulling them to the surface.

The serpent made another dash, its black blunt nose coming into view in the plant's glow. Enkidu jerked Gilgamesh back and his hand sprung open. The snake snatched the plant, with it the light, then dove back into the water with a fading screech.

Gilgamesh fought and thrashed and kicked.

Enkidu hauled him up.

When they broke the surface, both gasping for breath with ragged beards dripping salt water, Gilgamesh roared, "Why did you pull me up?"

Enkidu's mouth gaped, then closed. He took a slow breath. "Should I have sacrificed you to that creature instead?"

"It took the Plant of Life."

They swam towards the boat, still upside down but with a sopping wet Urmah on top slapping his tail irritably on the wood.

Enkidu's eyes shuddered closed as he made it to the vessel then reached out to pet Urmah. "I know."

Gilgamesh caught up and gripped the boat's side, bobbing alongside it. "You ate the other piece before the serpent attacked, though?"

Enkidu took a breath so long, it raked across time, touched eternity. He dashed his face away, his voice dropping to a whisper. "No, the monster got it too."

Gilgamesh stopped kicking, letting his body sink into the water.

Reality hit him harder than the waves, more intensely than any weapon or beast or god.

The plant was gone.

And Enkidu would die.

In a few days' time.

He licked his lips and tasted the salt of his tears mingling with the sea water before he released a roar from the depths of his soul.

A roar loud enough the gods would have to hear it.

CHAPTER TWENTY-TWO

A MARK MADE

ENKIDU BOBBED AGAINST THE BOAT, his fingers running mindlessly across Urmah's nose as the cub butted into this hand. Urmah vibrated with nervous energy. He knew something was wrong; he'd learned Gilgamesh and Enkidu's emotions enough to gather something was amiss, but he couldn't understand what threatened them now.

After Gilgamesh cried out, he wept.

His body shook, and a moan spilled past his lips, echoing across the water.

Enkidu placed a hand on Gilgamesh's shoulder, but he shrugged him off, turned away.

Kicking his legs to stay afloat, Enkidu nuzzled Urmah who'd crept closer. The lion's fur was damp and dragged over his skin. Enkidu didn't care. He tucked an arm around Urmah's neck and buried his face against him.

Enkidu would die.

Perhaps Gilgamesh's relentless faith had bled into him. Hope had burned in his heart, timidly like coals separate from the fire, but still waiting to catch flame.

Now the water of reality dumped on it so intensely the flames didn't even have time to sizzle.

With a sigh, he released Urmah and approached Gilgamesh again. The man shifted towards him, his eyes lined with red.

"We need to right the boat." Enkidu's voice didn't sound like his. It was like someone else had taken over. Someone whose heart didn't thunder in his chest and who didn't also want to sob and scream. "So we can return home."

Gilgamesh's brows pulled together then he smacked a hand against the sea. Spray flicked over Enkidu's cheeks. "What's the point?"

"We did everything we could."

"And we failed."

All the fury that had driven Gilgamesh forward, led him to fight monsters and yell at gods and demand the impossible, had gone. His voice was a whimper, his shoulders drooping into the sea.

Eyes stinging, Enkidu batted his lashes to fight tears. They couldn't both break down here. There was a long journey left to return to Uruk. Enkidu wouldn't live long enough to reach it.

His breath caught in his chest.

He'd never see Akirru again. Never attempt to play the flute.

He wouldn't return to see how much Usun had grown. To play a game of Twenty Squares with him or admire his sword work.

Never again would he step foot in the cedar forest where he'd come into life.

He'd die in a strange land, leaving Gilgamesh alone to face his fate.

Enkidu felt small. It was a strange sensation for him. The gods had created him at his adult size and even among the beasts in the woods, he'd towered. Only the trees reached above him.

Now he was a speck of sand in a massive world.

Nothing.

A name that would soon be forgotten.

Light gleamed in the sky, burning intensely. Gilgamesh wept and didn't look up, but Enkidu raised his face.

"Let me take you home now." Utu's voice vibrated through him.

"You've come this far for us?" Enkidu asked. "Have things changed?"

If Utu had traveled across Death's Sea and come into godless lands, perhaps he brought news with him. The gods had taken different sides over Inanna's choices. Perhaps the gods would stand opposed to her and all would not be lost.

Gilgamesh lifted his chin, his cheeks wet with tears.

"No," Utu said, his light dimming before brightening again. "But I'll save you both the journey."

Enkidu swallowed against his tightening throat. Knowing he'd one day die had been a worry, a mosquito buzzing at his ear. But to understand that he had only days left, that the gods could number his breaths remaining, that was another matter.

"You bastard," Gilgamesh seethed. "Did you set the serpent on us?"

"Gilgamesh," Enkidu gasped.

"I told you,"—the sun gleamed so brightly, Urmah ducked his head beneath his paws—"you wouldn't discover what you sought on this journey. I didn't let you take it without warning."

"You said I'd change things!"

"And you will, but not this."

Gilgamesh's dark eyes flashed, and he bared his teeth. "Fuck you! May you all die one day. May people forget your names and burn your temples and decapitate the heads of every statue in your image."

"Gilgamesh enough." Enkidu stared at the man he loved with his mouth gaping.

He was begging for Utu to smite him and— Enkidu gasped. His thoughts held truth, and he knew it.

You're right. Utu's voice glistened in his mind. *He doesn't wish to live without you.*

Enkidu's heart gave a painful thud. They were about to lose each other. After all their journey and fight, Enkidu would die, and Gilgamesh would choose to join him rather than carry on through the world alone. He swam closer to Gilgamesh and grabbed his hand. "Please, for my sake, don't do this."

Gilgamesh turned towards him, his eyes glistening. He studied him. The browns of his irises were warm. His lips unfurled, and he tightened his fingers. "Enkidu." He swallowed then mouthed the rest, like he couldn't bear to speak the words. *I can't.*

The sun gleamed behind them, but Utu remained silent.

"You're King Gilgamesh of Uruk. Lugal. Mine." Enkidu moved close enough that their bodies grazed. He remembered the first time they'd touched, when they'd fought before his city. How the King's weight pressing on Enkidu had sent his pulse racing. He'd loved Gilgamesh, in some small way, from the first moment he'd seen him looking grand and imperial on his throne. From the moment their flesh had scraped.

He smiled, and it spread as warmth filled him.

It came from the well of love they'd shared.

Enkidu hadn't had time. He'd only lived a short while.

But in that time, he'd loved massively. An ocean of it. Gilgamesh had once teased him and said he loved every pitiful creature he'd come across. In some ways, he had.

It's the reason they had Urmah.

The reason they'd freed the Stone Ones from eternal torment.

Possibly why he loved Gilgamesh.

But, oh, how he loved him.

"You're two-thirds god," Enkidu whispered, his voice curling with a tease. "Defeater of monsters and doer of many great deeds. Your name will go down in history, Gilgamesh." Enkidu's fingers trailed up Gilgamesh's arms, grazing over coarse hair and following the lines of his muscles. As he spoke, Enkidu realized his words were true. Perhaps that's how Gilgamesh changed things. It wasn't through his actions, but his story. If he died, that went with him. He needed to return home to Uruk, to his family, to his life. "You must live, for my sake if no other."

Gilgamesh swallowed. His throat bobbed in Utu's gleam.

He sighed, pressed a kiss to Enkidu's forehead, then nodded.

Enkidu grabbed Urmah and urged him closer. The lion had grown too large for him to carry comfortably anymore. He wrapped an arm around Gilgamesh's back and looked up towards the sun's glow. "Thank you, Utu. Take us home."

A moment later, they stood, clothing and fur dry, their bags somehow magically restored, on a dusty road. The cedar forest curled around it, thick trees standing stalwart against a wind that whipped hair off Enkidu's neck.

"I leave you here." Utu sparkled in the sky. "To give you time before you approach the city."

Gilgamesh didn't pay attention enough to find offense at the implication that they were too weathered and worn to return to Uruk. Utu spoke true, though. Gilgamesh wore the rags of his sole remaining tunic. It was gray and ripped and damaged. His beard bunched wildly around his face. Dark circles swept under his eyes.

Enkidu had to look as terrible.

Only Urmah appeared healthy and glossy, his mane lengthening around his neck to give him a golden beard. Enkidu reached down and scratched the lion's ear. He was a good boy. Loyal to the end.

He'd suffered through nearly a year of misadventures and dangers. Though he'd probably never get into a boat again. Enkidu chuckled then kissed Urmah's head before standing.

Gilgamesh stared ahead, his expression blank. He still had the height and muscles of a divinely born man, but he hunched and all the boasting that puffed his chest had gone out in a great heave.

"Home," he whispered, "is this way. We should clean up."

* * *

Once they'd both washed, their threadbare packs slung over shoulders again, Enkidu and Gilgamesh walked alongside Urmah on the road. Gilgamesh wouldn't look at Enkidu. He wept on and off, using his shoulders to wipe his puffy face.

When they reached a hill's crest where they could see

Uruk in the distance, tucked within the Id-Ugina River's bend, Enkidu quit walking. "Let's stop here."

Gilgamesh turned. "We're almost home."

"I don't want to go into Uruk." The city's bustle had always bothered him. If he had one last night, he'd rather spend it out there in the quiet. "Besides, that's not my home."

"Would you rather return to the cedar forest? We could linger there tonight."

A rabbit leapt ahead in the bush and Urmah's ears pricked up before he bounded away. Enkidu grabbed Gilgamesh's hand, waiting until he loosened enough for him to hold it before speaking. "You are my home, Gilgamesh. If I'm with you, I'm at peace."

Gilgamesh choked over a sob. "I feel the same, yet I couldn't protect you. I-I tried, Enkidu. I did and—"

"I don't care."

Gilgamesh met his gaze. "You don't care that we couldn't break the curse? You don't care that some bitch is going to snatch your life away because she's not getting her way?"

The heaviness of his words settled like stones on Enkidu's shoulders, but he shook them free.

He had cared. At some point it felt monumental that Inanna had cursed him and he'd die young. What purpose did a short life serve?

Then they'd gone on this journey.

He'd freed the Stone Ones from eternal suffering, rescued Urmah, saved Usun, helped the Wolf protect his pack, and loved Gilgamesh. He'd loved this beautiful, fierce, foolish, brilliant man with every drop of his soul. With everything he had to give.

He didn't regret it.

Gilgamesh wouldn't forget him. He'd promised, and Enkidu believed it, had believed in him when he'd been arrogant and frustrating and obnoxious. Now he trusted him with anything and especially with holding his memory.

"Perhaps I won't die," Enkidu whispered. Gilgamesh's eyebrows jumped, and Enkidu reached out, ran fingers over his gritty cheeks. "Maybe the gods pressure Inanna so she lifts the curse."

"If not?" Gilgamesh gasped. "Do you know what today is?"

Enkidu leaned on him, so his horns scraped his face. Gilgamesh reached up and curled fingers around a horn, as Enkidu knew he would. He smiled into the man's shoulder.

Fear didn't hold him any longer.

He could face his death, but he couldn't stand one more minute of Gilgamesh grieving him before he was gone.

"Yes, this time last year you said you wanted me in the wild again."

Gods, it was hard to believe those two men, drunk and stumbling in the palace courtyard, freshly vowed to the other, existed only a year before. They'd changed so much since then. Enkidu would still say yes to Gilgamesh. He'd say yes to him fierce, to him weeping, to him teasing, to him refusing to use Urmah's name, to him tucking around him as they lie down to sleep.

The sun set in the distance.

Soon the stars would come out.

The same stars that watched as Inanna cursed Enkidu.

He might have one night remaining, and he knew how he wanted to spend it. "Make love to me, Gilgamesh," Enkidu whispered over the skin beneath Gilgamesh's ear. "Out here in the wild."

Gilgamesh gripped his shoulders and took a shaky breath. "This might be it, though and—"

"Please." Enkidu leaned back until he could see peach reflected over Gilgamesh's eyes. Suddenly he saw the man's every detail. The way his lower lashes curled until they touched the softer skin beneath them. A freckle that blended in with his hairline. The indentations of his lips.

He was beautiful.

"Give me this one night. I want a few hours with you like my demise doesn't hang over us. Pretend, for my sake, that we succeeded, that tonight is the first night of forever?"

A single tear broke free from Gilgamesh's eye and slipped down his cheek, landing in his beard. He sighed then kissed Enkidu's forehead. "For you, I'd do anything, love."

Enkidu smiled.

All the heaviness slipped away from his body.

This was all he wanted, the only remaining thing life held that appealed to him. One night with Gilgamesh. If it was his final one, it was exactly how he'd want to spend it. In the distance the sun slipped away, Utu retiring to grant them privacy. Enkidu walked Gilgamesh to the hilltop and pulled him down to sit at his side.

CHAPTER TWENTY-THREE

MY HAND IN YOURS

CRYING HAD LEFT Gilgamesh's sinuses dry, his cheeks and lips puffed as he sat beside Enkidu. He'd never failed before —not like this at least.

All his life he'd fought the gods.

His father's death at Inanna's hands handed a city to him when he was younger than Usun, a child who had to learn to survive among gods older than time. Leaning into his god's blood, his heritage, to play up his strengths and disregard his weaknesses was survival.

Then he'd met Enkidu.

The purest, most authentic being that ever existed.

Words didn't come out of Enkidu's mouth that he didn't speak from his soul. He'd captured Gilgamesh's attention like the heavens once had. With Enkidu, he'd found purpose. Something more meaningful than legacy or manipulating gods.

Then Gilgamesh's arrogance had damned him.

He'd vowed that he'd break the curse.

And he'd failed.

Gilgamesh had destroyed monsters, traveled to lands

no other mortal had seen, faced gods, and grown the grandest city in the world. And none of it mattered.

He remembered his mother's words from so long ago. He'd stood in her temple, water trickling, the air humid, asking her if he'd achieve an immortal name.

You shall gain what you desire but lose that which matters more.

Gilgamesh flared his nose to fight back more tears that threatened.

He'd trade it all now—all the glory and legacy and every mention of his name that might continue into history. His mother was the goddess of prophecies. Those words weren't a mother's fretting but truth he'd ignored. He'd fought with every bit of strength he had, physical and emotional, to change fate. It hadn't been enough.

He would lose Enkidu by morning.

He swallowed hard and forced his jaw to loosen as Enkidu rested his head on his shoulder.

Urmah shook free from a bush and prowled over next to them while licking his whiskers clean. He dropped beside Enkidu who scratched his ears until the lion's breathing slowed.

He'd promised Enkidu that he'd give him one night where he pretended they'd succeeded. If they'd done so, he wouldn't be broken and weeping. He'd laugh, tease Enkidu, press kisses to his neck, watch the last wash of lavender fade from the night's sky.

Perhaps what Enkidu said had merit.

The gods were not in unison. Utu had defied his father and sister. The gods had allowed them to traverse their territory. Maybe a change was happening—not something Gilgamesh could affect but something out of his control.

Maybe Gilgamesh couldn't break the curse, but another would.

For the night, he'd have to pretend that was the situation, for Enkidu's sake.

Gilgamesh took a deep breath and decided to let the future keep itself.

He pressed a kiss to Enkidu's hair, his lips grazing over a horn's smooth surface. "What was your favorite part of our journey?"

Enkidu looked up at him. The evening had darkened, but Gilgamesh could still see the hazel green and golds of his eyes. Enkidu smiled, forming lines in his cheek. "Rescuing Urmah. Yours?"

Gilgamesh nuzzled his nose into his neck. "Oh, probably when we had to kill a bunch of eternal stone monsters because you're a pitiful sap."

"I'm not pitiful."

"Not denying you're a sap, though?"

Enkidu smiled. "We all have our weaknesses."

Gilgamesh grinned back and tangled fingers into the man's curls, angled his head so he could kiss him properly, found a horn and gripped it. Gilgamesh had endless flaws. Next to Enkidu, he became more aware of them, but Enkidu's love radiated so deeply it made him believe he could be better.

Enkidu had accepted him even when he wasn't.

Now Gilgamesh wanted to love him like their souls could twine. As the kiss ended, Enkidu's nose brushed Gilgamesh's. His eyes were soft in the dim light. Gilgamesh chuckled. He'd gotten to love this man who'd followed him through one ridiculous adventure after another.

Through deserts and seas, facing monsters and gods,

he'd held this man's hand and believed they could do anything.

Gilgamesh kissed him again, harder. Enkidu's hands slid around his back. Here was a man who could match him, who could handle his strength, who could put him in his place and love him just as fiercely.

He pulled Enkidu into his lap.

When they'd first made love, Gilgamesh had done so with uncertain movements and worry. He'd had time since, exploring and learning and loving. Now he knew what Enkidu liked, where to pull skin between his teeth, how hard to grip his hips, and what every nuance of a groan meant.

He slid Enkidu's tunic off his shoulders so his chest's sculpted form became accessible. As Gilgamesh brushed knuckles across hair, Enkidu moaned, and Gilgamesh fought a smile as his hand slid farther down.

Enkidu ground his hips forward, pressing their bodies together, and Gilgamesh gritted his teeth to fight reacting. He wouldn't be rushed on this night. He planned to treasure every furl of Enkidu's lips between his teeth, every taste of his skin.

Gilgamesh leaned forward and flicked his tongue over Enkidu's nipple then dragged it between his teeth.

A gasp, more beautiful than music, left the man's mouth, and his hot breath grazed Gilgamesh's neck.

The first time they'd had sex, Gilgamesh was far too gentle. He'd learned since that Enkidu liked it when Gilgamesh's hands were rough, his kisses bruising, his thrusts demanding.

Gilgamesh gripped Enkidu's thighs and lifted him higher into his lap. Enkidu's tunic fell, draping over his hips. Gilgamesh rolled him onto his back into the soft grass then traced his body with his tongue.

He tasted of the earth, grassy and sweet.

Gilgamesh scraped his teeth along his ribs and grinned as Enkidu's abs clenched, his hips driving up.

He'd have to wait a little longer, though.

Gilgamesh intended to make use of the time they had. To treasure each touch of that night like time held no meaning.

With his love for Enkidu, it didn't.

He removed the rest of Enkidu's tunic and his loincloth. For a moment Gilgamesh skimmed his eyes down Enkidu's body, the dark hair and heavy muscles, the hard length of him as eager as Gilgamesh was.

Enkidu was more beautiful than the stars slowly peppering the sky, more majestic than the gods' garden, more perfect than eternity itself. Gilgamesh had seen nothing as alluring as his body bare in moonlight, his arms stretching behind his head, propping himself up to watch.

Gilgamesh smiled and bowed between his legs. He kissed a thigh, then gripped both of Enkidu's legs hard enough that he whimpered. Gilgamesh trailed kisses down his leg until he reached his length and drew it into his mouth.

"Yes," Enkidu whispered. He talked during sex which Gilgamesh might have found annoying with another in the past. With Enkidu, he loved hearing his rough voice whisper directions and encourage him forward. "Harder."

Gilgamesh complied. He snaked a hand down Enkidu's leg as he picked up the pace, stopped long enough to slide his fingers into his mouth, wetting them, as Enkidu watched with hungry eyes, then returned to his task.

Enkidu directed him, and Gilgamesh obeyed.

There was only one situation where Gilgamesh willingly bowed, and it was beneath this man's raspy directions as his hips bucked and his sweat-slicked skin stretched before him, gloriously touchable.

Enkidu tensed, his body going rigid.

For a moment, Gilgamesh considered drawing him to his release, feeling the warmth of it against his flesh or the taste of it on his tongue. He wasn't done enjoying him yet, though, so he pulled back.

Enkidu sighed loudly enough that Urmah readjusted, yawning before curling back up.

For a moment Enkidu lay still, his chest rising and falling rapidly.

Damn, he was beautiful.

Perfect.

He rose to sitting and kissed Gilgamesh roughly, dragging his teeth hard enough across his lips that the tang of copper bloomed across his tongue.

"You're not even undressed yet."

Gilgamesh grinned. He enjoyed sex, but watching Enkidu's face scrunch, feeling his fingers tighten in his hair, seeing him lose himself was the best part.

"Nothing, really?" Enkidu asked as he walked on his knees closer until he could grab Gilgamesh's hips. "No biting remark to throw at me?"

A chuckle spilled out of him, and he lowered his mouth to drag his teeth over Enkidu's ear. "If you want me to bite, love, just give the command."

Enkidu laughed, and it rang out, spilling across the empty hill and wide world beyond. He removed Gilgamesh's tunic slowly, peeling each section down reverently.

Gilgamesh didn't rush him or take over. He allowed

Enkidu to kiss his body, glide fingers gently over muscles so he shivered, pass endless minutes removing fabric.

When he finally had him bare, Enkidu blinked up at Gilgamesh and smiled. "I love you, Gilgamesh. I wish you could know how much."

He lowered at that moment, taking Gilgamesh into his mouth and stealing his words. Gilgamesh wanted to reply that he understood. That he felt the same.

But he didn't possess Enkidu's capacity to speak and fuck at the same time. With Enkidu's thick lips wrapped around him, Gilgamesh couldn't do more than grunt in reply.

Enkidu laughed, and the vibration rang through Gilgamesh's body. He grabbed Enkidu's horns and plowed into the man's warm mouth.

A breeze whipped over the valley, causing goosebumps to rise over Gilgamesh's chest. The sensations were all too much. Every nerve had reached some pinnacle. Perhaps this would kill him. Gods, that would be glorious.

Enkidu pulled back, his lips glistening and swollen. Gilgamesh wanted to roll him over and slam him into the earth, drive into him, smack their bodies together until their sweat combined.

Before he had a chance, Enkidu reached into his bag and pulled out a crock then opened it. He scooped cedar oil out, letting it drizzle down Gilgamesh's chest. They'd avoided using the precious oil as they'd run low, however a little lingered, and Enkidu used it up without hesitation. He pushed Gilgamesh back to the ground, then climbed over his lap.

Gilgamesh readjusted where he could grip his hips and spoke, his voice husky. "Changing preferences on me now, are you?"

Enkidu laughed, grabbed another generous scoop of oil, and finished what Gilgamesh's fingers and mouth had started earlier. Then he slid himself down onto Gilgamesh, pulling their bodies together.

It was Gilgamesh's turn to groan, for his eyes to flutter closed.

Enkidu didn't move, and Gilgamesh opened his eyes to find him looking down at him. Moonlight haloed his hair and horns while it kissed the curves of his body. He looked like he belonged among the stars as the sky's navy unfurled behind him.

"What is it, love?" Gilgamesh asked.

A tear trailed Enkidu's cheek, and Gilgamesh sat up. He tried to pull away, but Enkidu clung closer to him, pressed a kiss on his neck. "Don't leave."

Gilgamesh wrapped his arms around him and peppered kisses on his shoulder. "Never, love. I'm at your side forever."

Which may have only been one more day, but Gilgamesh tried to forget about that. Instead, he held the man, felt his breaths rise and fall. He lifted his face, their noses brushing.

"I'm sorry."

"Don't be." Gilgamesh's voice was scarcely more than a whisper, but he held him in his arms. This night was about Enkidu. Gilgamesh's worries and fears and grief could wait. "Tell me what's wrong."

"Nothing is wrong." Enkidu kissed him, slow and lingering so their lips clasped to each other. He grazed rough fingers over Gilgamesh's nipple and everything in his body that had softened tensed again. Enkidu began to move, and Gilgamesh wanted to ask him to stop, to tell him what was the matter, but he was back to the fact that he couldn't fuck and speak at once, and oh Enkidu felt so godsdamned glorious. Warm and tight and eager as he rolled his hips.

"It's that I love you," Enkidu said, his pace picking up. He kissed Gilgamesh's cheek. "I've loved you since I first saw you. And no matter what happens, I shall love you until the Great Below collapses and names are gone and this world"—he groaned—"ceases to exist. Nothing can take that away."

Gilgamesh slid his hands across Enkidu's back, kissed his neck then grabbed his horns to urge him forward, faster.

Enkidu leaned his head back, offering Gilgamesh a better grip.

Their breaths and moans tangled together like the grasses.

Gilgamesh finished with a moan that left his entire body trembling. Enkidu batted tear-glistened lashes and looked down at him. Gilgamesh cradled his face, then kissed his brow, once over each eye. He rolled him back into the grass, pulling their bodies apart, and bowed between his legs again.

His thighs were sweat dampened and cedar sweet. Gilgamesh took him into his mouth and started a rhythm. Enkidu, for once, offered no direction, and instead drifted fingers into Gilgamesh's hair. When he came, Gilgamesh tasted the sweet warmth of him and didn't release him until his love lay sprawled over the earth with his eyes closed.

He rose, wiping his mouth and looked down at Enkidu.

With how still he was, he could be dead. Gilgamesh shuddered then pushed the thought away as he lay beside him. "Enkidu?"

"Hmm?" His reply was sleepy, his eyes not opening.

"If I could make you see how much I love you, the force of it would ricochet back and kill us both."

Enkidu's eyes snapped open.

Around them the world had gone dark, the moon full and creamy in the sky. A fresh year ushered in, and it was like the earth knew it, prepared for it.

Gilgamesh's gaze remained fixed on Enkidu, though.

"I have loved you," Gilgamesh whispered, "from the depths of my soul. I would fight the gods for you, climb into the Great Below, or to the world's highest peak for you. You are wonder and goodness, and I swear to you, no matter what happens, I won't forget. My life is at your command. I'll never shame your name again."

Enkidu smiled then rolled over so he could hug Gilgamesh. "I know."

Gilgamesh ran fingers through the man's sweat-damp curls and kissed him between the horns.

After a few minutes, he sat up, lifting Enkidu with him. He looked through his bag, then remembered he had no fabric left. Instead, he ripped his tunic's hem to wipe Enkidu down. The man tutted. "That was your last outfit."

"We're almost home."

Enkidu went still for a moment and the slicing pain of grief dashed through Gilgamesh. Enkidu may not live to make it back to Uruk, even though the city's glow from lamps glistened in the distance.

Gilgamesh swallowed, but Enkidu laughed, wiped himself off, then Gilgamesh, and helped him back into his clothes. His fingers brushed along Gilgamesh's body like he might never touch it again.

Once they were both dressed, they sat together on the hill. Urmah opened bleary eyes then walked over and laid his head in Enkidu's lap before falling into a slumber again.

Enkidu smiled gently down at the lion then raised his face to the heavens. "Tell me about the sky tonight."

"I've told you about this one before."

Enkidu released a contented sigh and rested his head on Gilgamesh's shoulder. "Tell me again."

Gilgamesh wrapped an arm around his back, cherished the weight of the man's body, then lifted a finger to point at the first constellation. "If you look there, those stars that curve together, they're called the Plough."

CHAPTER TWENTY-FOUR

LET US GO TOGETHER

Warmth shrugged around Enkidu. His muscles had grown loose, and his body was pleasantly sore. Gilgamesh continued pointing out constellations. Enkidu had stopped listening to the specific words, but he closed his eyes and listened to the rumble of his voice, the vibration echoing into his chest.

Enkidu's breathing grew deeper, and he rhythmically scratched Urmah's head. The lion snored quietly. In a few minutes all three would fall into sleep's arms, drift into the world of dreams.

Tomorrow they could face when it arrived.

For now, Enkidu was happy.

Gilgamesh pointed. "That's the brightest star in the sky this time of year."

Enkidu wanted to reply that Gilgamesh was the brightest being in his life. That he loved him so fiercely he'd go on a foolish journey, fight monsters, and face gods all to do so at his side. How he wished he could press the joy Gilgamesh had given back into his heart.

Gilgamesh's thumb brushed gently over Enkidu's hip,

and the drowsiness grew. He slipped into sleep once, then twice, then a peacefulness came.

"Enkidu."

He jerked around.

The dark sky glistened around him. Enkidu floated above the world, separate from his body. Below, Gilgamesh held him where his body curled against the man, and Urmah was tucked into his side. Gilgamesh looked down at Enkidu, smiled, and pulled him closer, kissing his forehead before lifting his face to the heavens. His eyes traced over the stars he loved so much.

Enkidu tried to move towards him, but he was stuck in place, floating above the world. He was dreaming, perhaps. Below he was still alive, his chest rising and falling with slow breaths.

Gilgamesh smiled, softly, in that only-for-him way that warmed his heart.

"Enkidu."

The voice called again. It was soft and melodic. Enkidu turned towards it. Among the heavens, a woman's face came into form. Her eyes glistened with starlight, her freckles a patch of dark clouds, her lips formed among the trees in the distance, her tunic the forest flowing beyond.

"Do I know you?" he asked. Something about her felt familiar.

Her eyes glistened. "Well, do you?"

A memory flashed through his mind. An image that had always been there, but he'd not been able to access. He lay naked in the cedar forest, new, his eyes peeling open the first time to a smile that gleamed like silver sunlight before it dashed away.

"You're Aruru," he said, certain of it. The goddess of creation. The divine that created him.

The trees curled up into a smile. "I'm your mother."

Enkidu gasped and would have stumbled back had he a body to do so in. "I was created for Gilgamesh. I have no parents."

"Ninsun requested I create someone for her son, yes. However, you are my child with whom I'm very pleased. I've come for you."

Enkidu frowned and looked back where Gilgamesh held him with that soft and hazy smile on his face. "I don't understand."

"Inanna plans to kill you at dawn." Aruru's voice went as hard and sharp as a blade. "She doesn't intend kindness. You will suffer."

He shuddered. It was strange to float above himself, to dance among the heavens Gilgamesh loved so much. From below they were majestic, but hovering among them their beauty stole Enkidu's breath. "I don't wish to leave him."

Aruru's features flashed, then she shifted, shrinking until she took on a human-like form. Thick dark curls draped over her shoulders framing her wide lips and large eyes. Only her nose was delicate with a splash of freckles across it. "You will leave him either way, Enkidu."

Throat tightening, he turned away from Aruru. He'd known this would come, that he'd lose Gilgamesh. Yet, some part of him had clung to hope that the gods might spare him. And he wasn't ready to leave Gilgamesh. He never would be. "I wish for every moment I could have. You're a goddess, you must understand my heart."

She moved closer, walking across the air. She stood as tall as Enkidu, but her eyes were a deep liquid brown filled with the wisdom of millennia. "Of course I do, son. You have loved him purely, and I can feel how deeply. However, do you not think it will hurt him more to watch you suffer a cruel death?"

Enkidu looked back again. Gilgamesh had his face raised so he appeared to look right at Enkidu. His heart lurched.

I love you, he whispered into the wind. He wanted to stay and say goodbye but not if it came at the cost of Gilgamesh's pain. He didn't doubt Inanna would torment Enkidu until his end to enact her wrath on Gilgamesh. Sometimes love called for sacrifices. Akkiru had taught him that. Enkidu wouldn't burden Gilgamesh with more pain just to steal a few more moments.

He wished he could reverse time and avoid angering Inanna. He wasn't sure he could commit to undoing his vow to Gilgamesh, though. Even if it cost him his life, he'd make it again.

"I never would have created you if I'd known Inanna would grow wrathful with you."

"No, don't say that." Enkidu whirled around to face his mother. "Don't say I wouldn't exist, that I wouldn't have lived or gotten to love him."

Aruru smiled. "Were you happy with your life, short as it was?"

Enkidu's chest ached. It was unfair that he had such little time. Yet, he didn't regret it. He'd lived, felt sunlight warm his skin, ran until his lungs ached, laughed so tears formed over his eyes, and loved. He'd loved so deeply. "I was."

"You'll come with me, then?" She outstretched a hand.

"What about Gilgamesh?" Enkidu's voice stumbled over his name. "He'll suffer."

Some part of Enkidu had held onto the idea that he might overcome the curse and remain at Gilgamesh's side.

He trusted him to keep his word, to not fall back into his wrathful ways. But he'd be miserable if Enkidu died.

"He cannot have both, Enkidu. I could remove his pain, but only if I removed the love he has for you and the memories you've shared."

Enkidu's breath rushed out of him. He should love Gilgamesh enough to agree. Send him home confused about why he'd left, but with his heart free from the anguish of losing him. He wasn't sure he was selfless enough to do that. There were some sacrifices he couldn't make. He wanted Gilgamesh to keep a piece of him, to remember him.

"There's something else you're not considering." Aruru cocked her head. "It's his love for you that's made him a better man. If you take the pain, you take all the good that's come from it."

Enkidu swallowed and closed his eyes, blocking out the world for a moment. "There's no way I can overcome the curse, is there?"

His mother's lips furled in, her brows pulling together. "If only you knew the arguments the gods have had over this topic, the sides that have formed. If I could stop Inanna's curse, we wouldn't be having this conversation. However, I've made a deal with Anu. We have plans for you, Enkidu, that have been prophesied but not yet enacted. Your purpose isn't over yet."

"What are the plans?"

She stretched her hand out again. "Let us go together, and I'll explain everything."

Still Enkidu paused.

Looked back once more.

At a king who sat beside his lover in ragged, worn clothing after finishing a journey he'd taken to save the man. A god-born man who'd humbled himself for love's sake.

At the tender smile he still wore.

Enkidu closed his eyes, and for a moment he could feel Gilgamesh's arm steady around him, how he held his sleeping body upright, the rhythmic rise and fall of his breath, Urmah's warmth on his leg.

Goodbye, my love.

He turned and accepted his mother's outstretched hand.

CHAPTER TWENTY-FIVE

A WIND BLEW THROUGH

GILGAMESH sighed happily as Enkidu's gentle snores matched Urmah's. Above, the sky glistened. He'd always loved the heavens, but something about it drew his attention, had him staring into nothingness like there was something he should reach for.

There was nowhere else he wanted to go, though. Enkidu slept peacefully in his arms, his city stood safe and gleaming in the distance, and for a moment it seemed time might stretch forever.

A wind blew through the valley, rattling trees and howling. A chill entered the air, and Gilgamesh frowned. Enkidu released a great sigh, a sound that matched the wind, then his body went still.

Gilgamesh froze, though his heart pounded until it vibrated. He shifted, and Enkidu slumped onto his chest.

"Enkidu?" he whispered.

Enkidu slept deeply, that was all. Gilgamesh didn't want to startle him. He'd speak a little louder, the man would rouse, then they'd both laugh. It was time for them to make camp and lie down.

"Enkidu." He spoke firmer.

Enkidu didn't reply.

Gilgamesh swallowed against his pounding heartbeat. He moved and Enkidu slid down his arm. Gilgamesh snagged him to keep him from banging his head, then laid him gently on the grass.

"Enkidu!" he shouted. Urmah jumped up and yowled like he'd join the cry. Gilgamesh grabbed Enkidu's shoulders and gave him a shake, then a harder one. "Enkidu, wake up."

Enkidu's expression had softened, his lips parted, his lashes splayed across his cheeks.

Gilgamesh pressed fingers to his neck and waited.

And waited.

No heartbeat thudded comfortingly back.

With another yowl, Urmah butted his head into Gilgamesh's hand before lying across Enkidu's chest. Gilgamesh growled and shoved the lion back. "Don't touch him."

Urmah stumbled then shrank to the ground, his eyes going wide, his shoulders rising to his ears.

No matter what happens—even if it breaks me—I'll honor your name in my actions. I swear it.

He'd said those words to Enkidu.

Gilgamesh stuttered over his breaths and brushed a strand of hair off Enkidu's cheek. His skin had grown cold in the wind, and Gilgamesh's fingers stilled over his flesh. He was always warm, flushed with heat and brimming with life.

No longer, though.

Now he remained perfectly still.

Enkidu was—

Gilgamesh threw his head back, yelled, roared, and

screamed. He shouted until his mouth hurt, until his voice ran out.

Urmah stared at him, remaining so still not even his tail swished.

When his voice grew too hoarse to continue, Gilgamesh bowed his head over Enkidu. He let his hands drop, his fingernails sinking into the dirt. A year of running, and Inanna's curse had caught them regardless. Caught them when he wasn't prepared, when he couldn't fight. Tears spilled down his cheeks, falling over his lips and dripping onto Enkidu's ragged tunic.

He'd died in rags.

Gilgamesh's throat closed for a heartbeat, not allowing breath in.

He'd dragged him on this damn trip, and nothing had come of it. Instead of prolonging his life, Enkidu had spent his last year tired, dirty, and in danger. He'd died like a nobody rather than exalted as a hero.

Lip quivering, Gilgamesh brushed Enkidu's curls behind his ear, attempting to loosen the tangles. Oil shimmered in a streak on his cheek. Gilgamesh lifted a piece of his tunic and tried to wipe it off, but it only smeared, spreading over his unmoving lips.

He stopped. He was making everything worse.

Bowing his forehead to Enkidu's, he startled at its cool touch. Gilgamesh held onto one of his horns and wept, his tears streaming down Enkidu's cheeks.

Gilgamesh didn't know how long had passed when he looked up at the cub who still lay watching, his ears twitching.

"Urmah," he spoke, his voice full of gravel. "Come here."

The lion rose only enough to crawl forward on his belly. Gilgamesh had frightened him. If Enkidu were there, he'd be upset over that. Gilgamesh swallowed down another rainy season of tears that longed to spill out.

When Urmah arrived, Gilgamesh outstretched a palm. The lion sniffed at it, then he slowly moved beneath his hand so Gilgamesh could scratch his head. Once Urmah stood, Gilgamesh bowed his head towards the scrap of a mane that hadn't grown in fully yet. "I'm sorry. I shouldn't have done that, and I promise you, I never will again."

Urmah licked his arm, his rough tongue dragging down the muscle. Gilgamesh pulled him close and wept into his musky fur.

When he was certain he'd calmed Urmah fully, he turned back to Enkidu. Lying down next to him, he took his hand. It had stiffened already, his fingers curled, shaped to Gilgamesh's hand. He burrowed his nose into Enkidu's neck, wrapped an arm around his waist, and lay with him, Urmah curling between their legs, until the sun came up.

As Utu stretched across the sky, Gilgamesh forced himself to his feet.

He ripped apart their bags.

The crock fell and cracked, what little cedar oil remained seeping into the earth.

Gilgamesh kicked the vessel hard enough that it tumbled down the hill then shattered fully. He fed the bits of dried meat to Urmah, then sewed the bags together before laying the fabric out beside Enkidu.

He didn't look like he was sleeping. He lay too unnaturally, his lips too firmly pressed, his hand still curled.

Urmah leapt upon Enkidu and licked his cheek. Gilgamesh bowed and gently pushed him back. "He's gone."

Urmah whined and butted into Enkidu.

Gilgamesh only sighed, then got behind the man, lifting

him beneath the arms to move him onto the makeshift pallet. It wasn't a good one. His body would drag along every stone and stick on the road, but Gilgamesh couldn't carry him because of the stiffness and he sure as shed wasn't leaving him. He'd give up and lie down and die beside him, except he'd promised Enkidu he wouldn't.

Godsdamn him and his stupid promises.

He got Enkidu onto the pallet, Urmah crying loudly the entire time, then began the long slow journey home.

By the time they reached the city gates, the sun had fallen.

People stopped and gasped as Gilgamesh walked through the gates and into the gleaming city. He scarcely noticed the crowd. He should be walking alongside Enkidu, thrusting their arms in the air, declaring their victory.

Someone startled, dropping a pot of water.

It shattered, and the liquid spilled onto the path.

Gilgamesh didn't even look up at her face. He didn't care.

The city shimmered and gleamed. It was a crown amid the desert, the world's grandest city.

It meant absolutely fucking nothing.

As he continued through the city, people gathered along the road. Word must have spread. They recognized him now, eyes wide as they watched him dragging a dead god-born man alongside a nearly grown lion who growled at anyone who came too close.

Gilgamesh would have praised Urmah could he have found the words.

As he passed shining, reflective mosaics and water pots, he understood people's dramatic reactions. He appeared as wild as he'd once imagined Enkidu. Dust covered his body and clung to his ripped and thinning tunic. His hair and beard tangled and splayed violently. Urmah prowled like he hunted, and behind them both, he dragged Enkidu on a pallet made from fabric scraps.

When they finally reached the palace, Gilgamesh could have wretched. Shamhat stood at the dais wearing a rich purple tunic, her jewelry glistening. Officials and soldiers and court members stood alongside her as well. But Gilgamesh's gaze caught on the man next to Shamhat.

Usun had grown in the year they'd been gone. He towered over his mother now, and a shadow of hair trailed along his lip.

He was no longer a child.

Now a young man stood in his place, rapidly filling in his broad frame.

Shamhat's mouth gaped. She looked around before snapping her fingers at a few officials including Hirin who all joined her in walking down the steps and meeting Gilgamesh. She bowed before him, but he couldn't return the gesture, couldn't find the heart to kiss her hand or greet her. If he moved too much, he'd see Enkidu. See him gone. Dead.

"Enkidu is to have a proper burial in a royal tomb." His voice boomed, echoing off the palace and washing over the silent crowd. "I'm ordering a temple built in his memory as his divine right."

Shamhat's mouth opened again, closed, then she rolled her shoulders back. "You've heard your king."

Hirin blinked rapidly and gestured for soldiers, some of Gilgamesh's closest men, to come. They bent down by Enkidu, grabbing the pallet's edges. Gilgamesh raised a hand to stall them. He bowed beside Enkidu.

He was gone.

This was his body, his mahogany curls, his thick, elegant fingers.

But his spirit wasn't with it anymore. Gilgamesh leaned over, regardless, and pressed a kiss to his forehead, touched a horn one last time, then rose, nodding to his men.

They picked Enkidu up and took him away.

Urmah watched with wide eyes, his head swiveling back and forth between the two men he'd never parted from.

"Urmah, you stay with me," Gilgamesh said firmly.

Somehow the king's voice had returned to him in Uruk.

The lion yowled once but walked alongside Gilgamesh, though his eyes remained fixed on where the crowd parted to allow space for the soldiers carrying Enkidu's body away.

Gilgamesh swept his gaze across the people, not meeting any eyes until he found the warm brown of his wife's.

Her eyebrows inched up only slightly. She was still a master at controlling her expression before a crowd. "Your king has walked among the gods and done so for Uruk's benefit." Her voice hummed steadily—a Queen's tone full of authority. "He'll retire now."

She offered her arm.

For a moment, Gilgamesh didn't take it. Dust puffed off him whenever he moved, but she didn't budge. He took her arm and led her up past a staring Usun, through the palace doors, past the front courtyard, then into a hall towards his room. Urmah loped alongside him, his gaze dashing back and forth, his posture low and tensed.

"This creature comes with you?" Shamhat asked softly.

"He's mine."

She nodded, the gold on her headpiece dancing and reflecting around the space.

When they reached his room, Gilgamesh was grateful that Shamhat opened the door and ushered him in. He didn't have the heart to open it. The last time he'd been there, he'd teased Enkidu, kissed his lips, made him promises he wouldn't keep.

As they entered, Urmah stepped over the fine rugs and found a corner to curl into.

Shamhat clicked the copper-inlaid door in place and turned around. "Was it Inanna?"

Gilgamesh parted his lips to answer, but a cry spilled out.

He dropped to his knees.

Shamhat fell with him, caught him, hugged him tight against her slight frame. He should have pulled away and not sullied her beauty with his travel-worn dirtiness. But he couldn't. Aside from Enkidu, she was the only person he had.

He wept, his nose flaring, tears getting sucked in with his ragged breaths.

"Oh, Gilgamesh." Shamhat rubbed his back and burrowed into him. "What happened?"

"I failed him." It was more of a wail than spoken words.

He fell heavily on her, and Shamhat struggled under his weight. He'd always been too big for the world, his personality too much. Only one man could bear the full weight of him.

Shamhat tightened her grip, braced against the floor, and held him.

"I'm here with you, Gilgamesh. I'm here."

He clung to his wife and grieved the only man he'd ever love.

* * *

Water trailed down his mother's temple walls. Gilgamesh wore rich colors again, a fringed sash tied around his hips and shoulders, bracelets and rings that shimmered over his tanned skin.

For seven days, he'd not slept or eaten beyond the food Shamhat forced on him.

Instead, he'd paced the palace at night, went to the courtyard he'd had the first honest conversation with Enkidu in, climbed to the roof and stared at the stars. Urmah followed him like a shadow. Gilgamesh even dragged him up to the roof. There he scratched his head as Enkidu once had when they sat leaning on each other discussing constellations.

Gilgamesh wondered if Enkidu had been truly interested or only listened for his sake.

He had so many questions left to ask.

So many unfinished conversations.

Even though the official mourning period had ended, grief still howled and screamed through him. He felt like a ghost that had taken residence in the body he walked about in. He answered inquiries, attended the burial, and spoke with advisors.

But within, he wept and wailed.

He'd allowed stylists to poke and prod and cut and curl him back into the shape of a king. As he walked into his mother's temple, he appeared the polished ruler of the world's finest city once more.

His heart, however, bled, slipping down his bones and pooling in his stomach. It was a wonder he continued forward. It felt like a cruelty of fate that he continued breathing, moving, existing in a world that Enkidu did not.

Blinking past tears he refused to show, he stepped into

the inner chamber and dropped incense into a basin before lighting it.

Water rushed down the walls' sides as the smoky scent perfumed the air.

The incense's cedar smell filled the room.

Gilgamesh swallowed against a lump in his throat.

"Son."

Gilgamesh turned but didn't meet his mother's eyes. Ninsun stepped forward, her hooves not disturbing the water but gliding through it like a ghost.

"You knew, didn't you?"

She stopped walking. "Knew?"

He raised his face. Gilgamesh had vowed to Enkidu not to return to his brash and angry ways. He intended to keep that promise. However, Enkidu would have to forgive him this single moment. Especially when he couldn't forget that his mother had only bothered to show up to share news about the Wolf's death which caused Enkidu even more pain. "You knew he'd die. From the very beginning you knew what he'd mean to me, and you knew how it would end."

Ninsun looked down. For a goddess, she appeared small and insignificant.

Gilgamesh stepped forward, his hem trailing over the water. "I stood here asking you to interpret a dream, and you gave all that talk about losing me. I thought you meant when I died one day, but that wasn't it, was it?"

"Please, Gilgamesh. I did as you asked, I—"

"You could have warned me," he roared. This wasn't just about Enkidu. It was the fury of a child thrust into a man's position, a king left alone, a person abandoned by his mother a thousand times in his life.

Ninsun blinked tears away. Good, he wanted her to cry.

Someone else fucking should besides him and Shamhat. In the end, Shamhat was the only genuine family Gilgamesh had ever had. Her and her partners had welcomed him back in the way they'd once absorbed Enkidu. Never again would he take Shamhat for granted or cease to appreciate all she did for Uruk, for the palace, for him.

"You know I can't share prophecies with mortals," Ninsun said to the tile beneath her hooves.

Gilgamesh snorted, curled his hands into fists then released them. So many gods had altered their rules, but his own mother wouldn't. He'd come in here with his prophecy arrogant, boastful, and foolish. He deserved a fall. But she knew how desperately he'd love Enkidu, how it would hurt to lose him. She could have warned him not to enrage Inanna, not to draw her wrath upon Enkidu.

She'd remained silent.

Her silence was the cruelest blow he'd ever taken.

"Gilgamesh, please understand—"

"I understand. When you wept and spoke of losing me, you knew I would stand here one day, and what I would come to say."

She whimpered, and tears spilled over her cheeks. "Please don't do this, son."

He frowned at her, the woman who'd birthed him then abandoned him to the divine's and the court's cruelties. She could have fought for him, protected him, but she hadn't. He knew her excuses, but he now understood they weren't enough. When someone loved another, they took risks for them.

For whatever reason, his mother hadn't been able to take those risks. Instead, she'd allowed Inanna to kill his father without a fight, allowed Inanna to oppress and berate him, allowed the divine to treat him like a bull, good for beating into the work they desired.

Gilgamesh understood love now.

It would run through a mountain of fire to save the other.

Sail across a sea of death.

Dive into the depths without hesitating.

Even if it was a lost cause.

"I love you, I do, I just—"

"I understand what I need to do now," Gilgamesh interrupted. "I need to speak with the gods."

His mother looked like a shattered pot, all wrinkled lines where there shouldn't be any, tragedy where peace usually reigned. "Yes."

"I ask you to arrange that. Besides that, I'm sure you know what I've come to say."

"Please don't, Gilgamesh. I beg you. All I've ever done for you was meant out of love. I've made mistakes, yes, but—"

"You're the goddess of prophecy. Tell me, does your begging actually change anything? In my experience,"—his voice wobbled—"I've found it does nothing."

She swallowed, and it echoed around her temple room.

"Goodbye, Mother."

Gilgamesh turned and walked out, knowing he'd never return again.

CHAPTER TWENTY-SIX
GAMES AND GODS

THE COURTYARD at the Queen's palace differed from those at the King's. Gilgamesh hadn't seen the place in decades. Shamhat encouraged Meritkara and Akkiru to decorate and influence the space. Gilgamesh could see both of them in its design.

Gardeners allowed the trees and plants to grow a little wilder in it. Musical instruments sat in baskets scattered about. Children laughed and teased and ran after one another. A group of mothers whispered in one corner and stopped as Gilgamesh and Urmah stepped into the space.

He understood why Enkidu liked this courtyard so much.

He'd expected the experience to be harder. Instead, it reminded him of everything he'd loved about Enkidu. How his body uncoiled in nature. How he gravitated towards animals and children and tender-hearted things. The way he laughed with his full body.

A smile slipped up Gilgamesh's lips.

He still wept every day. He imagined he would for a great long time.

But some beauty of their memories together seeped through all the misery. He stepped under a roof, and the group of young men seated around a game of Twenty Squares jumped up, their mouths parting as they stared at Urmah before they hastily bowed. "Lugal."

Gilgamesh nodded to them and shifted his eyes to his son. "May I have the next game, Usun?"

The boy blinked rapidly before bowing again. "Of course, my king."

His voice had deepened but still wobbled with higher tones. Soon he'd be a man. Gilgamesh had lost so much time with his foolish striving, with fighting the gods, with believing he could control it all.

No more.

The others cleared out and Gilgamesh sat across from Usun at the board. The boy busied himself with resetting the game and placing the knucklebones before Gilgamesh. His eyes kept darting to Urmah, though.

Gilgamesh lifted the bones and tossed them before moving the chips. Usun would likely beat him. He'd never had much opportunity to play games at his age. He scarcely remembered the rules.

For several minutes, they played in silence. Gilgamesh longed to fill it. He didn't know what to say to a child he'd spent so little time with.

Usun finally spoke. "Is that lion truly tamed? Like a dog?"

"No wild creature is ever truly tamed." Gilgamesh's heart rippled and his tongue felt heavy in his mouth. Enkidu never had been. The gods hadn't designed him for this world, truly. He'd hated civilization. Among the wild was the only peace he'd ever found. And with Gilgamesh.

"However, yes, as much as a wild thing can be. He was Enkidu's."

It was Usun's turn but his attention had drifted from the game to the lion. "How did he tame him?"

Gilgamesh swallowed. Thinking happy thoughts of Enkidu was one thing, discussing him another. However, he longed to fix this brokenness with his son while he had the chance. He didn't wish to allow the boy to grow up and become another brutal, broken man who hadn't felt one of his parent's love.

"He found him as a cub... rescued him, actually."

"A rescue?" Usun's eyes brightened, and he sat straighter. There was a little of the boy Gilgamesh remembered remaining in him, eager for a story.

Gilgamesh had those.

He had dozens of unbelievable stories he could tell. Adventures filled with dragons and fire and near-death experiences. Every single one of them he'd experienced at Enkidu's side.

He scratched behind Urmah's ear and nodded. "Enkidu and I had made it into the divine realm. It was a desert. The sun burned our backs as though Utu punished us for trespassing."

Usun pulled his arms around his knees, his eyebrows rising with the tale and the smallest smile brushed across Gilgamesh's lips.

"That's when Enkidu heard a cry. We followed it, me with my axes free, Enkidu with his sword raised, then we stepped into a valley of death."

Usun gasped. Gilgamesh found his tongue unfurling. The story spilled from him like it had burbled at the surface, waiting for an opportunity to overflow. When he finished that one, Usun asked questions which prompted him to discuss the scorpion guards, the mountain of fire, the burns they'd endured.

Usun sat enthralled, his chin lifting off his knees occasionally when he sucked in a breath or asked a question.

The sun slid steadily across the sky as they continued talking, the game forgotten.

"You miss Enkidu." Usun's gaze darted across the courtyard. "People say—" His eyes dashed back towards his father and red spread over his nose. "W-well, nothing. I mean, Enkidu told me people love to talk when they aren't doing anything interesting themselves. That's all it is."

A feeling pulsed through Gilgamesh's heart, a sharp pain blending with love's warmth. Gods, that was the man he loved to a finger. Always seeing through everything, loving anyone but unafraid to call their shed what it was. "Enkidu was wise. Tell me what people say."

"It's nothing." Usun grabbed a game piece and bowed his face over the board.

Gilgamesh grabbed the boy's hand gently until he released the piece. He understood Usun's reaction. Once, if he'd heard others gossiping about those he loved within his palace, he'd sever heads. He wasn't that man anymore. Too much had changed. It was funny that he'd promised Enkidu he'd change for his sake, but he found that he'd done so naturally. He'd learned that a person he loved more than his own soul could die without the world breaking in two or rain pouring to flood humans out of existence.

Instead, life carried forward.

His heart kept beating after it had broken.

In the end, only a few things truly mattered. Others could whisper and gossip until they used their final breaths for all he cared. What mattered was that he loved his family, kept his word to Enkidu, protected Uruk, and held his beloved's memory so it burned brighter than Utu's rays.

"I am not who I once was, Usun." He pulled his hand away, giving the boy space. "I promise, you can tell me."

Usun's brows pulled together, but he nodded. "It's only that people say the gods gave you Enkidu as a reward, and they took him away as a punishment."

Gilgamesh dashed his face away. His eyes stung, and he fought, but the grief won, a tear streaking his cheek. He wiped it away with a knuckle. "Perhaps they're right."

"Do you think," he whispered, "that makes the gods cruel?"

With a sigh, Gilgamesh turned back towards his son. "The gods are like us. Some are cruel, others kind. It's a rare soul that's truly compassionate."

He'd loved such a rare soul. Would love him until his dying day which he often hoped wouldn't be too long in the future. In the meantime, he'd keep his promise.

"There's somewhere I want you to go with me, Usun. Will you?"

"Yes, Adda."

Gilgamesh froze. His and Usun's eyes met. Never had his son called him father. He swallowed grief and pain down and rose then offered a hand. "Then come along, son. Just don't be afraid."

A frown marred Usun's expression but he accepted his father's hand and walked alongside him and the lion.

* * *

Utu gleamed like the sun spilled out of his form. He and the other high gods either couldn't or refused to push their form into a truly human-like shape. Utu had carried Usun, Urmah, and Gilgamesh to some mountaintop where there was nothing to see but sunlight and fog.

Standing next to his father, Usun trembled but remained upright. Urmah growled next to him, unhappy to be among the gods again. Hundreds scattered around them.

They all glowed and glittered and shimmered.

Some took the forms of humans, others of beasts or a mix of the two.

The greater gods, including Anu with his silvery light that reflected over everyone, took no form at all.

In the back of the crowd, shrouded in a slip of watery light and whistling wind, his mother watched him. He didn't look in her direction.

Inanna sat on a boulder, her long legs crossed, her wings pressed behind her shoulders. Gilgamesh clenched his teeth. He'd promised Enkidu no more retribution and, more importantly, his son was with him. He had to protect Usun, and this meeting was the first step toward that.

Yet every drop of blood in his body longed to get himself killed by tearing the flesh from her skin.

"You've requested this audience, mortal king," Anu's voice boomed like thunder. "We've granted it to restore peace among the divine."

Gilgamesh's chin tilted up. He and Enkidu had disrupted their damn peace, and he was glad of it. That's not what he came there for, though. Screaming at his fate, demanding more than his piece, were desires he'd shucked somewhere along his journey. His focus sat on higher things now. Usun released a shaky breath, and he reached out to put a hand on the boy's shoulder.

"Thank you for your time." Gilgamesh kept his voice even. He knew he wasn't equal with these divine beings, but he hadn't come as a god. He'd come as a mortal king, and he knew how to be that. "I have two simple requests for changes you might make, Anu."

Enlil hissed, his body forming into a dark cloud. "Why should we bother to listen to some foolish mortal's request?"

The sun gleamed, and Utu's voice roared. "You'll listen to him, or we can finish what we began."

The air filled with energy, lights flashed, the mountain trembled. Usun swallowed but, to his credit, remained standing tall, his fingers curled into Urmah's mane.

"We should listen," a goddess said, her eyes like stars, her tunic streaked with brown and green like a forest. "Because it's the right thing to do. Perhaps some of us"—this comment she directed at Inanna—"should try that for once."

Anu thundered, and the gods all settled. "We listen because I've agreed to do so."

Gilgamesh had been a king long enough to understand the situation. With the way the gods were arranged, nearly half of them stood opposed to Inanna now. A war brewed among the divine. Anu listened because it might prevent a fight he may not win.

Anu's energy shifted towards Gilgamesh, and another boom of thunder split the sky.

Gilgamesh forced his thoughts to stall as he wrapped an arm around his son.

The star-eyed goddess watched Gilgamesh. There was something sad in her expression, something mournful in the breeze swirling around her, a howling wind of echoed grief. "Go ahead, mortal king."

Gilgamesh nodded. "Again, thank you each for your time. My requests are simple." In his sleepless nights,

Gilgamesh had spent endless hours thinking through everything he and Enkidu had discussed on their trip. The unfairness of gods, the Great Below's cruelty, the pain they'd seen in others. From that, he'd formed a plan.

"First, I ask that you give mortals something to hope for beyond this lifetime. An afterlife—some place they can see their loved ones again." His voice broke, and he cleared it. "Second, I ask that you pass a law that no more children with god's blood are brought into the world."

"He has no right." Inanna snapped up, her wings spreading.

Her father sent a gust of wind in her direction, an outstretched hand insisting she sit, which she begrudgingly did.

Gilgamesh licked his lips. "Enkidu and I could only travel into your realm because we both possessed god's blood. But we were mortals, mere men. We didn't belong there. God's blood is a curse for a mortal. It makes him hunger for too much. Men should serve the gods, not seek to become them." He knew he spun this story to appeal to as many present as he could, but he needed them to understand it, to see its importance.

Anu nodded. "Your mother shared the requests you would make with me before you arrived."

Gilgamesh attempted to keep his eyes from darting to the woman where she stood with her head bowed.

"I believe both ideas are wise," Anu said.

"But Father!" Inanna dashed up again.

"Sit down, daughter. You have caused enough grief."

Inanna's eyes flashed. She looked around at the other gods, then dropped onto the boulder with a frown.

"We'll have a vote. All in favor of the mortal king's proposals."

Gilgamesh held his breath. In the interim, he listened to Usun's steady breathing and the scratch of his fingers grazing Urmah's head.

A variety of shouts of approval sprang from the group.

"Those against," Anu said.

Inanna stood. A dozen others shouted.

But it was far less than those who'd agreed. Gilgamesh released a sigh and his shoulders dropped.

"Very well." Anu shifted towards the mortal king once more. Gilgamesh felt small, a speck of dust looking at the heavens. He would never be a god, but he'd somehow, impossibly changed history. "We grant your requests."

Utu moved forward, his gleaming light blocking out the other gods. "I'll return you home now."

Gilgamesh nodded and gripped his son's shoulder.

But for one moment, the sparkling eyes of a goddess he had no name for broke through Utu's gleam. If he didn't know better, he'd almost think there was something loving in her expression.

As their feet landed on his mother's temple roof in Uruk, Usun released a trembling breath. Gilgamesh patted his back. The boy had done well. He'd make a fine king one day after he'd had plenty of training. That would start this week. It was time for the child to shadow him and learn the role.

He wouldn't be a child for much longer.

"Thank you, Utu." Gilgamesh bowed nose to knees which Usun echoed.

Urmah yawned then began licking his fur. Gilgamesh wished for a moment he'd been born a lion with such simple needs and desires.

"You've done well, Gilgamesh. I am sorry for your loss, even if you don't wish to hear the sentiment from me."

Utu's light ached to look into. Gilgamesh pulled his tongue from his mouth's roof and shook his head. "Thank you kindly for that. It's more than many gods might offer."

Utu gleamed brightly for a moment then disappeared back towards the sky.

Gilgamesh stepped next to his son. From their height they could see the great city they ruled, the people whose lives just gained a hope they didn't know about yet. It was a story Gilgamesh needed to spread alongside every tale of Enkidu he could remember. He needed them all pressed into tablets so the world would never forget the man. Never forget the good he brought. Never forget Gilgamesh's love for him.

"What do we do now?" Usun turned towards his father. He still trembled, and a breeze whipped hair off his forehead.

Gilgamesh smiled at his son. "Could I hug you, Usun?"

The boy frowned, then he wrapped his arms around Gilgamesh. The King startled at the impact. He'd had so little touch in his life, so little love. Enkidu had taught him he could find it, though. He'd start here with his family. He clasped the boy within his arms.

"We start with this," he said. "The rest we take one day at a time."

Urmah rubbed his head on Gilgamesh's thigh, and he reached out to pet the beast. After eating the Plant of Life, Urmah would likely live far past a regular lion's lifespan. Gilgamesh scratched his head, gave his son one more squeeze before releasing him, then looked out beyond the city's walls and the river, out to a smudge of green in the distance—the start of the cedar forest.

I'll keep my word, always. Gilgamesh mouthed the words, and he thought of Enkidu's laughter, his sparkling eyes, the way he'd changed history despite living such a very short time.

I promise you.

Gilgamesh turned and directed his son down the stairs and towards their future.

CHAPTER TWENTY-SEVEN

THE LEGACY OF GILGAMESH

THE FIVE-YEAR-OLD SITTING at the end of Gilgamesh's bed spoke as fast as a leopard moved when chasing prey. He couldn't keep up with all she said anymore. Once his brain had been quick enough to argue with anyone—mortal or divine.

However, time passed, and with it his mental acuity and strength left him.

In the last month, he'd quit getting out of his bed. Urmah lay next to him and released a massive yawn then curled back down. His mane was gray streaked now, his fur patchy, his body thin.

Time hadn't been kind to either of them.

Once Gilgamesh had been the world's largest and most fearless man.

The world's most ambitious king.

Then he'd met a man who matched him.

Gilgamesh swallowed. Nearly a century had passed since he'd loved and lived alongside Enkidu. He could still remember his eyes, their forest-wild color. His curls' texture. The shape of his horns.

When he tried to put it all together, his mind faltered.

Time had stolen many things.

But not his memories of his beloved. The statues around Uruk of Enkidu had once been a favorite place for him to spend afternoons, where he'd share stories of their adventures or remind others why they should leave offerings at the new pair of temples.

One for Utu and one for Enkidu.

The gods had kept their words and removed their overbearing presence from mortal life. Now people served them, but didn't interact with them, which was for the best.

"Then she broke my hand drum!" the girl cried out and crossed her arms, her lip furling out.

Gilgamesh knew the girl's real name, but he'd always affectionately called her Egi. She reminded him so much of Shamhat with her sharp mind and fierce personality.

Gods did Gilgamesh miss Shamhat. She'd been the last of her partners to pass. He'd mourned them all—the family she'd built for him whom he'd cherished. But he'd grieved none as fiercely as his wife and queen.

"What did you do, then?"

Egi blew a puff of breath that fluttered hair out of her eyes. The child had removed her braids. Such a strong-minded youth, that one. "I kicked her, and that's why I can't play in the courtyard tomorrow. It's not fair."

"Hmm." Gilgamesh nodded but didn't respond. She'd eventually have to learn to temper herself, harness her strengths. But she was young yet. Gilgamesh knew he shouldn't have a favorite grandchild. He'd loved them all, knew their names and interests and sat through endless games where they'd best him. But when it came down to it, Egi had always held a special spot in his heart.

"There you are." Usun stepped into the room and

frowned at his great-granddaughter. Usun's shoulders had curved in more in the last year, age catching up to him. His ivory beard was still thick and glossy, though. "I thought we agreed to leave Adda to rest today."

Egi moaned. Gilgamesh tried to sit up but found he couldn't manage and dropped onto the bed. Urmah groaned. "Leave her be, Usun. Let an old man have his joys."

Usun's stern expression dropped, and he patted Egi's head. The girl bounced down and walked over to her great-great-grandfather, then wrapped her small arms around his neck. She kissed him softly before whispering, "When I kicked her, I pretended she was the old mean Ferryman, and I was helping you and Enkidu free the Stone Ones."

Gilgamesh chuckled and brushed a hand over her dark hair. "I'm sure you were just as brave."

She gave him a smile as wide as her cheeks then pounced out of the room. She reminded him of Urmah when he was young, so playful.

"You overindulge her, Adda." Usun frowned but his eyes sparkled.

"She's so much like your mother."

Usun took a sharp breath. "That she is. Is there anything you need to be more comfortable?"

"I'm fine, son." He reached for Usun's hand, gave it a feeble squeeze. Usun leaned down and kissed his father's head. "I've had guards stationed just beyond your door. Should you need anything, you call and I'll come."

"I love you, son."

Usun smiled. "I love you too."

They'd had a lifetime to build the truths behind those words. Usun readjusted the blankets, gave Urmah a pat, and left. Gilgamesh stared up at the ceiling for a long time, willing sleep to come. His body's pain stole what respite rest might offer. He reached over to pat Urmah's head.

When he touched the lion, he knew.

He turned his face towards the creature.

No more rising of breath, no gentle affectionate growls, no movement at all.

Gilgamesh swallowed.

He'd faced grief so many times, and it never got easier. With great effort, he rolled towards Urmah and tucked his face into the lion's mane. He smelled of the wild, and Gilgamesh smoothed his hair down.

"You were a good boy," he whispered past tears. "The most loyal companion. Enkidu once said I'd love you one day. He was right. I hope you're reunited with him now." He lowered his voice even more, so he almost didn't speak. "I'm jealous of you, tell you the truth."

He kissed him, tucked beside him, and fell asleep.

Life had gotten unbearably tiresome. One being he loved after another leaving. And he was done living it.

* * *

Gilgamesh blinked his eyes open. He stood in a cave. Water trickled in the distance. His breath came out in a mist.

He lifted his hands to warm them with his breath to discover he could do so without hurting. Stretching his arms before him, he smiled. He was strong again, his muscles defined, his body buzzing with energy.

"Hello there. It's all right now, you've arrived at— Oh."

Gilgamesh's heart stopped then lurched into his throat. Even after nearly a century of not hearing it, he'd know that voice in a moment.

He turned slowly.

Standing before a rushing river, Enkidu held an oar embedded with jewels. He wore a navy tunic and gold shawl. His hair was brushed back, his horns curling elegantly into dark curls, his beard trimmed.

Gilgamesh took a short, painful breath.

He wanted to force his body forward, but the shock cemented his boots to the cave floor.

Enkidu gave his head a shake and gripped the oar tighter. "You might feel overwhelmed right now. You've died, but don't worry, you've come to a good place."

Blinking like he could make Enkidu's image disappear, Gilgamesh frowned. This was Enkidu, yet he spoke to him like a stranger.

"Do you not recognize me?" Gilgamesh's voice echoed off the cave, thundered. He'd rather fall into Death's Sea and give up everything if Enkidu didn't remember him.

Enkidu's hazel eyes shuddered shut for a moment, then they opened, and he cleared his throat. "Of course I do, Gilgamesh. Did you have a good life?" A smile, kind but polite. "I've heard stories about you."

Shock stole any immediate reply from Gilgamesh. He stood three large strides from the man that haunted his dreams every night and filled his memories. Yet the distance between them felt greater than death.

Gilgamesh stepped forward. "I hope you've heard all the stories I've shared about you."

The smile widened some. "Yes. You made me sound braver than I actually was in life."

"Surely you know you were always the bravest of the two of us."

Enkidu chuckled quietly and looked down then gestured to a boat behind him. "My role now is the Ferryman."

Gilgamesh scrunched his face. "You've taken that bastard's role?"

A flush of color spread across Enkidu's cheeks, but he still wouldn't meet Gilgamesh's eyes. "Well, I hope to have a better legacy. I ferry souls into the afterlife. You petitioned the gods and changed humanity's fate. But souls still arrive here in the Great Below first. It's my job to usher them beyond. That's what I'm here to help you with. You've died, Gilgamesh." He raised his face. "I'll take you to the Beyond."

Gilgamesh stared at this man. Now that he saw him, he wondered how he'd ever forgotten his appearance. He recognized every dimple and expression and line of his body. Yet, Enkidu spoke to him like he was a stranger. Throat tightening, Gilgamesh struggled to swallow. He didn't understand how he could feel so much if he was dead. He'd rather be alive still, in pain, lying in bed and dreaming of Enkidu than standing before him unre-membered.

"Have you forgotten about us, Enkidu?"

He moved closer, and Enkidu frowned. "Why would you think that?"

"You're speaking to me like I'm a stranger."

Enkidu closed the distance between them so Gilgamesh could see the individual hairs in his beard, how they gleamed in the cave's silvery light. He sighed. "You've lived a very long time, Gilgamesh."

Tears burned Gilgamesh's eyes. He'd lived far longer than he would have liked. Yet, in all that time, he'd never forgotten Enkidu. No, he'd made it his life's legacy to honor Enkidu's name and the promise he'd given him. Yet, time had pulled Enkidu from him. Now he had a different role and didn't care for Gilgamesh anymore.

Gilgamesh wished his soul had ceased to exist at his death.

This was far crueler.

He'd spent endless decades thinking of all the things he'd say to Enkidu if he had another chance. Now, his voice was a choked whisper when he spoke.

"I have never forgotten you." He swallowed down tears. "Every sunrise I thought of how it reflected across your eyes, and each sunset I remembered sitting beneath the stars together. Do you know how many grandchildren I have now, Enkidu? And I always knew which ones you'd have a soft spot for. Not one thing happened over my years that didn't make me think of you. I raised Urmah his entire life and loved him as you would have. I've kept every single promise to you, but"—his voice broke—"you're going to tell me you've forgotten the love we shared?"

Enkidu lifted his face. "You truly mean what you've said?"

"Of course," Gilgamesh hissed. He couldn't decide if he was angry or sad. Both. He felt so much of both, he wanted to burn the world.

"I thought, maybe..." Enkidu looked back at the glistening river before returning to face Gilgamesh. His brow furrowed, his lips folding, so a dimple formed below them. Gilgamesh knew that expression. He wore that face when he regretted something. "I thought perhaps you might have found someone else, or something else. It's been a long time for a mortal."

Gilgamesh stepped closer without breaking their locked gazes. "I told you when we met, I was no mere mortal."

Enkidu laughed softly. "The mighty King Gilgamesh. Yes, I remember."

Gilgamesh moved forward until their arms grazed. He

reached for Enkidu's hand but stopped short of touching him. He wouldn't without his permission. Enkidu slipped their fingers together and sighed. Gilgamesh's body burned with a million sensations. He'd waited a century hoping he might see this man again.

"I have not had one day," Gilgamesh said, "not one hour, when I didn't think about you. I kept my word and lived, but a piece of my heart died with you."

Enkidu leaned closer. Their noses touched, and Gilgamesh shivered.

"You'll want to go to the Beyond. Everyone you love who's passed is waiting for you there, and it's nice. My work is here. Souls arrive in this place but they need to be ushered past their earthly connections so they can move on to a better place. Sometimes they struggle and linger." He swallowed and looked down. "I know how much you dreaded the idea of going to the Great Below. Most of my time is here, working with new souls. I only travel to the Beyond when another soul is ready to travel. Spending an eternity in this cave would make you miserable." He dropped his hand, stepped back, and pointed to the boat.

Gilgamesh wanted to take the man and shake him until his teeth clacked. "The person I love is here." His voice thundered around the space, echoing against the empty cavern. "Do you think I would choose some fucking palace if spending eternity in this miserable cave with you was an option? Do you think I'd just go off to whatever the fucking Beyond is, if it meant leaving you again? Enkidu, if you knew how I grieved you. How I never got over it, you would understand how godsdamn ridiculous you are being right now."

Enkidu tilted his head and studied him. Then he laughed so hard that he held his stomach.

"Something humorous?"

Enkidu rose, a smile still stretching out his face, his eyes sparkling. He stepped up to Gilgamesh and wrapped an arm around his back. Gilgamesh sank into the touch as he grinned at him. "You're still the same stubborn, irreverent man I fell in love with all those years ago."

"Well, you're still a sap, clearly. Who convinced you to take this stupid job?" Gilgamesh's words held no heat, though. His hands wandered up to the small of Enkidu's back. Having him in his arms was the only thing that mattered.

"I like this job," he whispered against Gilgamesh's lips.

Gilgamesh nodded but drifted his face closer until their lips grazed.

Kissing Enkidu was better than becoming a god.

It was better than a legacy that would outlive him.

It surpassed any Beyond.

He didn't want beyond. He wanted this. Him.

Reaching up, he curled a hand around a horn, and Enkidu groaned.

When they pulled apart, Enkidu smiled at him. "Are you sure? Would you really want to join me in ferrying? It's not a romantic afterlife."

Gilgamesh traced fingers over the man's beard, across his cheekbone. "It is the only life I've ever wanted, after or otherwise."

Enkidu smiled. "I have missed you every moment, love." Gilgamesh's fingers stilled as he spoke. "Whenever someone appears here, I've hoped it would be you, and as time's passed, I've feared it would be you and you wouldn't love me any longer. That you would find the way I feel for you still to be too much."

Gilgamesh snorted. "Do you remember who I am? I'm the definition of too damn much."

Enkidu's smile slowly grew, like the sun rising over a hill. "Come on, there are others waiting for you who'd like to see you. Urmah arrived earlier." His cheeks flushed. "It was good to see him."

Enkidu led them to the boat, and Gilgamesh slung an arm across his shoulder as they walked.

"Did you worry your little beast would forget about you too?"

"Oh, he remembered me." Enkidu chuckled. "Flipped the boat as he fought me over getting into it, though."

"I don't believe he ever forgave us for dragging him across Death's Sea."

"It would seem not."

They entered the boat and sat. Enkidu reached out and grabbed Gilgamesh's hand; with his free one, he pushed the oar into the water and set them onto the rushing stream. It became dark and Gilgamesh tensed.

But his hand was in Enkidu's.

"You say people I love wait for me," Gilgamesh said. "Who?"

Enkidu chuckled. "Shamhat, for one. She's annoyed with you. She thinks you overstayed your time in the mortal realm."

"As usual, she's right," Gilgamesh grumbled.

The cave was dark, but the boat sloshed pleasantly through the water and the heat of Enkidu's fingers branded into Gilgamesh's hand. He never wished to release the man again.

"Of all the people that have passed through here and told me tales about you," Enkidu said, a smile in his voice, "there's one who spoke the most fondly of you and asks me regularly if I've seen you."

"Who?"

Enkidu shifted closer and pulled his oar into the boat, slowing their progress. "A young grandson of yours."

"Nigba." Gilgamesh's voice wobbled over the name. The boy had come into the world small and weak, his cries scarcely more than a whimper. Usun's third child who lived only six years. Gilgamesh had doted on the boy. Nigba had loved Urmah, loved to lie on his warm body and hide his face in the lion's mane. Gilgamesh had held the child as he passed, as his last weak breaths left his body that had fought so hard and lost.

"Is he well in the Beyond?" Gilgamesh asked.

"Everyone is healthy in the Beyond. He was delighted to see Urmah this morning. I don't know which one pounced on the other first."

Gilgamesh smiled. The idea of the child and lion reuniting made him sad he hadn't witnessed it.

"So, you figured it out." Enkidu's whisper echoed around the cavern. "What really matters in the end."

Gilgamesh lifted Enkidu's hand and kissed his knuckles. He wanted to hold that hand to his lips until he'd memorized it again. Wanted to touch him everywhere. Ask him a hundred questions. Kiss him until he couldn't answer them. "I had someone who taught me that, yes. A man far braver than me. Far kinder. Often when I interacted with my grandchildren, I wondered what that man might say or do. If I have any legacy, it's his."

Enkidu swallowed then leaned forward, resting his forehead on Gilgamesh's. His horns brushed Gilgamesh's flesh, and he reached out and pulled him into his arms, felt his heartbeat pound steadily against his chest.

Somehow, the two of them had stood cursed among the divine.

Yet, they'd endured the trials, suffered their losses, and came out victorious with their hands still clasped in each other's.

Among all the foolishness and fears, their love had created a legacy that would burn into forever, far after sand had buried their names and walls had crumbled.

Even once the world had changed irrevocably, that legacy–the love of one man for another–would burn as bright as stars and last as long.

AUTHOR'S NOTE

I was working on this series when I received a phone call that changed my life.

My younger sister passed away unexpectedly.

For months I plunged into a depth of grief I'd never experienced before. When I returned to this series, I was raw and emotionally bleeding.

This is a difficult book for me to read. I poured so much of my grief into it. While I'm no stranger to writing tragedy and grief, this is the first time I've worked on something that paralleled life as I was living it.

When I think of my sister, though, I think of her joyfulness, her rich laugh, her fierce stubbornness, and her easy acceptance of others.

Anna (who went by Katie throughout her entire childhood) was one of the most life-filled people I've known. If she did something, she did so fully. She was a scientist, a pilot, and a vegan. She cared deeply about social issues and had the grit and tenacity to put actions to her words.

She loved deeply.

She was loved deeply.

We miss her tremendously.

I hope this book, tragic as it was, also felt hopeful. And that it does some small measure of justice to the original myth that has endured such a long time in human memory.

Gilgamesh and Enkidu came to me in a season that has embedded them and their story in my life in such a way that I know they'll stay with me forever. I hope their love and stories and the hope they share stay with you as well.

With that, I leave you with the actual words of Siduri, the Wine Maker and her take on a well-lived life from almost four-thousand years ago:

Humans are born, they live, then they die,
    this is the order that the gods have decreed.
    But until the end comes, enjoy your life,
    spend it in happiness, not despair.
    Savor your food, make each of your days
    a delight, bathe and anoint yourself,
    wear bright clothes that are sparkling clean,
    let music and dancing fill your house,
    love the child who holds you by the hand,
    and give your lover pleasure in your embrace.
    That is the best way for a man to live.

-The Epic of Gilgamesh

ACKNOWLEDGMENTS

I've waffled between writing long or short acknowledgements for this book. Working on this series through one of the darkest seasons of my life meant that so many support people stepped in. I could pen endless paragraphs of thanks to everyone who helped, but I'm opting to keep them concise.

With deepest gratitude to my editors Milly and Natalie who gave so much energy to this project; to Dr. Andrew George who helped with the world building of this book; to Chaim, Stefanie, and Florian who created the design and art; to Megan for proofreading; to my therapist Erin who provided insights on grief I infused into this book; to my early readers who helped launch this series; and to my wonderful, supportive family and friends who loved me through all the trials of creating this.

Thank you all greatly.

Words do not suffice.

www.ingramcontent.com/pod-product-compliance
Lightning Source LLC
Chambersburg PA
CBHW070411310726
48977CB00003B/635